CW01236855

DIARY OF A CAT

DIARY OF A CAT

Mayumi Nagano

Translated from the Japanese by
Yui Kajita

MACLEHOSE PRESS
QUERCUS · LONDON

First published in Japan as チマチマ記 (*Tiny, Tiny Diary*)
by Kodansha Ltd, Tokyo, in 2017

First published in Great Britain in 2025
by MacLehose Press, an imprint of Quercus
Part of John Murray Group

1

Copyright © 2017 Mayumi Nagano
English translation copyright © 2025 by Yui Kajita
Publication rights for this English language edition arranged
through KODANSHA LTD., Tokyo.

KODANSHA

The moral right of Mayumi Nagano to be
identified as the author of this work has been
asserted in accordance with the Copyright,
Designs and Patents Act, 1988.

Yui Kajita asserts her moral right to be identified as the translator of this work.

All rights reserved. No part of this publication
may be reproduced or transmitted in any form
or by any means, electronic or mechanical,
including photocopy, recording, or any
information storage and retrieval system,
without permission in writing from the publisher.

This book is a work of fiction. Names, characters, businesses, organisations, places and events are either the product of the author's imagination or used fictitiously. Any resemblance to actual persons, living or dead, events or locales is entirely coincidental.

A CIP catalogue record for this book is available from the British Library

HB ISBN 978 1 52943 532 0
TPB ISBN 978 1 52943 533 7
Ebook ISBN 978 1 52943 534 4

Typeset in Warnock Pro by CC Book Production
Printed and bound in Great Britain by Clays Ltd, Elcograf S.p.A.

MIX
Paper | Supporting
responsible forestry
FSC® C104740

Papers used by Quercus are from well-managed forests and other responsible sources.

Quercus
Carmelite House
50 Victoria Embankment
London EC4Y 0DZ

John Murray Group
Part of Hodder & Stoughton Limited
An Hachette UK company

The authorised representative in the EEA is Hachette Ireland,
8 Castlecourt Centre, Dublin 15, D15 XTP3, Ireland (email: info@hbgi.ie)

1.

Early Spring • Breakfast • *1*

2.

Spring • Lunch • *45*

3.

Early Summer • Dim Sum Party • *85*

4.

Summer • Lunch and Snacks for the Tiny Tots • *123*

5.

Autumn • Picnic • *165*

6.

Late Autumn • A Hearty Feast • *199*

7.

Early Winter • A Special Gathering • *235*

8.

Midwinter • Snuggling at Home • *265*

The Horai Family

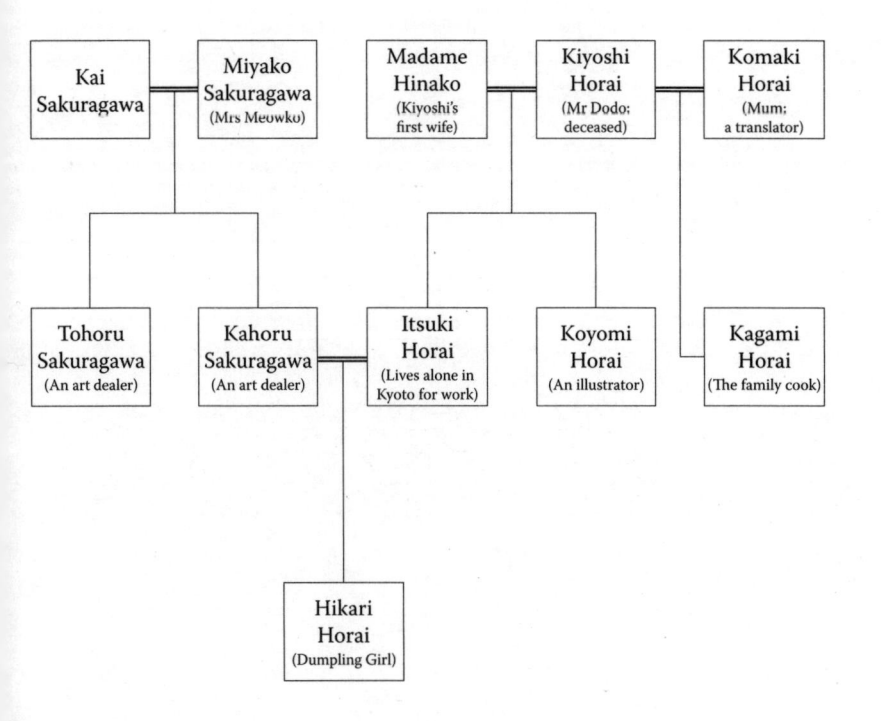

- **Kai Sakuragawa** ═ **Miyako Sakuragawa** (Mrs Meowko)
- **Madame Hinako** (Kiyoshi's first wife) ═ **Kiyoshi Horai** (Mr Dodo; deceased) ═ **Komaki Horai** (Mum; a translator)

Children of Kai & Miyako Sakuragawa:
- **Tohoru Sakuragawa** (An art dealer)
- **Kahoru Sakuragawa** (An art dealer) ═ **Itsuki Horai** (Lives alone in Kyoto for work)

Children of Kiyoshi & Madame Hinako:
- Itsuki Horai
- **Koyomi Horai** (An illustrator)

Child of Kiyoshi & Komaki:
- **Kagami Horai** (The family cook)

Child of Kahoru & Itsuki:
- **Hikari Horai** (Dumpling Girl)

1

Early Spring

Breakfast

Chicken and burdock roots simmered with apples
Broccoli sprinkled with dried whitebait
A bowl of brown rice

Grandad's name is Tamaki, and Mum's name is Komaki, so they decided to call me Chimaki. Basically, we're "thick roll", "little roll" and "rice dumpling" respectively.

Mum Komaki is a translator, and she writes on the side. She has a popular column called "Komakoma-ki", or "Itsy Bitsy Diary", in the free magazine published by Tekona, who sells home goods and crafty things in her shop. So I'm going to try penning my own "Chimachima-ki", or "Tiny Tiny Diary".

First, let me start with how I met Grandad.

It was a cold evening at dusk, and it looked like snow. Now that he's eighty, Grandad hardly ever helps out with the family business, but that day he took on a delivery run since it was just in the neighbourhood. They're called Matsu

EARLY SPRING

Sushi, but they don't do nigiri – their speciality is catering and bento boxes. When there's a flurry of events like banquets and memorial services, they get so busy that they need extra pairs of hands to cope with all the deliveries.

Grandad retired a long time ago, passing down the role of head chef to his son, Tsukune. Nowadays, he pitches in only when they get orders from their old, familiar customers. When a ninety-year-old neighbour says they've got a sudden craving for his anago sushi, fresh-faced Grandad simply *has* to call on them, toting a box of sushi topped with saltwater eel.

On his way home that night, Grandad swerved into a side alley instead of heading straight back. He had a mind to pop by Ukiyo-bune, just for a little bit, to grab a bite of some steamed tofu – a big favourite of his. In fact, that was the real reason why he stepped forward to deliver the sushi. The job was just a convenient excuse.

Steamed tofu is a special treat for Grandad, who's not supposed to eat a lot of eggs. You mash tofu and egg in a suribachi mortar until it's thick and gooey, then you pour it into a bowl and put it in a bamboo steamer. Once it's cooked enough, you splash on a bit of sake and eat it piping hot, blowing on it so you don't get burned. It's good with a spot of wasabi, too.

It tastes like a dream on a chilly night; some people even call it "paradise tofu". Grandad was planning to slip into the

BREAKFAST

diner and enjoy it in secret. Ukiyo-bune is a friendly joint where all Grandad has to do to have a steaming hot bowl of tofu served up to him is take a seat.

He was about to cross the threshold with a spring in his step when his eyes – rather keen for his age – happened to fall on us. There was a lamp with a paper shade standing outside the diner, with a gap of about four inches between the bottom of the lamp and the ground. That was where my baby brother and I had been sleeping since the night before.

The lamp's electric light gave us a little warmth, and it shielded us from the rain, too. A reassuring shadow to keep us hidden – just like they say, "It's darkest under the candle stand." We'd taken cover there when we saw Denden looking daggers at us. He's the grumpy, pot-bellied one who rules the streets around here. Grandad picked us up, brought us home with him, and we got our new names.

As you can guess from my name, I have pointy ears (if you look at me from the front, the white pointy triangles look like chimaki, those sweet rice dumplings wrapped in bamboo leaves that you have for Children's Day in May). The back of my ears is marbled with the colour of the caramel on custard pudding, and my eyes are a shade of aqua, neither green nor blue. My fur is mostly creamy white, except for one spot on my belly that's shaped sort of like a swirl, the same colour as my ears.

EARLY SPRING

As for my brother, the tip of his nose is white, as if he's dipped his face in a box of flour; other than that, he's chocolate brown all over. Sometimes, the light makes it look like he got sprinkled with cocoa powder. Tsukune – Grandad's son, now the head chef of Matsu Sushi – came out from behind the counter, took one look at my brother, and said he looks like an ohagi, those mochi rice balls wrapped in red bean paste, but Mum had already made up her mind that his name was Norimaki, or "seaweed roll".

By the way, for a while after we were born, we lived with Mademoiselle Rocco, who used to call us Marble and Chocolate. My brother probably doesn't remember much about her, though, since he was just starting to have baby food back then, and I hardly ever think about her now.

Norimaki and I strayed from Mademoiselle at a busy airport around New Year's, and since then, we've been wandering around by ourselves.

We were still wearing collars at first (though Norimaki was still such a tiny kitten that he didn't even have a name tag yet). But one time, at a restaurant parking lot off the national highway, a stranger – who looked like a travelling performer – warned us that some random roughnecks might slit our throats in our sleep if we went around wearing fancy-schmancy collars like those. He was living with a truck driver in their dekotora: a huge, blinged-up truck that looked like a shiny palace.

BREAKFAST

The truck driver's other companion, Jonathan (that's how he introduced himself), looked like a tough guy, with thick black hair that jutted out the top of his head in a flattop style, and he could stand on his hind legs by propping himself up with his long tail.

He was clever with his hands too – he could do tricks like unscrewing the cap off a plastic bottle or opening a new box of sweets. He even knew how to work the car stereo. Apparently, he'd had some service monkey training once. So he took off our collars for us right away.

Maybe they were swindlers, but at least we still have our throats intact. They gave us a lift in their flashy truck to the drug store in the next town over, and they fed us some pumpkin and boneless ham, so it's all good.

Even if we still had our collars, we couldn't have gone back home anyway. Mademoiselle Rocco moved out of her flat before leaving for her trip. We're lucky we got picked up by Grandad when we did. Norimaki was starting to get sick, snot bubbles dripping from his nose, so Grandad's a real lifesaver.

The first thing Grandad treated us to was fluffy surimi balls made of cod. He mashed some cod, mountain yam and locally made flour in a suribachi until it was nice and fluffy, then scooped the dough into balls with a spoon and dropped them in a clear broth flavoured with kombu kelp and bonito flakes.

EARLY SPRING

He let them cool down in a bright red bowl and served them to us just like that.

My little brother was feeling tired and weak, so he left some of the fluffy balls uneaten and went to curl up on Grandad's warm belly. Already feeling right at home, he fell fast asleep with a contented smile.

Grandad's place is cramped, with tools everywhere, so he called Mum, who lives nearby, and she decided to take us home with her. Mum's place is rather big, a Western-style house with lots of doors. Judging from the footsteps and voices, I guessed there must be lots of people living here.

That night, we slept in a basket. My brother was out like a light. Once I settled down a bit, I peeked out through the crack under the lid and found a little girl peering back at me. As soon as we locked eyes, I knew I'd met my rival.

"This one's got a mark like persimmon paste. Wouldn't it make more sense to call him Sasadango instead of Chimaki?" the girl said to someone out of sight, sounding like a real know-it-all. What she meant is that the mark on my belly – the one *I* think of as a creamy caramel cake – looks like persimmon paste. You can tell she's not the straightforward type by the fact that she opted for persimmon paste instead of something more common, like white bean paste mixed with miso.

A chimaki is a steamed dumpling made from sticky rice

BREAKFAST

and rice flour, wrapped in bamboo leaves. You don't put paste in it. Sasadango, on the other hand, is a bamboo-wrapped dumpling filled with some kind of paste. But Mum insisted that Chimaki is a good name.

From then on, I secretly started calling the little know-it-all "Dango Hime", or "Dumpling Girl". When the third term is over, and April comes around, Dumpling Girl will be in fifth grade of elementary school. If I went to school, I'd be in junior high, so a couple of years ahead of her. But considering how girls are a little bit more grown up than boys around the same age, I'd say we're evenly matched.

As she turned her back to me and started going upstairs, I called out her new nickname a few times. I didn't say it out loud, of course. She soon spun around and said, "Haramaki!"

Belly wrap. She's a sharpshooter all right.

That same night, Mum rummaged in the cupboard and brought out two shallow bowls for us with camellias painted on them: white flowers for me, red flowers for Norimaki. According to meow-rules, you can trust people who give you a nice bowl to eat from.

In this house, we can go pretty much anywhere we like. The rooms that are off-limits are locked. I'm not a big fan of adventures, so I rarely go up to the first floor. Norimaki still takes time to clamber up the steps. Plus, he can't get back down on

EARLY SPRING

his own. So most of the time, we spend our days either in the kitchen or the little dining room at the end of the corridor.

There's plenty of space for us to play games in the corridor, even though there's a fridge there and a boiler that heats up the whole house. It has wooden flooring, partly made of decorative sheets of yosegi wood with a sort of mosaic pattern fitted in here and there. If you look at them from a distance, they can look like the scales of a snake, so sometimes Norimaki freezes in his tracks when he sees them. It's funny – every so often he stops with his back paw hanging in the air, as if he were playing a game of Grandmother's Footsteps.

Next comes the small storeroom, hidden behind an accordion curtain. That's where they keep the kitchen trolley and the chair that's used both as a stepladder and a place to take a break from housework. Mum set up a den for us there.

This house has two dining rooms: a small, casual one where everybody usually eats, and another one with a long table. That's where they like to have classy meals when they have guests over. It's right next to the living room, which has a large window that opens out onto a terrace on the south side of the house.

When there's a big gathering, both Dumpling Girl and us brothers are supposed to keep away from the grown-ups' territory. As long as we behave, though, we can pop in a little bit. But swinging from people's legs and curtain-climbing are a no-no.

BREAKFAST

As for Dumpling Girl, she's supposed to pass by the mirror in the corridor before saying hello to the guests. Mum and the others remind her to pull up her socks properly, too.

Her socks have her school emblem embroidered on the side, on the bit that's folded over just below the knees. It's a monogram designed with blue pimpernels, a cross and the name of a saint that starts with an E, but it's been washed so many times that the threads are coming loose, and now it looks more like a skull. Dumpling Girl calls it "the curse mark", and she usually wears her socks rolled down like a dashimaki omelette so that it's hidden away.

It's not that she doesn't like the mark. She keeps it covered so that the curse will be at its most powerful when the time comes to use it. She hasn't told me yet what kind of occasion she has in mind.

The other day, she rolled those socks down to her ankles and showed me a purplish bruise on her shin. An impressive badge of honour. Its colours were a mix of azuki bean and strawberry, though some of it was turning green. Actually, it was a fake bruise – she'd rubbed a sweet potato peel against her skin to dye it reddish brown and touched it up with ballpoint pens and coloured pencils. A work of art.

"It was a nice purple bruise at first, but then it started turning green," she said. For her, this was a serious problem.

I told her, "You know how sweet potato tempura go green

11

EARLY SPRING

sometimes? I think it's like that." But I'm not sure if she got me.

There are shelves and drawers all over the kitchen. My brother and I aren't so shameless as to poke our noses everywhere, hunting for bonito flakes and dried fish. But I've figured out what's stored where and I have almost everything down pat. Norimaki, though, still goes around opening drawers and tipping headlong into them.

One of the chairs in the small dining room has a square seat cushion on it, the well-worn cover decorated with sashiko stitching. It's a patchwork of deep indigo and white fabrics dyed using the aizome technique and sewn together to make gourd-like patterns. Since no-one sits there, it's become a favourite spot for Norimaki and me. But, until two years ago, it was Dad's seat.

Dad's name was Kiyoshi, but his friends called him Dodo all his life. The kanji for *Kiyoshi* (圭) is made up of two characters for *do* (土), stacked on top of each other: that's how you get *Dodo*. Plus, it's a riff on how he was an open, confident kind of guy who didn't shy away from anything, which is one meaning for the phrase "dodo to shiteru" in Japanese. The nickname also stands for that thing you say when you want to calm down a horse – "doh doh", as in "whoa" – because he was born in the year of the horse.

Mr Dodo's chair looks heavy, and the armrests are carved

BREAKFAST

into horse heads. The left one is called Melos; the right one is Troy. Troy is pretty battered – an older American shorthair named Tatsumaki used to live in this house, and he had a habit of sharpening his back teeth on it.

Since we came to this house, I've fallen in love with small horse mackerel in the mirin-boshi style: sliced open, marinated in mirin and soy sauce, and dried in the sun. Grandad brought some for us the day after he found us, when he dropped by at Mum's to see how we were settling in. The rest of the family ate the fish, too, placing the slices on top of their bowls of rice.

It was *amazing*. Grandad made it himself, so the flavour was pure and simple, and he'd made sure to pluck out all the tiny bones so it was safe for us to eat. He'd sprinkled a generous dose of sesame seeds over the fish, which gave off a mouth-watering aroma, and broiled it over a fire real quick. When it's warmed up, the flesh gets nice and soft. Grandad cooled some down for us brothers, and I sank my back teeth into one. The sweet and salty juices seeped out of the tender fish and pooled in my mouth.

My baby brother took a bite from Grandad's bowl at first, so ever since then, he's liked having mirin-boshi with a bit of rice stuck on it. In fact, just this morning, he trotted up to Kagami to pester him for some rice while he was working in the kitchen.

EARLY SPRING

Kagami is the household cook. He told Norimaki to wait a little; first he had to get the breakfast ready for the people who were going out. So Norimaki went back to sit politely in the corridor with the heel of one paw resting on the toes of the other. A smart gentleman who was passing by complimented him on his surprisingly good manners.

I don't know who he is, but he gave us a warm smile. My little brother looked pleased with himself. The gentleman had silvery hair, which he wore swept back.

From the look and colour of his skin – smooth and shiny like simmered soybeans – he seemed to be East Asian, but given the way he dressed, in a fashionably washed-out flannel shirt and a slim knit jumper in maroon, he could've easily been a Jean or a Paul walking down some narrow street in Paris. He looked quite old, but younger than Grandad.

I was surprised to find there was still someone I hadn't been introduced to in Mum's house, even though we've already been here for about ten days. Then again, who knows how many people actually live here?

Dumpling Girl was on the phone, leaning on the fridge door; she was talking to her father, who's living by himself now for work, somewhere far away. I tried to ask her who the elderly gentleman was, but as soon as I said "Hey", she flopped her round felt hat over my face.

She gave me a pout that said, *Later. I'm asking him*

something important now. The topic of discussion was who would attend the parent–teacher meeting just before the end-of-term assembly. It sounded like her dad was thinking of having someone else go in his place, but she wanted *him* to come, and neither of them gave in, so the call went on and on.

Our Mum, Komaki, is Dumpling Girl's granny. Which makes Dumpling Girl's dad our big brother.

That said, he's not Mum's real son. Mr Dodo married twice, so he had a first wife and a second wife. Mum was the second one, and now she's a widow.

But nobody calls her that in this house; if you hear "widow", you might picture a really old lady, but in fact, she hasn't turned sixty yet.

Sometimes she tells people, "But I already have a grandchild in elementary school, you know," and gets a kick out of seeing their surprise.

What really shocked me was that the first wife, Madame Hinako, owns the atelier annex connected to the main part of the house, even now; and not only that, she makes the journey here every day from her own house nearby. Plus, she's even renting out the room above the atelier.

Madame Hinako is seventy now, but she still drives around in her car and casually goes on solo trips. She'll go out anywhere as long as there's a man who's worth her time there, whether it's the theatre, or the races, or a bar. I

EARLY SPRING

still haven't figured it out: is this fun, light-footed Madame Hinako actually a bunch of trouble who's hard to handle, still hanging around her former husband's house? Or is it just that Mum's so laid back she doesn't mind at all, so she's happy to let Madame Hinako do as she pleases? Are they both too cool for school or simply thick-skinned? Either way, one thing I can say for sure is that they've got style.

Madame Hinako is Dumpling Girl's real granny, but they're more like accomplices, the way they go about swapping secrets and jokes and plots. They like to join hands to take down their target – by which I mean Madame Hinako's son and Dumpling Girl's dad, of course. Though they're holding a truce right now because he's far away.

Norimaki and I haven't met him yet, but he's supposed to be coming home for a visit while Dumpling Girl is on spring break. His name is Itsuki.

We had a little chat with him on the phone:

"I'm Chimaki, and this is my little brother, Norimaki. Grandad found us under the lamp outside Ukiyo-bune one night when it was starting to snow a little, and he took us in. Nice to meet you."

"Meet you," Norimaki echoed.

"Good to meet you too," he replied. "Hope you'll make friends with Hikari." (That's Dumpling Girl's real name, by the way.) "Don't go outside, though. It's a pretty busy street with cars passing by all the time. Just play in the house and the garden. And watch out for the big lout who looks like a bear and that other one who resembles a grumpy lioness. Be careful you don't get too close to the hedge."

A straight talker. Itsuki seems like a great guy. The only mystery is where his wife could be – that is, Dumpling Girl's mum. She doesn't seem to be living in this house, and I haven't heard anything about her so far. It's a delicate question, though, so I can't just go around asking anyone.

Mum's house doesn't have any rooms with a tatami mat floor. It's because it was built by Mr Dodo's father to be rented out to people from other countries. Those kinds of rental houses used to be popular back in the day, apparently.

How long ago do I mean by "back in the day"? Well, it's when there was an airline called BOAC, and it used to be hip to go about town carrying a bag with their logo on it.

You might wonder how I know such an old-timey story: I heard about it from Jean Paul (I'm friends with him now, and that's what I call him). He said he's been to London on a BOAC flight.

Anyway, when Itsuki was old enough to go to elementary school, his father, Mr Dodo, talked things over with *his* father, the owner of the house, and moved in with his family.

"A house can last for a long time, huh?" Jean Paul murmured.

EARLY SPRING

He sat on Mr Dodo's chair, letting me and my brother snuggle on his lap. But nobody told him to move aside – or seemed to notice he was there.

Since it's a Western-style house, the kitchen is Western, too. It's got a huge oven, probably big enough to roast a whole spring chicken, and a four-ring gas hob – not so common in Japanese homes. The wrap-around counter with all its shelves and drawers is in the shape of a U, with the sink in the middle facing the window.

It's Kagami who cooks for everyone. His name's written with the kanji for *mirror*, but I always picture it in the simpler katakana letters. When he has to write his name somewhere, he draws a mark instead: it looks like that round, bald head that grows on the tip of a spring onion stalk.

Don't ask me why he chose a spring onion head for his symbol. It looks pretty similar to the blue onions on a Meissen plate. Sometimes he draws it like a crown and puts his initials on it. This family's last name is Horai – written with the kanji characters for *treasure* and *come* – so his full name is Kagami Horai. It's supposed to be a really lucky name.

The Horai family has a particular tradition when it comes to naming their kids. They always put the kanji of the day of the week they were born in there somewhere. Mr Dodo was born on a Saturday (土曜日), so he has the *do* kanji, which means *earth*, hidden in his name, Kiyoshi (圭); Itsuki was born on a

Thursday (木曜日), so you get the *moku* kanji, which means *tree*, in Itsuki (樹); Dumpling Girl was born on a Sunday (日曜日), so she's got *nichi*, the kanji for *sun*, in Hikari (曜).

But there's one exception to the rule, to protect the family fortune: even if someone was born on a Wednesday (水曜日), which has the kanji for *sui*, meaning *water*, they would never use any kanji with a water radical. That's why they have relatives with names like Hide (求) or Izumi (泉), but no Nobu (江) or Migiwa (汀). They say the water radical – that's the three little strokes on the left side of the character that looks like a water current – would wash away the treasure. No-one knows which one of their ancestors made this up, and there's no real basis for the idea, either.

This family tradition is a lot trickier than having a zashiki warashi haunting the house – one of those spirits that look like children and can be quite mischievous. Mr Dodo's grandad had an extravagant name: Nishiki (錦), which is the word for those magnificent silk brocades with elaborate patterns woven from threads of gold and vibrant colours. His sisters were Kin (金) and Gin (銀), or gold and silver respectively. His brothers' names were auspicious, too: Asahi (旭) and Nozomi (望), or the rising sun and hope. But when it was time to name *his* children, he picked ordinary kanji.

My guess is that the family had already used up all the lucky characters, so he had to make do with more mundane ones. Take Mr Dodo's dad's name, Kashiki (炊): that's the kanji for *cook*, as in cooking rice. I'm not sure how well it works as a human name. But I'd say it's still better than aunt Fuku (服), which means clothes, or the other aunt named Nabe (鍋), which means pot, as in hot pot.

Kagami, who was born on a Friday, is Mum's real son. It's amazing that his name – the kanji character for *mirror*, so elegant and mysterious – still hadn't been used in the family by then.

Though he'd lived away from Tokyo for university, he came back when he graduated and took on the family's cooking duties instead of starting work at a company. He takes care of groceries and grows aromatic vegetables in the garden.

With her work, Mum Komaki doesn't have much time for cooking, so she counts on Kagami to put food on the table.

Besides (this is a secret, so don't tell anyone), cooking isn't really Mum's strong suit, even though she's the daughter of a family who runs a catering business.

"I mean, think about it," she'd say breezily, "a knife is a kind of weapon, so it used to be a man's job to wield it in the first place. That's why the flair for cooking only gets passed down to the men in our family."

Even though she can't cook, her taste buds are hard to

please – she's been eating tasty food ever since she was little, after all.

Mr Dodo liked to invite his friends over for meals, but Mum Komaki got by without cooking, thanks to Ms Fu.

From what I've heard, there used to be a live-in cook at the Horai house named Ms Fu, who was around since Mr Dodo was little. Auntie Fu was born in Shanghai, and her specialities were handmade shumai and gyoza. She was quick to learn Western-style home cooking staples, too, just by watching other people. The Horai family called Ms Fu's cooking "Fuinese Cuisine".

Jean Paul remembers Ms Fu's cooking, and his personal favourite was her "Bavarian fried pastry". First, she would prepare a white sauce using plenty of cultured butter, imported from abroad, then stir in some dry-roasted shrimp and mushrooms. Next she sandwiched this sauce in some wholegrain bread that she'd baked earlier and dunked it in milk. Once the milk had soaked into the thickest part of the bread, she coated it in flour, egg and panko breadcrumbs, then deep-fried it in a pan.

"You eat it steaming hot – cut into thick portions while you can still hear the sizzling. She made it with different fillings too, like mince meat in white sauce, or marmalade. All delicious." Jean Paul pretended to line up some freshly fried pastry in front of him, miming like a master storyteller.

EARLY SPRING

After Ms Fu passed away, the Horais managed to get by somehow, sometimes asking for help from a housekeeper who didn't live in, or getting deliveries from Matsu Sushi; the rest of the time, someone in the family would step in to cook.

But since it usually caters for special events like celebrations or memorial gatherings for the deceased, the Horais felt a twinge of guilt at eating Matsu Sushi fare on an ordinary day; besides, if they ate it too regularly, it wouldn't feel special anymore when they *did* want to order in for some kind of occasion. So, more often than not, Mum and the others made do with bento boxes and ready meals from the local supermarket.

The thing about a housekeeper – especially a veteran one – was that they would only cook in their own particular style. The one the Horais hired from time to time would make everything sweet and salty with sugar and soy sauce, then finish it off with mirin or sake. Sometimes she'd add sesame oil or vinegar, depending on the menu. Her dishes went well with rice, but the flavours were too strong for the Horais' tastes.

So they found another cook: one who'd trained as a nutritionist. Unlike the seasoned housekeeper, who stuck to her sweet-and-salty style, the nutrition specialist made the sort of meals you'd expect to be given for school lunches or in hospitals. Everybody could tell they were eating a well-balanced diet, but they simply didn't feel the spark in it.

BREAKFAST

Eventually, Kagami came home from college to look for a job. For the first time in years, he was back in the kitchen in his own house. He'd sharpened up his cooking skills while living by himself, and he put them to good use.

Most families would get worried if the son was having trouble finding a job, but not so in *this* house. Every time Kagami got a rejection, the whole family breathed a secret sigh of relief.

When autumn rolled around, and he still hadn't landed a job, he finally decided to become the cook for the Horai family, and he entered into negotiations over his salary with Itsuki, the present head of the household. They settled on the level of pay and benefits a college graduate would receive for his first job.

That day, Mum opened the very best bottle of Condrieu white wine especially for her son.

Mum usually works on her translations or writes late into the night, so she doesn't show up when everybody else is having breakfast. Mademoiselle Rocco was like that too, back when Norimaki and I used to live with her. She was an actress, and her plays always started in the evening, so she came home late and basically slept through the morning.

Since we were brought to the Horai house, the two of us have been spending the night in the little storeroom that's separated from the corridor by an accordion curtain. They

EARLY SPRING

laid the softest quilt for us in a basket that smells really nice, like a mix of pine needles and green apples – and that's where we snuggle down.

When she has to work all night, Mum comes downstairs when everybody's asleep to make hot cocoa for herself. We hear her padding closer in her felt slippers, and she peeks in on us as she's passing by. My baby brother is usually fast asleep, but I'm only pretending.

You should see the way he sleeps. He lies flat on his belly with his front and back legs stretched out, like when you slide down a grassy bank in the summer. You grab a big round satoimo leaf and use it like a sleigh to go whizzing over the grass. At first you lie on your belly, and once you get used to it, you can stand up on the leaf.

Norimaki was born in the beginning of winter, so he doesn't know what it's like to go sleighing on the grass yet. But I guess he's already riding like a pro in his dreams.

Mum bends down and tickles his side, saying, "You're a funny little guy." He curls up into a ball, then after a little while, goes back to sprawling out. In the morning, I ask him what he was dreaming about, but he doesn't remember a thing.

The first one to wake up in the house is Kagami. He's already in the kitchen before dawn. My brother and I come out from our basket and try to get his attention. Since he's prepping for breakfast, he doesn't really play with us, but he doesn't scold Norimaki for swinging on his leg.

Kagami is slim and he has slender fingers. The strands of his hair are thin, too – soft and smooth. But he wears funny-looking glasses with thick black frames that look like someone drew them with a big felt-tip marker. I can't say it looks too good on him.

Still, I think he's actually really fashionable. Whenever he's at the kitchen counter, he wears a crisp, spotless white shirt with pointy collars. The stitches around the buttons on his cuffs have a nice design, sewn with pale aqua blue thread, which stands out against the white.

When the morning light falls on the nape of his neck, it makes you think of cool fresh milk inside a glass bottle, or the clear colour in between the patterns on a white porcelain bowl. Most of the time, he wears grey, melange or black slacks.

This morning, he was making chicken soup in a big enamel pot. It was still dark outside; the house was quiet. The only sound was the soft bubbling of the simmering soup. Kagami stood in front of the pot, his expression serious. His hands moved gracefully like a tea master.

My little brother was at the window above the sink, and he climbed onto a teapot without a lid (the lid went missing

EARLY SPRING

some time ago, and Kagami's been looking for it). Since the window frame is about four inches thick, Norimaki needs a bit of extra height to peer outside. But it wasn't dawn yet, so all he could see was the dark. Somewhere far away, a train was rattling by.

Norimaki spotted something, and all of a sudden, his body narrowed and fell right into the teapot. It's the kind that's shaped like a European pear, so it tapers at the top. I thought he'd make a racket, but not a peep came out.

I went over to check on him and found him curled up at the bottom of the teapot. It was a perfect fit for him. He'd already forgotten what he'd seen that had surprised him so much.

At half past six, breakfast was served in the small dining room. The sky had been slowly paling for a while, and it was fairly bright already. Maybe the way I'm writing makes the timeline confusing, but this is supposed to be a scene that followed right after Dumpling Girl's call with her dad, from the same morning I was telling you about.

Kagami started introducing the breakfast menu for the day. He doesn't normally bother, but there was someone new at the table this morning.

A young man named Sakuragawa had moved into the room above Madame Hinako's atelier over the weekend. Norimaki and I don't know much about him yet, so we've been keeping our distance. He hasn't said hello to us, either.

BREAKFAST

"Gobo burdock roots became a popular vegetable to cultivate during the Edo period, when people started to make gobo mochi with it. They steamed the gobo until it became soft, then grated it and kneaded it together with sticky rice to make chewy cakes, and ate them deep-fried. I imagine they enjoyed these mochi with black sesame miso paste. Rice was hard to come by for the common people back then, so burdock roots became a major source of glucide. In other words, they're not just any vegetable: they're a crucial carbohydrate, practically a staple crop. This dish with chicken and burdock roots feels light on the stomach, but it's packed with a surprising amount of calories. On top of that, about half of the glucide doesn't get digested because there are no digestive enzymes for it inside the body. That makes it a convenient way to fill up the stomach, and even though it's high in calories, there's no need to worry about gaining weight. I've simmered the chicken and gobo with apples and served it as a soup, so you only need to have the mushrooms and vegetables on the side along with a light serving of brown-and-white blended rice, and you'll have a nutritious breakfast menu with brightly coloured vegetables and plenty of vitamins and minerals. To absorb the fibre more efficiently, please remember to chew your food properly. Don't just shovel it in."

With that, Kagami went back to the kitchen and returned with a bowl of broccoli mixed with fried mushrooms to the

EARLY SPRING

table. He sprinkled dried whitebait over it. He was wearing a navy blue apron today, with HAVING SUITON SOUP AT A RAILWAY STOP written on it in white.

"The whitebait serves as a dressing. Even though these shirasu fish are so small, there's a lot of calcium packed into them. What helps your body absorb the calcium is the vitamin D from the mushrooms, but dried whitebait has vitamin D in it, too, so you could say that it's a small but practical ingredient. At the same time, it's also high in cholesterol, so you have to eat it with mushrooms or vegetables. Fibre traps in cholesterol and helps your body get rid of it."

"Makes sense," Sakuragawa chimed in, but he was just nodding along while leafing through a magazine, so he wasn't *really* listening. With a quiet "Itadakimasu", he started eating before Kagami could finish reeling off his explanation,

At that point I was still under the impression Sakuragawa was nothing more than a tenant who rented a room from Madame Hinako, and it did seem strange that he sat at the Horais' dining table, looking for all the world like a member of the family. Well, no wonder – he turned out to be Dumpling Girl's mum's younger brother. That is, Sakuragawa is Dumpling Girl's uncle.

The Horais had invited him to stay as a sort of security guard for the family, since the only man in the house while Itsuki was away would be Kagami. So Sakuragawa gets to live

BREAKFAST

here rent-free, and to top it off, he gets free meals, too. Plus, he's at work during the day, so I don't know how he's supposed to be guarding the house. If you ask me, he's getting a little too much special treatment.

Even though he's a newcomer, he already sits in Itsuki's seat, like he's the head of the house. I thought he should be paying more attention to Kagami. If Itsuki were here, I bet he'd listen to everything Kagami had to say and thank him for all his efforts.

Sakuragawa's first name is Tohoru. He's twenty-seven, and he's an office worker. He's single for now. Judging from how he dresses – a thin, elegant broadcloth shirt and a perfectly chic tie (with a flashy design) – I'm guessing he's a bit of a playboy.

He cuts a nice figure, though. His hair looks effortless, for one thing: it's like he just let it dry naturally after a shower and ran his hand through it just once. Considering what I have to do to keep my topcoat in good shape, I think he must be going to a stylist who really knows their stuff.

Dumpling Girl told me about Sakuragawa's mum, Mrs Meowko (at least, that's what her name sounded like to me). According to her, Meowko was so cute back when she was a student that she had all the boys wrapped around her little finger. She went around having the time of her life, but one day, she suddenly married the one man nobody had

EARLY SPRING

expected her to choose: the no-nonsense, deadly earnest Kai Sakuragawa (Tohoru's dad, that is).

When I heard about Mrs Meowko, it made me think of the auntie with the same name at the tofu shop who used to feed some of her milk to Norimaki. Back when he'd just started living with Mademoiselle Rocco, Norimaki could only drink milk, so Auntie Meowko from the neighbourhood took care of us.

Auntie Meowko was a calico cat, but her baby daughters had soft and fluffy fur with spots, like cows. Apparently, when Mrs Meowko – Tohoru's mum, I mean – was young, every man who passed by on the street glanced back at her. She was just that gorgeous with that "willowy waist" of hers (but what *is* that, anyway?).

Norimaki had finally got the grains of rice that he'd been asking for on his mirin-boshi fish, and now he was munching on it. He was so excited that he did a little dance. But that sent the fish flying by accident, and it landed near Sakuragawa's feet. Chasing after it, he tumbled over, got confused and clung onto Sakuragawa's expensive-looking suit trousers.

Sakuragawa had been reading a magazine called *ApiA*. Keeping his eyes on the page, he bent down. Since he's tall, he has long arms too, and he easily caught Norimaki by the scruff of his neck.

BREAKFAST

Oh no! He's going to send him flying! But before I could think what to do, Sakuragawa put down his chopsticks, cupped his hand underneath my brother, and set him down on the seat cushion on Mr Dodo's chair. He gave Norimaki a little pat on the head.

"Don't run around like that when you eat. Calm down. You don't want to choke. Rice can easily go down the wrong way if you're not careful. A tiny tot's got to eat some veg and whitebait, too," he added, placing a broccoli head with whitebait sprinkles in front of Norimaki.

"When our Shinra was little," he went on, "gramps used to give her a bit of whitebait every day. Makes your cartilage strong, he said. They're tiny, but you eat the whole fish from head to tail, so there's a lot packed into them. Shinra loved broccoli, too. Go on, try it. It's good."

Norimaki's eyes went round, as if to say, "What's *this*?" He'd never seen it before. I'd tried both broccoli and dried whitebait at Auntie Meowko's, but not him.

"You can try it," I said, nudging him. He took one bite, and his face melted into a big smile. It looked like it hit the spot. With the second bite, he could taste how good it was even more, and he waved his front paws in the air in glee. Losing his balance, he plumped down on his bum and rolled backwards.

By then, Sakuragawa, and even Kagami, who usually has a poker face, were grinning. From that point on, they were going

EARLY SPRING

to have fun with my brother every time there was something new in season to feed him – I was sure of it. But Norimaki didn't seem to mind one bit, so I let him be. I sat next to him in Mr Dodo's seat and licked around my mouth.

Koyomi had come downstairs some time ago. We could hear her humming, so she was probably wandering around the kitchen or the corridor. Jean Paul told me she was humming an Italian pop song called "In Un Fiore". It used to be a favourite of Madame Hinako's – a big hit around the time she gave birth to Itsuki. She used to sing it for him as a lullaby (though it sounds to me like the kind of song that would wake you up).

Koyomi is Madame Hinako's daughter. It's not good manners to reveal a woman's age, so I'll just say she's Itsuki's younger sister and leave it at that.

Madame Hinako looks like a lush bouquet of flowers, like roses and peonies, even from fifty yards away, but Koyomi isn't like her, and she knows it. What's attractive about Koyomi is her frank, down-to-earth personality.

Like her mum, she has a keen sense of fun, and she draws playful pictures with splashes of colour. She's an illustrator. To sign her artwork, she draws the kanji character for her name (暦), only slightly skewed – and then, surprise! It looks just like her face.

Even though she's not related by blood to Mum Komaki,

BREAKFAST

they've been working together for a long time, and they get along well, too. Sometimes Koyomi illustrates the books that Mum translates. They're both big foodies, but neither has the time or the inclination to pick up a chef's knife.

Koyomi was in the kitchen, peering into the pot of chicken and burdock roots; she looked concerned about something. "Don't mess it up," Kagami called out from the small dining room, as if he could see through the wall. He could tell what she was up to just from the sounds she made.

When Kagami talks to Sakuragawa, who's close to him in age, he's all polite, but he's rude to his older half-sister. She doesn't mind at all, though. Apparently, when your brother is almost twenty years younger, nothing he says can bother you.

I get that, too – my baby brother's so little I never feel like getting mad at him.

"Such a tough choice," Koyomi said. "Should I forget about how fatty it is and eat the chicken *with* the skin to get a collagen boost? Or should I give up on the beauty perk and take a piece *without* the skin to drop the calories? It makes a big difference. And I just had anago sushi at a restaurant yesterday. Did you put in any sugar besides the apples?"

"No, the only sweetness comes from the apples," Kagami said bluntly. He wasn't grumpy or anything. He just doesn't try to be nice to people – that's the way he is. Even when he's in a good mood, he doesn't really show it. So far, the only times I've seen him laugh is when Norimaki does something silly.

Koyomi ladled some burdock roots and skinless chicken from the pot into her own bowl. She came over to the table and sat down next to Sakuragawa. Kagami, who was sitting across from him, glanced at her bowl.

"No apples?" he asked.

"I put on fat really quick from fruit sugar, so I'll pass for today. I won't be going out in the morning, and I don't have plans to do any exercise. I'll make up for it with broccoli, though."

"That's ridiculous. You should skip your three p.m. snack instead. Cookies and rice crackers and stuff like that don't give you anything but calories – at least apples thicken the soup and add a little bit of vitamin C. And before you start fretting about eating the chicken skin, you should know that you need vitamin C to produce collagen, and apples are rich in potassium, which helps your body flush out sodium. I didn't peel the apples, either, so you'll get polyphenol from it, too. That soup is healthy enough to drink up. It looks a bit dark, but I only used half a teaspoon of soy sauce. The colour comes from balsamic vinegar. The rest is just juice from the chicken and apples. That's why I set the table with deep bowls instead of plates. So that everyone can have it along with the soup and maximise their nutrient intake."

BREAKFAST

I don't know why, but Kagami got all worked up and rattled this off in one long breath. He might seem as calm as water, but if you pour water into a pot and light a fire underneath, it will always boil over eventually.

The bowl Kagami had picked out was shaped like a morning glory: a thin ceramic bowl with a pea green glaze. A pool of glaze in a different colour gleamed at the very bottom: a shade of burnt umber speckled with silver, like the bark of a sakura tree on a rainy day. You can tell he cares about colour palettes.

Koyomi wasn't interested in having an argument with her younger brother. "Are you mad at me? Did I say anything to upset you?" she asked.

After a pause, Kagami mumbled, "No, I'm not mad or anything."

"Really? That's alright, then. Thanks for telling me so much about the menu. Well, I'll dig in then. Itadakimasu."

She started eating, but she seemed distracted. Soon she put down her chopsticks and looked closely at Kagami across the table.

"Did Hikari write that?" she asked.

She was talking about the white lettering on his navy apron. He nodded. I don't know anything about calligraphy, but the letters looked neat, firm and crisp – not the impression you get from Dumpling Girl usually (who knew she had a talent like that?).

35

"She said she'd write me something for my birthday, so I gave her a request. I had it turned into a print block and dyed on my apron."

"That's your favourite poem?"

"I wouldn't say it's my top favourite. Words in a poem can cut into you wherever there's a kink, or a warp, so I just happened to be in the mood for it that day. That's all. It's a poem by Kenji Miyazawa – he wrote it in his mid-thirties, towards the end of his life, when he was developing fertiliser. That summer, the drought lasted for forty days. He ran around giving advice to the farmers about how to care for their rice and making enquiries at the weather station until he fell ill from fatigue."

"Hmm. I'll check out his poetry," Koyomi said.

"Here it is," Dumpling Girl piped up, holding out a book. (You can go straight into Kagami's room from the small dining room, and there's a fitted bookcase in the corridor in between. The books are mainly Kagami's, but they're mixed in with everyone else's.)

Koyomi opened the book right away. In the meantime, Jean Paul told me in a whisper about Mr Kenji and his work.

Mr Kenji was a famous writer who wrote a story called "The Cat Office". It's all about the Kamado Cat: that's what he's called, because he sleeps in the kamado furnace in the kitchen to get some warmth at night, and he's all sooty from the ashes. With his nose and ears blackened with soot, he looks like a tanuki – you know, a raccoon dog – so the other cats don't like him. His co-workers at the office are mean to him, and he gets so sad and sour, he can't even eat the bento box he brought for lunch.

He cries on and off for three whole hours after that. Poor Kamado Cat; poor bento.

In his poem "Having Suiton Soup at a Railway Stop", Mr Kenji talks about how he doesn't know what to do with the soup that his friend brings for him all the way to the railway stop, with suiton dumplings and scallops in it. He can't say he doesn't want it, so the bowl just sits in his hands.

He feels like he's eating fluffy lumps of clouds or something.

I thought about the soft scallop dumplings that Grandad makes just for us – I could keep eating those for ever. Norimaki called them "fluffies", and I picked up the habit from him. They're made with beaten egg whites. Grandad adds just a few drops of melted butter into the clear layer at the top of the soup. It smells so good I can hardly wait till it cools down – it really is a special treat.

But Mr Kenji can't eat the suiton dumplings that are as soft as a cloud. He's frustrated that he can't even make the rain fall for everyone who's been waiting for it; instead, all he can do is to stare at the clouds resentfully as they float across the sky, glowing white. That's why the cloud-like suiton weigh down on him, and he can't help thinking, "Just like I can't eat all the clouds in the sky, I can't eat your affection, either."

Mr Kenji's poems and stories are crowded with delicious meals, but the characters in them are always feeling too choked up to indulge in them.

Kagami left his seat and walked off to the kitchen.

"It's a fascinating psychology," Jean Paul remarked.

"Is Kagami feeling troubled because someone likes him?" I asked.

"Oh Chimaki, that's not it. The one offering the suiton soup is Kagami himself. He already knows how his friend will respond. But he still can't help making the suiton."

"For who?"

"If you can figure that out, you're all grown up already."

I didn't get it. I guess I've still got a long way to go.

After Kagami went to the kitchen, Koyomi thumped her elbow down on the magazine that Sakuragawa was reading.

"Hey," she said, "don't you know that it's considered a form of domestic violence not to show your appreciation for the food that your spouse has lovingly prepared, and it qualifies as grounds for divorce? Shouldn't you say a word of thanks, at least?"

BREAKFAST

Sakuragawa looked like he had no idea what she was on about. "But I'm single—"

"I'm talking about your position. You're sitting in the seat that's reserved for the head of the household, so you're expected to be attentive to the people who live here. Do you know whose fault it is that he's such a chatterbox this morning? He's anxious. He doesn't really show his feelings on his face, so it might be hard to tell, but he never talks that much – it's not normal for him."

"Well, Itsuki's just better at this sort of thing than me."

"Anyone can do it. As long as they remember how lucky they are to have a decent meal served up to them."

Sakuragawa listened for the voices coming from the kitchen. Dumpling Girl and Kagami were talking about her bento lunch. For the filling in the rice balls, she requested one with shrimps and broad beans, and another with scrambled eggs and dried whitebait, with plenty of broccoli on the side; she also asked him to tuck crispy chicken skin flavoured with lemon juice into the small gaps in between them.

"Back when we were in senior high . . ." Sakuragawa began, "I used to wait for Kagami on our way to school and grab his bento box. It was on the small side, but you wouldn't believe how good it was. Once you get a taste of it, you're hooked. I always thought that was his mum's cooking."

"What about your own bento?" Koyomi asked.

39

"Store-bought. I stopped buying them once I started stealing Kagami's, and used the money for something else. There's no shortage of stuff to buy when you're a high schooler."

"What a jerk. You've been making him cry since *that* long ago, huh?"

"Who, Kagami? Everyone gets him wrong – even you, his big sister. Have you ever seen that guy shed a tear? *I* haven't."

"So, you want to make him cry?"

"Sorry, I'm too old for that." With a silent laugh, Sakuragawa put down his chopsticks. He got up and took his dishes to the kitchen to wash up.

"Gochisosama – thanks. It was good," he said.

He sounded sincere. He might have been scanning the magazine the whole time, but he'd polished off everything; not even a grain of rice was left in his bowls. I'm not sure if Kagami was convinced, though.

Sakuragawa went straight from the kitchen to the front door. There's a guest toilet with a sink just off the entrance hall, where he could tidy himself up before leaving for work.

"You forgot something," Koyomi said, holding up the magazine he'd left on the table.

Kagami took it from her and hurried to the front door, calling out, "Senpai," as though Sakuragawa was still an older student – a habit from their time at junior and senior high. Norimaki and I trotted along behind him.

BREAKFAST

When he reached the entrance hall, Kagami stopped short, looking like a lost child. He was about to say something, but he swallowed back the words.

Sakuragawa came out from the toilet, put on his jacket and shrugged on his coat. The collars were trench-coat-style, but the coat had a slender shape overall, with a thin belt to match. More than anything, it was the colour that lent it style: a dark shade of Van Dyke brown, even though it was meant to be a spring coat.

"I don't need it," he said. "Could you throw it out?" He was talking about the magazine.

With a nod, Kagami rummaged in the pocket of his "suiton soup" apron and pulled out a stopwatch. "Next time, please spend five more minutes on mastication." He sounded like a manager on a sports team.

"Mastication?"

"The key to efficient fibre intake is how many times you chew your food."

It seemed like Kagami just couldn't stop talking today.

"Well, maybe you can negotiate with the bus company to add another stop closer to the house."

Sakuragawa takes the bus to work.

"You could always wake up earlier and walk."

"Or I could skip breakfast here and pop by some café instead."

41

EARLY SPRING

"Then you'd miss out on vegetables."

"I'll find a place with a salad bar."

Sakuragawa opened the front door. The wind was still chilly in the early spring morning. Norimaki shrank back. The frosty breath of the north blew right in.

"Would you . . . like to take a bento?" Kagami asked in a low voice.

"What did you say?"

"Only if you'd like." Kagami had followed Sakuragawa to offer him a bento lunch, but hesitated to bring it up because he noticed that Sakuragawa's business bag was slim and functional, clearly designed to carry only the essentials.

"I have a lunch meeting today," Sakuragawa said.

"So you won't need a bento. Have a good day, then," Kagami said, turning on his heel and starting down the corridor.

"I might ask for one tomorrow, though," Sakuragawa aimed at Kagami's back as he slipped out the front door. When Kagami glanced over his shoulder, the door closed with a light thump, and all we could hear were Sakuragawa's footsteps fading away.

Soon Dumpling Girl was at the back door, calling out, "See you guys later!" She takes the same bus as Sakuragawa from the exact same stop, but the next-door neighbour lets her take a shortcut through their garden.

BREAKFAST

Norimaki and I thought of following her out and seeing her off, but Koyomi held us back. "Not so fast," she said. "There's a bear out there. He's not scary, but you don't want him coming over and throwing his weight around. Norimaki would get squashed like a flat seaweed roll. His owner, Mr Maruko, keeps feeding him fatty meats, so he just gets bigger and bigger."

That got me wondering what the bear looked like, so I climbed up on the kitchen sink and peered out the window. I saw our chunky neighbour lolling around in the shade of the bordering hedge.

Norimaki clambered up on the teapot next to me. The bright patch of sun by the window made him squeeze his eyes shut and wiggle his nose.

Achoo!

His sneeze sent him tumbling into the teapot again.

2

Spring

Lunch

*Dry curry with spring vegetables
& brown rice with black soybeans
Mushroom pickles
Soya milk chicken soup
Or spring sandwiches with soft scrambled eggs
and plenty of watercress*

Mum Komaki is writing her Komakoma Diary column at the table in the small dining room. Norimaki is by her feet, tossing around his fluffy knit toy. We call it Squid, but it looks more like a monster. Mum came up with the name because it's black all over like it's covered in squid ink.

I wasn't there when Mum and Grandad gave him the toy. So I haven't seen what it was supposed to look like. By the time I saw it for the first time, the damage was done – or, as Norimaki likes to say, it had been "transformed".

Who knows what happened to it? Did it grow hair and feathers, or did it lose them? Did it spew out black ink, or blow out bubbles? Was it all of the above, or was it something else entirely? Anyhow, it turned into a mystery blob: a tangle of black yarn that could be anything from a dog, a bear or a frog to a vampire bat.

SPRING

The stuffing in Squid is uneven, so when you bounce it around, you never know where it'll end up. And Norimaki goes bouncing after it.

Sooner or later, his claws get caught in the loose yarn, and he goes into a panic, thinking it bit him. He opens his mouth in a big triangle and calls for help. Though I did already teach him that plushies aren't alive.

In Komakoma Diary, Mum writes about flowers and plants in the garden, yummy food, and anything else that pops into her head. Sometimes she shares, word for word, a question that Dumpling Girl asked, like this one:

"When you open a tin of corned beef, you use the little tool that comes with it, but does that tool have a name?"

Actually, I'd been wondering the same thing. You hook the slot in the tool onto the thing that sticks out on the side of the tin, roll it all around until the tin splits in two, and finally, you get at the beef. I've never seen that tool anywhere else – only on corned beef. The tins our crunchies come in are different, with lids that open up.

Mum didn't know what it was called, either. When she checked on the manufacturer's website, they said it's a "key".

"You learn something new every day," she said to Dumpling Girl. "Here's another bit of trivia while I'm at it. Did you know it's supposed to be '*corned* beef', not 'corn beef'?"

LUNCH

"How do you spell that?" Dumpling Girl asked, pulling out her "Mamemon" notebook.

"C-O-R-N-E-D. Same as corn on the cob."

"Why? Corn and beef have nothing to do with each other."

"Oh, but they do."

Hang on – before we go on, let me explain what this "Mamemon" notebook is all about. It's a collection of little curiosities and questions – or "gimon" in Japanese – that Dumpling Girl comes across. The pun doesn't stop there: if you write "Mamemon" in the Roman alphabet, you'll see that there's "ma" (French for "my") and "mémo" hidden in there.

At Dumpling Girl's school, all the students carry around whichever small notebook they prefer especially for jotting down their "Mamemon": that is, those little questions and discoveries from their daily lives. On *her* notebook, she's written "Mamemon" in big brush strokes, using the kanji characters for "bean" (mame) and "ask" (mon). It's so she remembers to ask lots of questions even about the tiniest things, she says.

Anyway, back to corned beef.

"At first, *corn* was a noun for something in the shape of a grain, so the grains of salt crystals are also a kind of corn," Mum went on. "*Corned* means that the meat was cured in grains of salt to preserve it. So, we should be calling it 'corned beef', but some people say 'corn beef', and in Japan, they pronounce it even shorter, like 'conbeef'. I like salt-cured

SPRING

pork better than beef, though. It's perfect for kakuni: you desalt it, dice it and braise it until it's soft and succulent. Kagami's kakuni is delicious with sake – a match made in heaven. Melts in your mouth like a first-rate fondant made by a chocolatier."

Dumpling Girl had been jotting things down in her bold handwriting, but now she looked up, furrowing her brow. That's the face she makes when she disagrees with something.

"Kagami always says soft foods are more fatty and sugary," she said. "So if you only eat soft stuff, it's bad for you. A healthy diet means having a good balance of different colours, shapes and flavours, and including a mix of hard and soft foods in your meals."

I get it: "A perfect blend of cruchy and moist." That's the phrase from an advert for posh meow-food. I'm happy with the normal kind, but I prefer to steer clear of the junky ones that are too heavy on the seasoning.

After Norimaki and I got separated from Mademoiselle Rocco, and we were wandering around by ourselves, we stayed for just one night at a bookstore off the national highway. The tabby who got his meals in the shop's office invited us in. His name was Nozaki, but no-one knew how he got his name, not even Nozaki himself.

Nozaki always ate crunchy meow-food with flaked corned beef on top. A blend of hard and soft.

LUNCH

The manager of the bookstore was a big fan of corned beef, so the cans were stacked high on the shelves in the office. Taking a closer look, I noticed not all of them had a picture of a cow on the label; a few had horses. The manager would briskly chop up some cabbage, stir-fry it with the meat, and eat it with a bowl of white rice. There was a trick to this stir-fry: if you poured in some soup instead of oil, the cabbage got softer, and the corned beef wouldn't burn.

Nozaki got the beef bits without the cabbage along with his crunchies. "Have as much as you want – don't be shy," he told us, but it was so salty we could barely get through a bite.

It's a nice day today – the sun's been out since the morning. It rises earlier now, between four and five a.m.

Kagami went to buy some fresh harvest from the Seishiro Farm near our house; they sell their vegetables direct to customers. Norimaki and I got to ride along in the front basket of his bike. Seishiro's parents own the farm now, but he'll inherit it when the time comes. He has a stringy beard around his jawline. It looks just like the moss that grows in the garage at Mum's house.

This morning, their harvest included leafy greens with the dirt still on, green tomatoes, ripe red tomatoes and bell peppers with traffic light colours, red, yellow and green. I heard Seishiro's family have been farmers ever since the Edo

SPRING

period. Besides growing vegetables, they have an orchard with kiwi vines and blueberry bushes.

When Kagami got back to the house and brought in his groceries, he gazed thoughtfully at the thermometer in the kitchen. Since it's getting warmer these past few days, he was wondering how best to store the fresh produce.

The leafy greens don't last long, so he'll probably blanch them in the course of the day and turn them into either ohitashi (with soy sauce and dashi dressing) or goma-ae (with ground sesame). Mum and Dumpling Girl like spicy ohitashi with a spot of mustard, and Koyomi likes the gentle sweetness of black sesame dressing, so I'm guessing he'll make both kinds, half and half.

For breakfast, Kagami cooked some chicken mince for Norimaki and me. He lowered the heat just before the chicken got too hard and crumbly, and stir-fried the fresh leaves until they softened in the fat that seeped out. The leaves he bought today had some yellow flower buds mixed in – rapeseed blossoms, maybe – and I liked the hint of bitterness they gave off.

Dumpling Girl grows edible dandelions on the veranda outside her room, as if she were some Parisienne. I don't get what's so special about them, but Norimaki loves her dandelion leaves in his salad. The dandelion salad is usually topped with hard-boiled eggs —separated into whites and yolks, pushed through a strainer, and sprinkled over the leaves. But one time Kagami put on a poached egg instead, and Norimaki did a little happy dance with a yellow moustache around his mouth.

Kagami doesn't really trust the fridge. It's pretty empty most of the time, and he mainly stores flour, sugar and grains in there. Though it's problematic that veggies go bad, he says it's just the course of nature for them to wilt over time. He thinks it's weird to expect vegetables and eggs to stay fresh for so long. It's only natural that the salad leaves you pick in the morning are limp by the evening.

Most vegetables will last for a while at room temperature if he wraps them up in newspapers without washing off the dirt and puts them away in a corner of the cupboard under the stairs. Eggs and apples, he buries them in rice chaff (in separate boxes, of course). Norimaki sometimes falls in and gets smothered in the chaff.

Kagami took half the peppers and tomatoes that he bought this morning and washed them in a big rain barrel outside. Then he wiped them dry and chopped them into one-inch squares. Next, he put them in a hanging net and dried them in the sun. His drying net is a vertical tube of netting with three mesh shelves inside it, each one about

SPRING

twelve inches in diameter; it has a handle at the top so you can hang it up.

He laid a piece of gauze on each shelf and placed the cut vegetables in neat rows. The blue tomatoes are for pickles, which means they only need to be dried whole for a short time, so he put them where they'll be easier to take out. When everything was ready, he hung the net where it would get plenty of sun, this time from a branch of the paperbush tree, which was past its flowering season now.

When this tree was in full bloom, the round heads of flowers looked just like paper wasps' nests. You wouldn't be able to tell them apart if you just looked at the shadows on the ground. Every time I passed by, I'd be on edge, looking out for black-helmet stingers swarming out to attack me.

Now, the drying net is swaying in the breeze. Norimaki has a wistful look on his face, like he wants to lie inside the net himself. But Kagami told him never to jump on it or swing from it, so he stays put like a good boy.

Kagami hangs up a gardener's shade cloth to give Norimaki something else to play with. Norimaki springs at it and swings back and forth. When he gets tangled up and yowls for help, Kagami frees him and gently tucks him into his apron pocket to calm him down.

Since Kagami's looking after Norimaki, I can take it easy. While they're doing their thing, I sit on the table next to

Mum, who's working on her manuscript, and I get on with my studies, too.

You might think it's a pity to hang a fresh harvest to dry instead of eating it right away, but vegetables get tastier when they lie around outside on a sunny day, just like we feel more cheerful when we've soaked in the sun. Grandad says you can get a rich dashi if you soak dried shiitake mushrooms in water, but with fresh shiitake, it's not quite the same: you can enjoy their nice scent, but you don't get as much flavour in the water.

Norimaki and I don't know the ins and outs of dashi flavours. But if dashi just means tasty water, most of the time we like any kind of water that's at room temperature.

At Mum's house, they collect rainwater in an old big barrel that a distillery was selling off. They've attached a tap to the side of the barrel, and underneath there's a ceramic basin, which Koyomi made herself, to catch the water. This tap is different from the ones inside the house; there's always a bit of water dripping from it, leaving a shallow pool in the basin.

Right now, the basin is dappled with light falling through the branches of the sakura tree, which are sprouting young leaves. But a little while ago, it was in full view of the sun, and the water was the perfect warmth for us. We gulped it down, and Norimaki's belly swelled like a peanut shell.

SPRING

When Mum came downstairs after everyone finished their breakfast, she saw Norimaki's belly as he was romping about and said, "Oh, someone was hungry," but it was actually all water sloshing around in there.

The rain barrel, which used to hold whiskey, is stippled with insect holes that are impossible to cover up. The hoops of the barrel are kind of loose, too. So it's not a watertight barrel; water keeps seeping out, and it's always damp on the brick base underneath.

Since that corner of the garden gets a lot of sun in the morning, Kagami placed a watercress seedling tray there at the beginning of spring. Now the watercress is starting to grow.

Mum picked some of the leaves, saying, "Let's have something nice for brunch."

Kagami had already made soft scrambled eggs at Mum's request and gone out. He's only responsible for breakfasts and dinners as the Horais' cook. Everyone takes care of their own lunches, so he can spend the afternoons however he likes.

There's a whiteboard in the corridor where everybody writes down their plans and whereabouts; for this afternoon, Kagami has written, "At Sacchan's → shopping." So he must be at Sacchan's or doing some shopping right about now.

When Sacchan came over the other day, Kagami introduced him to Norimaki and me as his "girlfriend". There's one thing I don't get, though. They used to be classmates – they went to the same schools, all the way through from elementary to senior high – but I know Kagami went to an all-boys school. So I'm not sure how Sacchan, who went to the same school as him, can be a *girl*friend.

But there's nothing mysterious about Sacchan himself; he's a nice person who brings a new knit toy for Norimaki every time he comes to visit. He's the one who brought Squid. He makes them all himself, actually; he's good with his hands. He specialises in designing electronic components, so he's got to be.

Sacchan likes Liberty prints, and he wears shirts that he also made himself, complete with handmade accessories. The little accessories are either attached to the clothes, or hidden somewhere that's not obvious, like in pockets and linings.

Most of the time, he dresses like Kagami: a simple jumper, for example, with run-of-the-mill jeans or slacks. So he looks like a boy, at least from the outside (though I don't know if a college graduate in his twenties who's already working can be called a "boy").

It's the fourth Saturday of April today. Dumpling Girl's at school. Instead of regular classes, she has a "Mamemon Meeting". At her school, there's a show-and-tell gathering once a month when everyone shares their Mamemon discoveries.

SPRING

When a student gives a presentation, holding up a photo, about how "there are two types of Chinese spiranthes: one with flowers that spiral clockwise, another that go counter-clockwise," the other kids ask, "What about snails?" and "What about conch shells?" And they scribble down those new questions in their own Mamemon notebooks to look into later.

The meeting finishes before noon, so she'll come home for lunch. Her dad Itsuki is back in Tokyo for the first time in a while, so Dumpling Girl is planning to cook something herself.

Itsuki works in the administrative office at a university in Kyoto. He was supposed to come back to Tokyo during the spring vacation, but he had to postpone it for various reasons. To make up for it, he took a slightly earlier and longer break ahead of the string of national holidays.

Since he couldn't come home for the parent–teacher meeting in March, Sakuragawa – Dumpling Girl's uncle – went in his place.

I overheard Mum Komaki filling Itsuki in on how the meeting had gone over the phone. A classmate who didn't know much about the Horai family had caught a glimpse of Sakuragawa and said to Dumpling Girl in surprise, "Your papa's so young." Dumpling Girl had replied, "I was born when my dad was studying abroad at sixteen. That sort of thing is pretty normal in France, you know."

LUNCH

According to Mum, Dumpling Girl really was born in a hospital in Paris. But they came back to Japan when she was a baby, so it's still silly how she prances around acting like a Parisienne.

Before she left for school, Dumpling Girl brought out a chair with a little side table attached to it to sit near Kagami in the kitchen. She wanted to pick his brains while having her breakfast – about the menu for the lunch that she was going to prepare for her dad.

She was drinking a mug of broccoli smoothie mixed with soya milk and maple syrup while nibbling on a piece of rye bread topped with a thin crêpe-like omelette and cucumbers.

"Don't you think dad's starting to get a bit flabby around his stomach? I want to come up with a healthy menu for him – but something that's easy enough for me to make. Is that too much to ask?" she asked.

Eventually, they settled on dry curry with spring vegetables. It would be showtime for the fresh tomatoes and peppers that Kagami got from Seishiro this morning. She would serve it with plenty of pickles and soya milk chicken soup on the side.

I'll copy down exactly what Kagami told Dumpling Girl: instead of using store-bought curry roux, which are solidified with oil, you can make dry curry with curry powder, salt and

SPRING

honey, so it'll only have a third of the calories of the curry that people usually make at home in Japan. If you look at the roux from the stores – the blocks of sauce base that you melt in the pot – they're actually about fifty per cent oil (!).

Sun-dried vegetables are good to eat as they are: no need to blanch or boil them. And you don't lose the vitamins that dissolve in the boiling water. Just broil the dried slices a little, and this tasty juice comes oozing out. Stuff them into pitta bread before the juice drips down, and you're all set.

Sun-drying vegetables and salt-curing meat are nuggets of wisdom from the old days when people didn't have gas or electricity and had to be frugal with their fuel.

If you pick more mushrooms and wild plants than you can eat in one sitting, you can lay them out in the sun until they're completely dry, and they'll keep for several days. Dry some slices of daikon or mountain yam in the morning, and they'll be nice and soft by dinnertime, so you don't even have to cook them. Kagami says if you mix dried burdock root, carrots and mushrooms straight into rice and cook the rice just like that, you'll get such a deep flavour, as if it was seasoned. One thing you'd better cook before eating, though, is kanpyo, those strips of dried gourd.

The tomatoes and peppers that Kagami put in the hanging net earlier this morning will be just dry and soft enough by the time Dumpling Girl comes back from school for lunch.

LUNCH

The sun will bring out the umami, the rich savoury taste, of the pure vegetables themselves. They'll get a bit wrinkled, but they'll be mixed with curry powder, so no problem.

"The curry will be so good they won't believe you made it, Hikari," Kagami promised her.

I hear a rumble in the distance. I can picture the bus with the red line running across its body making its way up the gentle slope and coming to a halt at the bus stop. I bet Dumpling Girl will be home soon, coming in through the back door after taking the short cut through the neighbour's garden. A perk of being a kid, I guess.

Though she likes to pretend she's a Parisienne, she doesn't mind being treated like a kid when it comes to taking the short cut. She races under the sakura trees in the next-door garden, swinging a tote bag for her gym clothes in one hand, and a school-specified bag carrying tools for her hands-on lessons in the other.

The Horai house's back door doesn't lead into the kitchen but the linen room next to it. Besides the laundry and drying machines, there's an ironing board and a desk with a sewing machine. You could call it a utility room. Like I said, this house was built to be rented out to people from abroad, so that's why it's designed like this.

Norimaki and I leaped onto the sewing desk to spy on the

SPRING

neighbour's garden from the window. (Since Norimaki is still too small to reach the desk with one jump, he aimed for the treadle first, then the chair, and finally the sewing machine itself.)

Our plan was to go and meet Dumpling Girl if our neighbour, the Bear, wasn't lolling around on the hedge like he usually is. (He looks like a middle-aged uncle with his potbelly, but he's actually quite young.)

But, too bad, Uncle Bear was stretched out like a seal, belly up. (Waiting for Miss Koharu, who lives two doors down from us, to pass by.)

Mr Maruko and his wife – Uncle Bear's parents, that is – live in the house next door. Mr Maruko loves nothing better than a ripe, fatty tuna or a finely marbled sirloin steak that melts on his tongue like butter. He's not the stingy type, so he happily shares food like that with Uncle Bear.

He's the polar opposite of my grandad, who thinks *real* meat has got to be sinewy and rock-hard: the kind that makes you clench your teeth in a wide grin when you chew off a piece. (I'm with Grandad on this one, but Mum tells him to go easy on the meat because he's not as young as he used to be.)

With tuna, too, Grandad prefers the sinewy red cuts. He says the finest way to have tuna sashimi is to arrange the bright red slices on a dish of ocean-deep indigo. Still, he can't resist those soft, melty foods like paradise tofu, either.

LUNCH

Mr Maruko went to the same elementary school as Koyomi; they were even in the same year. But now, with his flabby bulk and broad shoulders, he looks a lot older than her. Well, not that Koyomi dresses her age – sometimes she braids her hair and wears a denim pinafore dress.

Dumpling Girl is coming. I can see her in her spring uniform: she used to wear a navy felt hat when it was cold, but now that the new term has begun, she's switched to a violet cotton one. She hasn't changed her skirt yet, so she's wearing the winter navy one, but her knee-high socks are the same violet shade as her hat. When I had a look this morning, the school emblems embroidered on this new pair of socks still looked like proper pimpernel flowers, not skulls.

Mum finished writing two instalments of her Komakoma Diary earlier today. She had a good chat with Tekona, who came to pick up the manuscripts, then they headed out to the art museum on their bicycles.

Mum's bike is the sporty type, and Tekona's is a mamachari, a plain city bike with a front basket. Tekona has two daughters: nine-year-old Hako and six-year-old Kokona. Kokona, who was small enough to ride in the back seat of her mum's bike only a little while ago, started elementary school this spring.

When Kokona comes to the Horai house, she squeezes Norimaki and me in a bear hug, so I was relieved she wasn't

SPRING

with her mum today. I know she doesn't mean any harm, but she almost chokes us.

The title of the free magazine that Tekona runs is *Maman tekona*. Mum says it reminds her of the legendary woman named Mama no Tekona, whom poets sung about in the ancient *Man'yoshu* – that is, the "Collection of Ten Thousand Leaves", the oldest surviving treasury of Japanese waka poetry. This Mama no Tekona was too popular with men, and she killed herself because of it, so it's an unlucky title, according to Mum. Tekona brushed her off, saying, "I have my own darling already, so I'll be fine!"

"How about changing 'Maman' to 'Okan' at least?" Mum suggested. ("Okan" is another way of saying mum – it suits the middle-aged, gutsy type.)

"Non, merci!" Tekona said with a laugh.

For the next issue, she'll put Norimaki and me on the cover. So her "darling" (a photographer) came for a photo shoot.

I wanted to look classy in the pictures, but Beeper (she's actually called Lumina, but we decided to call her Beeper), who was perched on Tekona's shoulder, started making sounds like a fire alarm, a trick she's picked up recently. Norimaki and I arched our backs in surprise, and Darling took a snap right there.

Beeper has a pretty coat of feathers in cherry pink and

orange, and a sweet round face with cute button eyes. But if you look closely, you can tell that she's a wily one, and you can't let your guard down around her. Both her beak and talons are always sharp, ready for action. She's a peach-faced lovebird: a noisy, stubborn one who does as she pleases.

Mum's column today was about her watercress brunch. She read it out loud for me:

When water starts to warm, and the watercress grows thick and green on the water's edge in the garden, I get a sudden craving to eat an egg sandwich. Whip up some soft scrambled eggs (it's got to be melty and creamy), nudge it onto a piece of toast, and add plenty of watercress, blanched and dipped in dashi soup, on the egg. Put another piece of toast on top, then slice the sandwich in half.

The sweetness of the egg and the bitterness of the watercress mingle together to make pure bliss. A gift from spring, I think, as I munch on the sandwich. Using rapeseed flowers would feel even more like springtime, I suppose, but we have a lot of watercress in the garden – so watercress it is.

Jean Paul, who was lounging on Mr Dodo's chair, with Norimaki napping on his lap, let out a chuckle. "Really, I do wonder how old Komaki thinks she is. She talks just like she used to when she was a young girl."

When Kagami makes iritamago, or soft scrambled eggs,

SPRING

it's perfectly dreamy. It would pass as an omelette, too. His secret for getting that softness is to crack one extra egg to whip up the white into a meringue separately, then mixing the frothy egg white into the rest of the beaten eggs. The leftover egg yolk can be used in all kinds of ways. A quick and easy one is to make a batch of sweet dengaku miso, and slip in the yolk when it's still hot. The yolk gives the paste a nice colour and gleam, and adds depth to the flavour, too.

Then you can broil some awafu – chewy dough made from wheat gluten with millet grains mixed in to add texture – drizzle the homemade dengaku miso over the awafu, and serve with a small sprig of sansho pepper leaves. It's a classic item in the bento boxes at Matsu Sushi, and the recipe for the miso is a family secret. Kagami picked it up directly from Grandad. A tasty alternative is sandwiching salt-grilled anago eel with slices of awafu, coating it with the miso, then grilling it all together: another recipe from Grandad.

Norimaki and I aren't allowed to eat miso because it's too salty, so they just give us the anago. The saltwater eel, when it's in season, is plump and sweet, and it melts away in your mouth . . . Now that's what I call heaven.

Sometimes the leftover egg yolk gets turned into meow-food. Kagami stir-fries some mince chicken and mixes in the yolk; then he pours in some dashi soup and steams it until it's soft and fluffy. Even though it doesn't have any extra

LUNCH

seasoning, the sweetness from the egg and the rich umami from the chicken meat blend together, and one bite makes me so happy, I don't know how to describe it. I *love* listening to the juicy fat sizzling in the pan, too.

But Kagami wipes away the fat with a kitchen towel first before mixing in the yolk. He says if he doesn't do that, it will end up too high in calories for Norimaki and me. We don't need that much energy until we're old enough to go chasing after girls (I wonder when that will be?).

After looking over Mum's manuscript, Tekona said, "Whenever I make scrambled eggs, it gets hard and crumbly before I know it. It'll be nice if you could add a tip on how to get it so soft."

Mum looked a bit uneasy. Though she translates French cookbooks and books about handicrafts for work, she actually doesn't make her own scrambled eggs, let alone fine-tune the texture – but even her friend Tekona hasn't caught on to that, apparently.

All Mum does is wait with a slice of toast in one hand and pop on the beautiful eggs that Kagami cooks with perfect timing. When she has a go at cooking eggs herself, she doesn't have a special method of making it soft. Sometimes it happens by pure chance, though.

Tekona is from Nagano Prefecture, and she told Mum about what happens when she visits her parents' house.

SPRING

"You wouldn't believe how sweet my mum has her eggs, whether it's scrambled or rolled into a tamagoyaki. She puts in a little bit of milk and a big dollop of honey. There's a lot of beekeepers around my hometown, so they put honey in everything. Bee larva is an expensive delicacy, so they're more for special occasions – but honey is another story. Her egg dishes taste just as sweet as I remember them from my schooldays. She cooks up a storm with soba noodles too, every time I go back home. She says it's nothing like the soba in Tokyo that's been boiled in stale city water. The idea of calories doesn't even cross her mind."

Tekona is slim right now, but she doesn't want to put on weight in her forties like her mum did.

Mum Komaki told her that if she's that bothered, she could try cutting back on her drinking. It sounds like Tekona really enjoys her liquor.

When people come to the house to discuss projects with Mum, they always seem to be under the impression that she's some kind of domestic goddess, who takes care of all the small chores around the house alongside her translation work and then writes about them in her Komakoma Diary. She's good at putting on an act like that, so she hoodwinks everyone.

The books that Mum has translated line the bookshelves

LUNCH

in the corridor between the small dining room and Kagami's room. They have approachable titles like *Crafting at Home in France*, or *A Little Corner of Paris*, or *French Girls' Training in the Kitchen*.

Anyone who picks up one of these books is bound to think that translator is an expert on household chores, just like the author. Well, whaddaya know (that's what Grandad would say): Mum is no better at cooking or sewing than Dumpling Girl. She's good at using tools like pliers and hammers, though.

She's already written up the next week's instalment of Komakoma Diary, too:

When I see those heads of tsukushi, field horsetails, shooting up in the grass, I can't resist picking them. They're so easy to pluck, so before I know it, my hands are full with big bundles of stalks.

Back when I was little, I would fill up my hat with tsukushi shoots and bring it to my mother. She'd say, "You don't even like them that much," but she'd still boil the lot for me. She was right, though – I didn't like them if they were cooked in the ohitashi style, steeped only in dashi, soy sauce and mirin. It left a pungent bitterness in my mouth.

I preferred having them simmered in dashi, with beaten eggs poured in. When the eggs are half-cooked, you arrange the tsukushi in a flat pile on a thick but lightweight plate – something with a Nordic pattern, a loose drawing of birds and

SPRING

leaves, say – and gently place a scoop of egg on top, slow and steady so the egg won't fall apart. Voilà.

After that, she wrote about the cross-shaped purple blossoms of the night-scented gilliflower, and how she found a dead-nettle with white blossoms instead of the usual pink ones. She handed over this manuscript to Tekona, too.

Dumpling Girl came back from school. She got changed in her room upstairs and came down to the kitchen in an apron that looked like something from *Alice in Wonderland*. Lunch was planned for one p.m. She was already hungry, so she was thinking of stealing a bite or two of the sweets that Kagami had baked last night.

He had prepared about five thin sheets of dough, buttered them up, spread a layer of nuts between each of them, and popped them in the oven. They were cut into lozenge shapes, and each one was quite small. Just as Dumpling Girl was brewing apple tea for herself, Koyomi came in.

"Weren't you going to make lunch for your parents today?" Koyomi asked.

"Yeah, it'll be at one."

"But you're having sweets now?"

"Well, school made me hungry."

"Sure, but that looks like too much to me. Let me guess – you're telling yourself it's okay to eat one before lunch because it's a good source of protein with a nice balance of iron and fat, and it's a small piece? Like a logical French girl would say?"

Dumpling Girl nodded eagerly. "Can't I?"

"Baklava is the sweetest treat you can find. If you go back to its origins, it used to be an emergency ration for nomads in the desert. It's not the sort of thing to eat when you're feeling a bit peckish – it's designed so that you can stave off your hunger with only a small piece. A lifeline until you reach the next oasis. It's made with a whole lot of butter and honey, and nuts are practically made of fat, so it packs quite a punch. I mean, plants produce fruit to leave as much wealth as they can for their offspring, so it stands to reason."

"Bak-what?"

"Baklava. It's a classical kind of pie. You stretch out thin layers of dough, brush them with butter, cover each layer with chopped nuts and bake it. According to one theory, the pharaohs used to eat them in ancient Egypt. For Turkish baklava, I've heard it's common to use pistachios and a certain kind of butter made from the milk of sheep that fed on thyme. Though I don't know the exact recipe – you'll have to ask Kagami."

Dumpling Girl pulled out her Mamemon notebook and jotted this down. Talking about the thyme-eating sheep seemed to have reminded Koyomi of something; she started singing a slow song, murmuring "parsley, sage, rosemary and thyme" in a low voice.

SPRING

The doorbell rang, and Koyomi left off her singing to answer the door. Norimaki and I tagged along.

"Hi, Kahoru! Come on in. You're the first one today. Itsuki's not here yet."

A woman we'd never seen before stepped inside. She had shiny black hair that hung down just below her shoulders. The tips of her hair weren't straight if you peered closely, but when you stepped back and looked at it as a whole, they looked neat, like the needle leaves of a conifer.

She was stylish in her silvergrey blouse and smart trousers. She waved at Dumpling Girl, who had just finished writing in her notebook and looked up.

"Haven't seen you in a while, Hikaboo," Kahoru said. "How've you been?"

"Excellent. And you, Kahorun?"

"So-so, I guess. Sorry I couldn't come to the parent–teacher meeting the other day. I was on a business trip, and it was so out of the way. I was at a mansion whose owner died, and I had to stay there overnight to value their art collection."

"Don't worry. Sakuragawa came with me, so it was fine." Dumpling Girl calls her uncle Sakuragawa, just like I do. (Well, I'm the one mimicking her, actually.)

"Did you behave?" Kahoru asked.

"Which one of us?"

"Your fake papa, of course."

LUNCH

"Well, you know what the younger teachers at our school are like: they're the type to wear woollen tights in moss green or old rose or something, even when it's already the beginning of spring, and they bustle around in loafers that look like a pair of dachshunds. There's no-one for him to flirt with."

"In some cases, ladies like that are within Tohoru's range too, you know. The customers he attends to are the same, once they shrug off their fur coat and wipe off their make-up. Just a bit more plump – that's the only difference, really."

"Schoolgirls are out of the question, right?"

"That's the only way he doesn't swing. He's wholesome in that sense."

Jean Paul whispered something that was a big surprise to me. This woman named Kahoru is actually Sakuragawa's older sister; she's Itsuki's partner and Dumpling Girl's real mum.

Both Kahoru and Tohoru work at an art dealer firm that their mother, Mrs Meowko (I haven't met her yet, so I don't know her real name) inherited from her parents. But it's not like they're trying to keep the business in the family; anyone can get promoted based on their performance.

Kahoru is in charge of making purchases overseas, so she's often away on business trips, even when she's back in Japan. Tohoru's departments are online sales and customer management.

You might be wondering why Kahoru doesn't live in this

SPRING

house with Dumpling Girl. For one thing, she and Itsuki aren't actually married ; not only do they go by different surnames, they've actually never lived together. Since she flies around Europe and North America a lot of the time for work, she's based in Paris.

The real reason why the couple lives like that – Jean Paul says, "It's ridiculous, but also reasonable, depending on the way you look at it' – is this: Kahoru was born in the year of the fire horse. (Apparently, there's a superstition that a fire horse woman will end up killing her husband.)

Most people wouldn't take it seriously. You wouldn't expect someone like Kahoru to think twice about it, either – she just seems so progressive, flying around the world and negotiating deals with international collectors – but she's stuck to her belief that she should never live with Itsuki in a legal marriage, despite his attempts to persuade her otherwise. Well, I guess that goes to show how much she cares about him.

Dumpling Girl seems to be having fun with her family situation, calling her mum by a nickname and all. She's friends with Mum Komaki, and her room is right next to Koyomi's, who's like a big sister to her. She gets along well with Kagami, too.

"Who are these little guys? Are they newbies in the house?" Kahoru asked.

"Yup," Dumpling Girl said. "The white one's Datemaki because he has a yellowish swirl on his belly, and it looks like a fish-cake omelette. The tiny one's Norimaki. They're brothers."

Hey! That's not my name! I wanted to say.

I went up to Kahoru and introduced myself: "Hello, I'm Chimaki. Nice to meet you." My brother said, "I'm Norimaki," and gave a little bow. Though I suppose it must've sounded like "*Miaowmnya*" to Kahoru.

"Oh, clever boys," Kahoru said. "I hope you'll come over to my parents' place sometime. We have a gorgeous cat named Shinra (she's a grandma now), and three brothers: Chikuwa, Hanpen and Uzura. We call them the Oden trio, though, since they're named after those fish cakes and quail eggs that go in the hotpot."

After that, Dumpling Girl finally got started on her cooking. First, she brought in the vegetables that Kagami put out to dry in the morning. He'd already chopped the amount she would use in bite-size pieces before drying them, so they were ready to go.

She combined these with slices of the Jonathan apple that Kagami had dried in winter. Enough moisture had gone out of them to leave them the perfect level of softness.

Dried vegetables are quick to cook, so there's no need to stir-fry them for long. That's how you keep their natural umami. The brown rice with black soybeans was already in

SPRING

the rice cooker; Kagami had set the timer so that it would be ready right on time for lunch. So all that remained was to chop the garlic and the dried king oyster mushrooms, and stir-fry them all together with mince meat. Even with a fifth-grader taking the reins, it would be a decent meal.

Dumpling Girl is too short to see over the counter, so she got on a footstool to reach the chopping board. Norimaki and I decided to watch her hard at work.

When the meat started sizzling, and the sweet aroma wafted through the kitchen, it was the most mouth-watering, tantalising thing. The juice burst out and hissed in the pan, tickling my ears. Not that I was actually hungry. I'd had a big breakfast.

She cut down on the amount of meat for Itsuki's sake, and instead added finely chopped eringi mushrooms to make it just as filling.

"Sorry, but it's no use asking – you won't get any," she told us. "There's garlic and chilli pepper in here. And I'm about to put in some raisins and dried berries steeped in white wine. Kagami said Makimaki shouldn't eat stuff like that."

When she's talking to the two of us together, that's what Dumpling Girl calls us: Makimaki.

There are lots of things we're not allowed to eat. Kagami made two kinds of stickers – one black and another with a skull on a red background – and stuck them on the danger

LUNCH

zones, so it would be easy for Norimaki to see what to avoid. He put them on cans of cocoa and tea, too.

The thing that gives onions and garlic their unique smell thins the blood and helps prevent clotting in human blood vessels. It's great for older people, like Mum and especially Grandad. But if Norimaki and I eat it, it damages what makes up our blood – like poison!

I didn't know the details back then, but Mademoiselle Rocco did teach me that I shouldn't eat onions or garlic. I love the sweet smell of stir-fried or grilled onions, but they're bad for us. Same goes for garlic chives, onion chives and a kind of wild plant called long-stamen onion.

Mademoiselle Rocco didn't eat vegetables like that, either. She said the smell would seep into her skin, so as a stage performer, she had to avoid it. Rocco's speciality was menchi-katsu – deep-fried mince meat patties. Other than the crispy panko breading, it was made of pure mince beef and nothing else.

She would wake up around noon on her day off and roll a bunch of patties about the size of a ping-pong ball, piling them up in a mountain on a large plate. She'd tuck into them while they were sizzling hot, without even dipping them in sauce or mustard, and gobble down about five in a row. The pure umami of the meat was all the flavour she needed for hot menchi-katsu, she used to say.

SPRING

At night, when they'd cooled down, she'd have the rest with mustard soy sauce with a spot of vinegar. Rocco was skinny, but her stomach was a fighter.

There's no onion in Kagami's dry curry, either. He doesn't like how it makes the curry stickier and sweeter. His seasoning is simple: just curry powder and salt. No need for sugar, since there's plenty of dried fruit in it. He does drop a little bit of honey in the mix to give it a nice gleam, though.

The soya milk chicken soup was almost done, too. It was time for the finishing touches: slicing the chicken meat that Kagami had preserved in soy sauce, stirring it in, and sprinkling some coriander leaves on top.

"It smells amazing. Need a hand with anything?" Kahoru, said, coming in to check on Dumpling Girl.

"I'm alright," Dumpling Girl replied. "I just need to bring the soup to a boil, and that's it. Can you call Dad and tell him don't be late for lunch?"

"He says he'll be here in a minute," Kahoru said, holding up her phone.

Soon the doorbell rang. Kahoru went to open the door and came back, arm-in-arm with a man. I could tell he was Itsuki without being introduced. When he said hello to us, I recognised his voice from the phone calls. He crouched down and ruffled Norimaki's head. Norimaki's face melted into a dreamy smile.

I'd been worried for Itsuki because Dumpling Girl said he's got flabby, but to me he didn't look like he had any extra fat. And he wasn't hiding it anywhere, as far as I could tell. Compared to Sakuragawa, he wore his suit like it was the most ordinary thing. The way he carries himself, so easy and natural – now *that's* cool.

Dumpling Girl's lunch was to be served to her parents in the main dining room, which was usually reserved for meals with guests. It was a special occasion, after all – a rare chance for parents and daughter to share a meal together, just by themselves – and besides, the small dining room would quickly get too cramped once everyone came home.

Kagami was the first to show up. "I'm back," he said, walking in with his friend Sacchan.

Sacchan, whose real name is actually Sachiya, was wearing a Liberty print shirt as usual: rose pink today. In contrast to the flowery pattern, the cut was sharp and trim, and the faded indigo of the denim trousers complemented it nicely.

The university that Sacchan had studied at was nearby, and they had picked some yomogi mugwort from the garden on campus. They said they were going to make kusamochi with it: chewy green rice cakes. I thought you made kusamochi

SPRING

with soft baby leaves, but apparently the mature leaves around this time of year are better for their fragrance.

For the mochi dough, they were going to use brown rice flour from the rice miller. They'd got hold of some kinako – roasted soybean powder, that is – from the same shop, which gave off a pleasant scent. Then, while they were busy in the kitchen, Sakuragawa came home.

He had a work event in the evening today, attending a reception at a gallery that he was in charge of, so he had gone for a haircut in the morning. (Though he has the kind of hair that looks flawless just by brushing his hand through it, he still goes to the salon pretty often.)

"Hey, something smells good," he said. Of course, I thought he meant Dumpling Girl's dry curry, rather than the grassy smell coming from the boiled yomogi leaves that they were grinding in the suribachi bowl.

Kagami thought as much too, and said, "Hikari had a go at making dry curry. There's probably some left over. Would you like me to warm it up?"

Sakuragawa didn't answer right away. He slowly walked around the kitchen like he was looking for something. Sacchan was staring out the window, seemingly absorbed in crushing the leaves, but no doubt he was all ears.

After a little while, Sakuragawa said, "It's okay. I have to entertain clients tonight, so I better not smell like curry."

LUNCH

Kagami didn't know how to carry on the conversation, so he clammed up. But he couldn't go back to making kusamochi either, since Sakuragawa was still lingering in the kitchen.

"Can you help me out here, Zaku?" Sacchan couldn't take it anymore and called him over. Zaku is his nickname for Kagami, though only he uses it. I have no idea what "Zaku" is supposed to mean, and I've yet to find out where it comes from.

Kagami went over to him in an instant.

Sakuragawa left the kitchen for the small dining room. But he came right back.

"Hey ... why curry?" he said standing in the doorway, directing the question at Kagami's back.

"It's an easy dish to make well, even for a schoolkid like Hikari," Kagami said, sounding slightly offhand as usual.

"That's not what I mean. What I'm asking is, why didn't you think I was talking about the kusamochi?"

Kagami and Sacchan, who were both still facing the window, tensed up a little. Sacchan's back slackened first, and he nudged Kagami with his elbow. Kagami turned towards Sakuragawa. But he didn't say anything, clearly confused.

Sakuragawa had begun in a blunt tone; now his face softened just a touch.

"My mum was always at work, so I was gramps' little sidekick – I've grown up to have the same tastes and likes as him.

SPRING

That smell that wafts up when you steam grass, the aroma of roasting tea, the wholesome smell of sweets made with rice flour, things like that. I like fresh kusamochi in particular – that's something special."

With that, Sakuragawa turned and headed for the front door. He was probably going to his own room above Madame Hinako's atelier in the annex.

Kagami stared after him, his pale face expressionless; he pursed his lips, almost as if he was slightly angry. But there was a faint flush on his ear lobes now: a sure sign that he was flustered.

Koyomi had observed the whole exchange in silence while fixing a quick lunch of yogurt and cereal for herself. She threw a wink at me: *Did you see that?*

"That's the way he does it – a silver-tongued rogue who's got everyone dancing to his tune," she said to us. "Look how smooth and natural he sounded: you can tell he's serious trouble. I wouldn't advocate picking up his manners just as they are, but you boys are going to grow up to be hunters someday, so it wouldn't hurt to study the technique of a master."

Norimaki wasn't listening to her at all. He was too busy clambering up onto the chair, then the sink, and staring intently at the bag of honey-coloured kinako powder that Kagami had just cut open. He kept his distance at first, but

LUNCH

he finally decided it was time to take the plunge and have an adventure.

He's at that age when he simply wants to stick his head into open bags. He probably hadn't meant to make a big mess. Curiosity killed the cat? Nope, but he did get covered in powder from head to tail.

3

Early Summer

Dim Sum Party

*Small baos; steamed gyoza with lettuce & shrimps
or daikon radish & snow crab meat*

Sake manju buns with pumpkin paste & dried fruits

*Soba manju buns with black cane sugar
and hyuganatsu citrus peels*

Peach manju buns with satoimo taro paste

Chinese-style salad with shirataki noodles

Almond tofu with soya milk

It's been raining non-stop lately. All day, every day, rain, rain, rain – it keeps pouring through the night and into the morning, stretching on from dawn till dusk, and doesn't let up at night, either. The rain barrel in the garden is overflowing, and the eaves gutter is gurgling.

If it was a clear day, the sky would already be paling around three a.m. at this time of year, but the rain clouds get in the way. But still, Yoake and Higure – the crow couple who live in the horse-chestnut tree growing in the garden to the south of ours – fly out to hunt for their breakfast, "to be strong in the rain" (as Mr Kenji wrote in another famous poem).

It's because their only child, born in the spring, is hungry. If ever there was a pair of doting parents, it's this crow couple, the biggest mollycoddlers in the neighbourhood. Or, to be more exact, their "Junior", who should've flown the nest by now, is the biggest spoiled brat. The only thing grown-up about him is his large body; he can't even sit still in their nest when his parents are away. He gets frightened by everything and makes a racket cawing for his parents, disturbing the whole area. As if that's not bad enough, Junior's voice is just like his papa Yoake's: hoarse and gravelly like he's had too much to drink.

It happened earlier today, too. Tekona came to the Horai house on her bicycle, wearing a long black raincoat with a hood. When she reached the gate, Higure (Junior's mama) gave her a flying kick in the head. It was because Junior was scared out of his wits, thinking Tekona was a black, slippery monster like Kurokawa or Amefurashi. But *he's* the one with the blackest coat – he's such a joke.

Then again, I have to admit, Tekona did look suspicious in her black raincoat, all wet and glossy in the rain. I could tell it was her from her city bike, but if I hadn't known who she was, I would've stayed well away from her.

"I may look hideous, but it's made of kelp – good for the planet," Tekona explained when Mum Komaki opened the door and looked dubiously at her raincoat.

"I'm not falling for that. Are you sure you're not turning into a monster? I think I see scales," Mum said.

Big fat liars, both of them.

*

Tekona brought something wrapped in a stiff, light blue waterproof material, called a flower-coat. As you can guess from the name, inside it was a handful of blossoming branches. They looked like single-flowered roses or camellias, fairly big and white, with long fuzzy stamens that caught the eye. They weren't as fragrant as roses, but there was still a whiff of their sweet smell in the air.

When we went to Seishiro Farm with Kagami the other day, a similar scent was wafting from the kiwifruit orchard. I saw the Russian Blue who lives on the farm, Gindoro, stagger like a drunkard over to one of the trunks and flop down at the base of it, twisting around his body.

Gindoro usually puts on a tough guy act, so it's rare to see him letting his guard down like that. He's often seen prowling along the netting that surrounds the orchard, swaying his shoulders like a security guard. If a stranger happens to pass by, he'll hiss and give them a death stare. He glowers at Norimaki and me too, whenever we visit the farm.

Gindoro behaves himself when Seishiro is around, though. Seishiro found him in a pet shop under an elevated railway. He was a youngster back then, and along with his three brothers, he used to brag that they were the last descendants of a Russian aristocrat. Eventually, he was the only one left unsold. He was on sale at half price when Seishiro came by to look at some motorbike parts in the next-door shop and took him home.

EARLY SUMMER

Seishiro is fussy when it comes to his bike and things like the condition of the inner tube, but he's an old-fashioned, analogue type – that is, he's not tech-savvy – plus, he doesn't like to read, so he can't tell the difference between print that's been typed and lettering done by hand. He's the kind of person who would look at a document that anyone could see is handwritten and think it's something officially printed. He took the pet shop owner at their word and never doubted Gindoro's pedigree for a second. His partner, Rika, simply shrugged, saying a certificate like that can't be real.

Gindoro wears an extravagant collar: a turquoise blue band embroidered in silver thread, with a silver tassel attached to it. Seishiro and Rika bought it for him when they went to Cappadocia (not the one in Turkey, but a shop around here). The two of them seem to get along best when they're drinking together.

In the sense that he doesn't do any work, I suppose Gindoro does have something in common with nobility. Seishiro thinks Gindoro catches mice on the farm, but he's got it all wrong. Gindoro just steals the mice that someone else caught and takes all the credit for himself. That's why he's known as Gindoro, putting together *gin*, which means *silver* (as in mice) and *dorobo*, which means *thief*: in short, "mouse-thief". Seishiro just calls him Gin.

*

DIM SUM PARTY

Seishiro watched Gindoro rolling around by the kiwi vine, then turned his eyes on me. "Chimaki's keeping his cool," he murmured.

"Looks like he's still a kitten," Kagami said, and they both nodded.

"Our boy Gin's always like that this time of year – he hates getting wet, but as soon as those flowers open up, he makes a beeline for the kiwi orchard, rain or shine, and tumbles around those trees all day long. Luckily he doesn't care about the fruit, so he doesn't get in the way when it's harvest time. They're in the same family as the matatabi plant, so kiwis attract cats like a magnet. Well, we call them 'kiwi', but they come from onimatatabi, after all."

Even after hearing their exchange, I didn't get why Gindoro was squirming around like that under the vines. Maybe he'd pilfered a bit of sacred sake from a shrine somewhere, or a sweet steamed bun offered to a jizo statue on the side of a street, and got himself drunk.

Norimaki wanted to walk on the trellis that formed an open roof over the kiwifruits. I could just see him getting stuck up there and wailing for help, so I told him no. Seishiro gave us a small bag (that he'd used for digging up new potatoes) just in time, so Norimaki forgot all about the trellis, at least for the moment.

There's only room in Norimaki's little head for one object

EARLY SUMMER

of interest at a time. Once he gets distracted by something new, he forgets everything else.

The other day, the fabric that covers the underside of the seat on Mr Dodo's old chair ripped apart, and it opened up like a bag. All the stuffing spilled out. Mum went to get the tools to mend it, but when she came back, Norimaki had already slipped inside.

Mum tried to coax him out, saying it's prickly in there, but he only dug deeper and deeper. Mum brought the hat for the teapot from the kitchen – the one that covers the whole pot to keep the tea warm.

With its pillowy quilted cover, the teapot hat would be much comfier than the prickly hole under the chair. It even had a pom-pom on top, and decorative beads that caught the light and glittered. Norimaki threw himself at the hat, just as Mum had expected, burrowed into it and stayed there, mumbling something I couldn't make out. He sounded like he was swapping secrets with someone – but don't ask me who.

With all the rain these days, it's been tricky to sun-dry the vegetables. Last week, Mum had an idea and wrote it down in her Komakoma Diary:

On a rainy day, I feel like having steamed food. Fill up the house with billows of steam, as damp and intense as the deluge outside. Open the windows wide and, instead of a

DIM SUM PARTY

bamboo screen, hang a see-through cloth from the ceiling. An Indian-style one with golden thread woven into the border would be nice.

Light some incense sticks with a name like "Rain Tree" or "Nile", cool yourself with a heart-shaped fan – like the leaf of an aoi, the wild ginger plant – and imagine you're lounging in a tropical rainforest. If you have a dim sum party like that, it's sure to brighten up the gloomy days of the rainy season.

As soon as she read Mum's draft, Tekona was keen. Since she was going to the Kappabashi Kitchenware Town to stock up on things for her shop anyway, she decided to buy a bunch of portable gas stoves, pots and seiro bamboo steamers.

This issue of *Maman tekona* was supposed to have a special feature around the theme "What would you eat if there was a blackout, and you couldn't use electricity?" But the rest of Mum's column went like this:

When I picture a dim sum party, I want it all – I would make both Chinese bao and sake manju buns: some pure white, some with a roasty tint, some with thin dough, some with thick dough. I'd like some soft chewy ones with a little bit of piquant pork meat inside, marinated in oyster sauce and black pepper. It's the best when there's just enough meat in there to keep you wanting more – that way, you can savour the taste and texture of the dough around it.

For xiaolongbao that melts in your mouth like magic, my

top choice would be a juicy pork filling where the rich soup bursts out with your first bite, but I also like the ones where the pink and green of small shrimp and lettuce show faintly through the dough. In autumn, xiaolongbao with crab roe filling would be a special feast. Bao with chunky chestnuts poking out of the dough would be fun, too.

Another tasty snack is those steamed buns made of mashed pumpkin and coconut powder. With a tiny drop of honey, it's just sweet enough. Give it a sprinkle of ground black pepper. Pumpkin and spices make a perfect match. Of course, they also go well with a spicy sauce, or with sunflower seeds on top.

Hungry Mum likes to put down whatever pops into her head: that's her typical style. It should be Tekona's job to edit Mum's writing, but she doesn't do anything to tidy it up and goes right ahead with it.

Well, not that anyone complains. It's a free magazine that Tekona puts together for fun to entertain her shop's clientele, so she's free to print whatever she likes – and her shop attracts people who share her tastes. Actually, the magazine's going really well, with quite a few people saying they want to place their adverts in it.

So I'll keep on writing my Chimachima Diary too, not to be outdone.

*

DIM SUM PARTY

So, that was how the whole dim sum party scheme came about. It was meant to be a double bill, combining lunch and afternoon tea. Since this went beyond the contractual terms binding our cook, Mum agreed to pay Kagami a special fee.

Norimaki and I listened in on their planning:

"Here's the dilemma," Mum said. "Freshly steamed buns are out of this world, but we don't want to put on too much weight. What I'm saying is – I want you to make healthy, low-calorie dim sum."

"Here's the short answer: that doesn't exist," Kagami said, as blunt as ever. "Dim sum is meant to be a snack in between meals, so in terms of calories, it's already a surfeit. Just pick a side – either you curb your appetite, or give in to the temptation and accept the consequences."

"I know all that, but couldn't you work something out? I mean, this idea of a tea party – chatting over steaming seiro baskets on a rainy day – doesn't it have a lovely ring to it? Some people work up a good sweat doing exercise; for people like us who don't move around much, I feel like this kind of indoor activity is one way of making ourselves sweat."

"How does sweating come into this again?"

"Saving electricity. The idea is that to better survive the hot months while dialling down the AC, you have to sweat properly and train your body to cool itself. That's why we're getting together to eat, drink and have a merry time in a room

EARLY SUMMER

with the windows open instead of having the air con on, and working up a sweat in the heat and humidity. Though our biggest enemies are the mosquitoes, not the heat. You know we get those tiger mosquitoes in our garden? If we want to keep the windows open, we'll have to figure out what to do about *them*."

"Burning incense might not be so good for Chimaki and Norimaki. You're going to let them play around here while you're having the party, right?"

"Of course – I can't lock out our little kiddies. It's what they're used to. I'll check with Dr Yamao about the incense."

Dr Yamao is our vet. Norimaki can't say the word for doctor yet: he says *o-isa-shan* instead of *o-isha-san*. So I call her Miss Oisa.

The next day, Mum got a memo with the same dishes I noted at the beginning of this entry. It was Kagami's menu for the dim sum party.

"Let me start off with a caveat," Kagami said, shifting into lecturer mode. "The dough for most dim sum is made of wheat flour – and if not wheat, then rice flour or mochi rice. Which means there's a limit to how 'low-calorie' it can be. You have to either be careful not to eat too much yourself, or burn the extra nutrition you take in by exercising right after the meal, or just give up and let your body gain the fat. That's the sort of mindset you need."

"Wait a second," Mum cut in. "But that sounds like some sort of willpower test. It's supposed to be a fun party."

"Well, that's life. If you listen to the numbers, you'll see what I mean. Take steamed pork buns, for example – a single large bun packs about 420 calories. Roughly equivalent to a heaped serving of rice in a small donburi bowl. Five xiaolongbao with pork filling – which would be the average number in a medium-sized seiro steamer – come to about three hundred calories. That's sixty per piece, so it's on the low side for a meat dumpling. Carbohydrates turn into glucose first, then get absorbed by the body. But if that glucose isn't used, it sticks around. At your age, Komaki" – sometimes Kagami calls his mum by her name – "450 calories is the cap for one meal, so if you eat a steamed pork bun for a snack, you shouldn't need dinner. All the more so if you don't exercise. But you'll probably get hungry as usual when it's time for dinner, and you'll likely eat again in the evening. In that scenario, whatever you have for dinner would certainly tip you over the daily limit. The sad truth is that you lose your muscles if you don't work out every day, but your body can store as much fat as it gets. For most of human history, people went hungry, so they needed a body that could store up fat. If we enter another ice age, the survival of the species will depend on whether we can retain fat in our bodies."

"Never thought I'd hear *you* talk about keeping the species alive."

"I was making a general statement. I don't intend to personally."

"Thought as much ... Well, never mind, that's all up to you. Back to dim sum – if you use snow crab or small shrimp instead of pork or chicken in the filling, how many more can we have?"

"Instead of one bun, you can eat one and a half, at most. The problem is the dough rather than the filling."

"I guess it doesn't make any difference if you grind lotus roots or potatoes or something and knead that into the dough?"

"Potatoes and the like are pretty high in calories, actually. And they're starchy, too. At least meat has protein, which builds muscle and bone – that's another way to look at it."

"Is there any hope at all?"

"There is one thing: you could use daikon radish instead of normal gyoza skins. Daikon is mostly water, so you'll cut down on calories quite a lot. Slice them into thin circles with a mandoline, soak them in water, then wrap the fillings in them."

"Hmm. Sounds like the healthiest gyoza skin ever, but I'm not sure I want to go that far."

"It's not as bad as you think. Steaming makes the sweet

umami of the daikon seep out. It'll go really well with a sauce that has a bit of a kick, like something Thai or Sichuan. Texture-wise the daikon slices will feel different from pickled radish like senmaizuke, and you won't have to worry about the salt content either, unlike with pickles."

"If I had to choose between the dough or the meat, I'd pick the dough. I just *love* it so much. I could eat an empty bun and still be happy – whether it's bao or sake manju. I like the buns with red bean paste, too, of course, but I'd rather give up on the sweet filling and have more of the white dough instead."

"How touching."

"You know what Mr Kenji said: 'Made from wheat flour and a little pinch of salt / How good these plain white pancakes of Ihatov are.' He's talking about rice crackers in that poem – they turn into 'pancakes' in the world of Ihatov, his imaginary utopia – but I'd say manju buns would be nothing if it weren't for the dough. Look at those flower buns, hanamaki – funny they're the same name as Mr Kenji's hometown – they barely have any flavour, nor do they have a filling, but they're divine when you eat them fresh out of the steamer. I always have the first one plain; the second I dip in a bit of sauce. Something spicy with chilli oil in it."

"Just like yogurt bacteria have regional variations, the yeast that ferments and raises the dough has different flavours depending on the region, too. I heard there's a type of yeast in mainland China that derives from the time of the emperors. They say the xiaolongbao made with that particular yeast has a thin, resilient dough that melts away with the filling as soon as you put it in your mouth, sliding down your throat."

"Never underestimate the power of bacteria or fungi."

"By the way, about the dipping sauce I mentioned – nam pla fish sauce and doubanjiang paste are salty, so you have to watch out. For instance, there's 1.4 grams of salt in one teaspoon of doubanjiang. The ideal amount of salt intake for an adult per day is six grams; at your age, you should aim even lower, so if you want spicy, it's better to just use chilli pepper. If I go to the Asian market, I can find the spicier kinds that you like, Komaki."

"With your homemade 'low-calorie' dim sum, how many can I have? Eight pieces, at least?"

"If you're planning on having dessert, like custard pudding or tapioca, then six."

"You know, when I go to a Chinese restaurant where they bring out the dim sum on a trolley, I sit with four, five friends, and each of us orders a couple of different kinds, and before you know it, we've easily put away eight or ten pieces. On top of that, we get the sweets like mango pudding, and the syrupy soup with apricot kernel powder, and coconut yogurt with tapioca. Six pieces and a bit of dessert sounds really sad."

DIM SUM PARTY

"You can fill up your stomach with Chinese-style salad while you wait for the buns to cook. It's normally made with vermicelli, but my version uses shirataki noodles made from konjac. So it's just like eating a vegetable."

"Won't they smell like konjac?"

"They're the shirataki from Yatsuko, so no problem."

"Ah, that shop in Yanaka."

"I'll put in plenty of dried cucumber and daikon, so it'll be a crispy salad. Drying vegetables keeps the vitamins from breaking down. I could add some small shrimp, or snow crab meat that's been boiled and shredded, too. For the dressing, I'll mix lemon juice and black vinegar, with black pepper and chilli pepper to give it some zing – so it'll be better for you than sauces made with doubanjiang or sesame oil. I'll make crumbly chicken mince simmered in sweet soy sauce, but that's just for me. I can eat more calories than everyone at your girls' party."

"No fair! We all know you're a girl at heart, anyway. Maybe I'll invite Sakuragawa, too."

"He left for Shanghai yesterday. On a work trip."

"Oh, right . . . So you're up to date with his schedule, then?"

Sakuragawa had told Kagami that he wouldn't be needing his bento lunches for a while – that's how he found out about Shanghai.

*

EARLY SUMMER

Anyhow, the day of the party rolled around.

After putting away the breakfast dishes, Kagami stayed in the kitchen and buckled down to prepping the dim sum.

First, the sake manju: that is, white steamed buns that give off a faint whiff of sake because the dough is fermented with rice koji, an essential element in sake brewing. He made a filling with mashed pumpkin for these buns. Only a little bit of sugar went in the paste, while the sour-sweet blueberries gave it a nice tang.

The soba manju, or buckwheat buns, get their sweetness from black cane sugar. Kagami added a dash of soy sauce to the dark brown dough: a secret ingredient to deepen the flavour. He didn't fill it with azuki bean paste like they normally do; instead, he kneaded some peel strips from a citrus fruit called hyuganatsu into the dough, rolled it into little balls, and popped them into the seiro steamer. I don't know what citrus fruits taste like, but he told me that the sweetness of the dough and the gentle bitterness of the peel make a lovely match.

Tekona was so excited by the idea of steaming up the room with a row of steamers that she bought a set of tools for each person at the party – consisting of a portable stove, a bamboo steamer and a pot – and had them delivered to the Horai house in advance. Mum had actually ordered a set from Tekona's shop as an emergency kit to tide us over in

DIM SUM PARTY

case of blackouts, but Tekona sent the whole lot as an early midsummer gift.

It was raining again: the perfect setting. Tekona arrived in the same black raincoat she was wearing before. As she arranged the flowers she'd brought in a vase, Mum Komaki watched her skillful manoeuvres.

"The blossoms look like buttercups, but the leaves are different," she observed. "And if you look closely, the middle is round and fat like a sea anemone. Doesn't it look like a clownfish could live in there? Are these yellow flowers from the same kind of plant?"

"That's the male flower. They bloomed on time this year. The male and female flowers grow on separate plants, and the one you compared to a sea anemone is the female."

"Do the male flowers not bloom every year?"

"They do, but you never know when – sometimes too early, sometimes too late. They remind me of someone we know, but I'll refrain from saying who."

"Who?"

"I told you, I won't say it. The white, shaggy things are the stamens, and the bit underneath swells with the fruit. You'll see what kind when it grows bigger."

"Will I?"

"Of course. I think you like the sour taste. Lots of vitamin C."

"If it's flowering now, the fruit should ripen around autumn, right?"

"Around this time of year, you see the imported ones from the southern hemisphere in grocery shops."

"Ah, I got it now. The one with the same name as the bird — it has to be kiwi."

"Bingo. The flowering season is already over in orchards in Tokyo, but they're still in season over in my hometown, so my mother snipped some branches this morning and brought them for me. Ever since the bullet train line opened, she just hops over here whenever she feels like it without even asking what I'm up to."

"That's nice, though. I mean, she doesn't need you to show her around Tokyo, does she? I suppose she just wants to go wherever she likes."

"Oh yes, she's never fussy about it: she's happy with whatever tickets are available on the day in the box office, whether it's the theatre or concerts. She even gets those one-act tickets to see kabuki."

"She sure knows how to enjoy herself."

"She's just spontaneous — never plans ahead."

"Someone who doesn't plan ahead can't grow vegetables or take care of flowering trees. I'd say she's good at using her time effectively."

"Too much of a busy bee, if you ask me." Tekona inserted

the last branch into the vase and waved at me to come closer. "To tell you the truth, I was kind of looking forward to seeing how Chimaki would react, but he doesn't seem affected at all."

"Right? He *should* love it – I mean, they're basically the same sort of plant as matatabi. Kagami told me that they went to the kiwifruit orchard at Seishiro's the other day, but nothing."

"They say it's the same for lions and tigers, too – when they're little cubs, they don't even glance at it. I guess Chimaki's still a little boy, since he plays with his brother all day long."

I was offended. I don't *play with* Norimaki; I'm *looking after* him. He's still a baby, so it's a lot of work.

Just a minute ago, when I was looking the other way, he stuck his head out the window and got his head dripping wet from the rain streaming down like a waterfall from the edge of the eaves. He doesn't get that if he pokes his head outside, he'll get wet.

"Oh dear! You're drenched. Come here, pookie, let's get you dry."

Tekona spread out the big soft towel that she always carries in her handbag and put Norimaki on her lap. It's a fluffy gauze towel, so it feels really nice to touch. Though his head was the only part of him that got wet, Norimaki rolled onto his back, showing his tummy and blissfully closing his eyes. *He* doesn't have a care in the world.

*

EARLY SUMMER

I felt like going a little bit rogue, so I went to the part of the corridor covered with linoleum and played a game of flying slippers. The hemp slippers for guests in the summer are light, so they slide really well, but the woollen slippers that used to be Mr Dodo's favourite – with a tartan pattern of light blue, green and red that's supposed to represent some family in Scotland – are heavy with thick soles, so they don't fly far.

Somehow, nobody says let's put away those slippers, and Jean Paul, who comes by from time to time, wears them as if they were his. Whenever Mum finds those slippers left near the entrance hall or in front of the toilet, she says, "Oh, he's already back – I haven't finished my manuscript yet," and hurries to the kitchen to make tea (it was their daily habit to chat over tea when Mr Dodo came home from work). A moment later, she gets pulled back to reality and remembers that her husband is dead – that's what she told me anyway.

Mr Dodo, also known as Kiyoshi, passed away two years ago when he was sixty-seven. Unlike Grandad Tamaki at Matsu Sushi, who's turning eighty-one this year and still going strong, Mr Dodo died young, which made everybody grieve even more. But Mum has a different opinion.

"He crossed to the other side before his body got weak, and he didn't have to suffer through a long illness, so he's one of the lucky ones. I wish *I* could go like him, really. He got to

DIM SUM PARTY

visit Napoli and Capri, and dropped dead not long after he came back – I'm sure he's more than satisfied."

When Madame Hinako came to work in her atelier as usual, Koyomi invited her to the yum cha party.

"I don't snack between meals on weekdays as a rule, so I won't have the dim sum, but I'd love to come for tea. Kagami's brew is always delicious."

Spoken like the self-disciplined Madame that she is.

As for me and Norimaki, our breakfast today was a combination of small shrimp, simmered mince chicken and meow-food crunchies. So it wasn't like we were hungry, but when Norimaki got bored with his other games, he trotted over to the kitchen.

Actually, he's had his eyes on a new addition to the house ever since Kagami bought it about ten days ago. It's a basket for washing grains of rice, woven with plant vines; compared to a normal metal sieve, it's deeper, and the bottom is more rounded, which is more convenient when you use your fingers and the palm of your hand to wash the rice. It's probably a perfect shape for us to curl up in, too.

But Kagami is rather protective over that basket, and he hasn't let either of us touch it yet – not even once. He keeps it in a cupboard with a sliding door that I can't open because it gets a bit stuck, and you have to tug hard. And every time he

EARLY SUMMER

uses it, he goes to the trouble of taking it somewhere upstairs to dry: uncharted territory for us.

Or else he puts it away inside the hanging net, so we can't reach it. And as if that wasn't enough, he wraps it up carefully when it's dry and hides it away inside the same cupboard again.

It's a special basket for cleaning rice that's going to go in everyone's food, so it makes sense that we shouldn't play with it, but it seems like that's not the only reason.

"Well, that basket's made of matatabi vines, so no wonder he's so careful with it," Koyomi told me as she sat at the table in the small dining room with a newspaper spread out in front of her. "I heard you two didn't react at all to kiwi plants, but it could be any day now when you start your 'girl hunt', you know."

I didn't get it, though; I still have no idea what matatabi is. I pounced on the paper and demanded an explanation.

Koyomi understands simple meow-talk. "Some things are better left unsaid," she laughed, dodging my question.

Norimaki is dreaming of the day when he can curl up inside that basket while someone sways it back and forth like a swing.

Dumpling Girl got home earlier than usual because her school had a shorter day today. She came back soaking wet just as the rain was getting more intense. Water dripped from the hem and sleeves of her hooded raincoat, which is part of her school uniform (it's roomy at the back so that she can wear it over her backpack, and it's got a zip running down the side, so she can take things out of her bag without taking off the raincoat).

When she reached the back door, she pulled off her coat under the eaves, shook off the raindrops, and hung it on the coat stand; then, stepping into the linen room, she peeled off her drenched socks, towelled her legs, and put on a dry pair of socks and indoor slippers. Today she picked brown socks with red strawberries on it. She said she feels like something bright and colourful on rainy days.

Then she went up to her room to get changed and came downstairs in a denim dungaree skirt. She was still wearing her school blouse underneath; a cotton gauze shirt, which was her uniform during the summer.

Passing her by in the corridor, Koyomi told her, "Remember to stuff some newspaper in your wet socks. But not the one from this morning," and went into the linen room with a soya milk coffee in a wooden mug. Koyomi was on laundry duty today, so it was her job to take out the clean clothes from the tumble dryer, fold them up and sort them into separate piles, and iron the ones that needed ironing.

On days like today, when Dumpling Girl finishes early, she has a bigger breakfast in the morning and goes to school

EARLY SUMMER

without a bento box. And by the time she gets home, she's famished.

Kagami said she could start eating earlier than the rest, so she peered over the tray with the rows of white gyoza and manju buns, which were waiting to be steamed.

"It'll be my lunch, so I want something savoury, but I'll take a peach manju because it's cute," she said.

A spot of soft pink was brushed onto each cheek of the peach-shaped buns. When they're steamed, they'll plump up and look even more like a peach.

"Does this have white bean paste in it?" she asked.

"No, it's not bean paste," Kagami said. "It's made from mashed satoimo taro and yamaimo mountain yam. I added a tiny drop of maple syrup to make it sweeter, so I'd say one bun is about seventy calories. I would've preferred filling it with a white paste made from runner beans, but Komaki asked me to make it as light as possible, so I opted for satoimo – though it's just a small difference. The drawback is that it doesn't look as nice. Other ingredients that could make a white paste, like lotus roots or lily bulbs, are usually higher than satoimo in their nutritional values. That's how Japanese people got their nutrients in the old days. If you look at it from a historical perspective, we live in an abnormal age where people try to avoid high-calorie foods."

"You're so right," Koyomi jumped in. "Most public health

DIM SUM PARTY

insurance leaflets advise you to eat at least 350 grams of vegetables a day, but root veggies and legumes don't fit into the definition of vegetables in nutritional science. Let's say you make a curry with potatoes and chickpeas in it. You might feel like you're eating healthy, but it doesn't count towards your 'vegetable' intake, and you only end up getting more carbs and starch on top of the curry roux that's already fatty. And your nutritionist leaves a comment like, 'Next time, try swapping the potatoes and peas with spinach and broccoli.'" She paused in her rant. "Did you make the gyoza skins from scratch, too?"

"I would've liked to, but handmade skins always turn out thicker – there's no way around it. So I decided to use store-bought ones today. We've got snow crab meat and small shrimp for the filling, but since everyone's going to have their own steamer in front of them, I thought it'd be nice if they can wrap their own gyozas with their favourite fillings, so I've laid them out in these small plates. There's snow crab mixed with chopped dried daikon radish; okara soy pulp simmered with vegetables; pumpkin paste with lettuce and shrimp – they're all pretty good. I made small meatballs with pork too, for people who fancy meat. I'd recommend wrapping it with stewed hijiki seaweed or dried daikon strips, but if anyone thinks it's too much effort to wrap things, I can do it for them."

"No pork bao on the menu?"

"Well, a dim sum party without pork buns wouldn't be

much of a party, so I made small ones. They're more for enjoying the dough than the meat filling, though. This dish took the most work out of the whole menu. I did a few rounds of proofing and bench resting. For the filling, I used ten grams of meat."

"How many can I have, calorie-wise? Someone like me, I mean."

"I used less sugar so that each bun doesn't go over seventy, so if you're only having these, you can have six."

"Six? That's it?"

"There's an'nin tofu waiting for dessert too, you know. If you want to have that, six is the limit – or eight, if it's just the dough without any filling."

"How many calories would you get from the almond tofu? You make it with milk, right?"

"I used soya milk for today. If you have it without the syrup, one bowl would be forty calories. With the syrup and dried apricots on top, it goes up by eighty-eight calories."

"It jumps up that much just from the toppings?"

"I prepped the syrup in case anyone thinks the soya milk smells too strong. But it tastes good without it. The dried apricots are whole fruits steeped in sugar, so you can't avoid the calories there. If you just drizzle the syrup on top without any apricots, I'd say that's about twenty calories extra."

"Hmm, tough choice," Koyomi murmured with a sigh just

DIM SUM PARTY

as Mum Komaki called out from the living room. She wanted help with rearranging the sofa and side tables to make it feel more like a party. Koyomi went over to lend a hand.

Dumpling Girl was still trying to decide which pieces to take. There were five buns on her plate now.

"You move around more than the middle-aged people, Hikari, so it's alright if you want three extra buns or so. If you pick one without the filling, it's fine to have another one on top of that. Though just to warn you, they might feel a bit dry and rough inside compared to the pork buns you get in stores. These days, people prefer smooth and fluffy, so store-bought buns are heading more and more in that direction. They use a lot of sugar, margarine and shortening to get that texture. And as a result, they're packed with trans-fatty acids that can raise the bad kind of cholesterol."

"The buns keep getting bigger too, don't they? There's this shop near my school that sells a huge pork bun about the size of a baby's head, and there's always a queue in front of it. When I see everyone biting into their bun on the streets, it even looks like they're having candyfloss. You should see that shop around lunchtime in winter – there's *so* much steam billowing up from there that you'd think something's on fire and go to call the fire brigade. And when you walk through that alley in the summer, you're hit by this wall of hot, humid air. But I have to admit, their buns do look amazing. I try not to walk down that alley so that I don't cave in and buy one – but what do you think I should do to stay strong?"

"Try picturing yourself five years from now. What kind of body shape would suit you? An earthenware teapot, a smaller teapot, a cooking pot, a kettle – or maybe a sponge gourd, a pumpkin, a topinambour, an aubergine, a cucumber. None of them are better or worse than the others: just think about what shape *you* want."

"Topi . . .?"

It was time for Kagami to prepare the tea and clean up around the sink. He brewed a few different kinds of tea in glass teapots, including one where the leaves opened up like a lotus flower, and another one which gave off a golden glow when it caught the light at a certain angle.

Dumpling Girl decided to get out of his way and let him do his work. She opened one of the steamers over a bubbling pot and arranged her dim sum in it with a pair of tongs.

At tea time, Madame Hinako popped in from the door between the family's living space and her annex atelier, where she did her French embroidery work. The atelier had its own separate entrance, but she could also come in freely through this door.

Before we go on, let me walk you through how the family fits together again. For those of you who have everything down pat: feel free to skip ahead. The current head of the house is Itsuki, who's living on his own in Kyoto for his work (he's Dumpling Girl's dad); before him, the head of the house was Mr Dodo (Mum Komaki's husband).

Mr Dodo married twice in his lifetime. His first wife was Madame Hinako, who owns the atelier. Mum Komaki was his second wife. Itsuki and Koyomi are Madame Hinako's children. Kagami is Mum Komaki's only son.

Mum Komaki has been working as a translator for a long time, since before her marriage and she carried on after Mr Dodo's death, too. Madame Hinako, on the other hand, used to work at a trading company when she was single and quit her job after marrying to focus on raising her children. Eventually, Itsuki came of age and Koyomi graduated from senior high school. Then she made her "declaration of independence". Her reason: she found her calling.

"As soon as she has an idea, she acts on it – 'no time like the present' is like her motto. By the time she mentioned it to me, she'd already enrolled in an embroidery school in France, so of course, she doesn't care to listen to anyone's advice," Jean Paul explained with a chuckle.

Madame Hinako learned the art of needlework there, came back to Japan, and became an embroidery artisan. Collaborating with textile designers, she embellishes fabrics that turn into fashion collections.

According to Jean Paul, "embroidery" in Japan means

sewing patterns with thread (so someone who embroiders can be called a "sewist", too), but embroidery in places like Belgium, France, Italy and Spain is something you "weave". Madame Hinako doesn't only use thread in her embroidery; she also weaves in other things like beads, seashells, leather, feathers and small branches.

Her atelier is filled with colourful threads along with little bits and bobs she uses for ornament. They're kept in jars, and boxes and drawers. When the door to the atelier is open, Norimaki and I are free to go in and out as we please. We can even peer inside the boxes and drawers.

But we made a promise that we would never climb up on the big desk. In any case, it's coated with an essential oil that smells like oranges, which we're not a big fan of, but that desk is where she spreads out the precious fabric that she's commissioned to work on, so we mustn't get our hair all over it.

Madame Hinako was going out somewhere tonight, so she looked even more fashionable than usual, in a chocolate brown sleeveless dress and a long voile blouse in the same colour – chic and elegant. In meow-terms, I'd say she has the look of a Maine Coon or a Norwegian Forest.

The airy ruffle collars of her blouse accented her somewhat pointy face. You might not think so judging from how she looks, but she's really easy-going and not fussy at all.

DIM SUM PARTY

Since I was the only one who was waiting for her on our side of the door, she asked, "Where's the little one?" and went to look in the small dining room. Jean Paul was lounging there by himself, Norimaki napping on his lap. Everyone else was in the living room.

"Oh, you're back, dear. It's not even Obon yet," she said. (Obon, by the way, is when people honour the ancestors' spirits in the middle of August.)

As far as I know, Madame Hinako is the first person to notice Jean Paul's presence. I don't know why, but no-one else pays him any attention, let alone talks to him, whenever he's sitting in Mr Dodo's chair or walking around in his slippers.

It's as if he's invisible. Mum even thinks *I'm* the one moving around Mr Dodo's slippers.

"Well, who said we have to follow the calendar?" he replied breezily.

"I'm sure it's all the same to *you*, but unfortunately, we have our own plans on this side of the world. Did you know Komaki's having a party today? It's a girls' day in – all the ladies of the house and her friends are going to have a get-together and chat over tea to their hearts' content. I hope you won't sneak up on them and give them a fright."

"Luckily you're the only one who can see me, Hinako . . . except for my friends here."

He was talking about me and Norimaki.

117

"Really? Doesn't Komaki see you? I've never met anyone who's as whimsical as she is."

"She's more practical than she seems."

"But just the other day, I saw her talking by herself out in the garden, so I went to see what was happening – and she was actually complaining to the crows in the tree that their crybaby is too loud."

"Well, she's right – that couple lets their brat get away with anything."

"What couple?"

"The crows, of course—'

"How do you know they're a couple? They could be brothers, no? Crows all look the same."

"Never mind about the crows. Weren't we talking about Komaki? She might not look it, but she has her feet planted firmly on the ground, that one. So she doesn't notice I'm here."

"Aw, that's too bad. You'd like to chat with her, wouldn't you? She's good company."

"These tiny tots keep me entertained instead. They call me Jean Paul, you know."

"At least it's not Johannes Paul"

"You don't think it suits me?"

"Oh no, not in the least."

*

DIM SUM PARTY

Dumpling Girl picked up the steamer with her cooked dim sum and went to the living room. Norimaki and I trailed behind her. The furniture was arranged differently now, and the window to the terrace was wide open.

They'd lit incense on the terrace. Miss Oisa, our vet, said it should be safe to burn it indoors too, as long as the room is well ventilated, and there's no constant stream of dense smoke.

Norimaki sneezed when he saw the smoke coiling up from the incense in the distance – though I'm not sure if he was reacting to the smoke, or if the sight of it just made him think of something else.

After that, he started letting out a tiny sneeze every time he saw steam coming out of the steamers. It wasn't like his nose was itchy, or he didn't like the smoke: just that the steam made him sneeze by reflex somehow.

Dumpling Girl bit into the peach bun first. She's the type to start with her favourite food before anything else. I prefer hiding my favourites away for later.

Whenever she's savouring her meal, she has this calm and collected look, and she takes one bite after another without uttering a word. She did the same thing as she relished the dim sum.

The others picked out their favourite pieces and put them in their steamers, too. While waiting for the buns to cook, they followed Kagami's advice and dug into the shirataki noodle salad.

Koyomi sat down next to Dumpling Girl. Dumpling Girl pulled out her Mamemon notebook, where she'd jotted down the "topinamboo" that Kagami mentioned earlier, and asked Koyomi about it.

"Are you sure it's not 'tochimenbo'? He kind of mumbles when he talks, so you might've heard him wrong," Koyomi said.

"Do you know what a tochimenbo is, then?"

"I've heard of it, at least."

"What language is it?"

"It comes up in Natsume Soseki's book, *I Am a Cat* – so it's Japanese. There should be a paperback on that shelf over there, but I don't see it now. Maybe someone's reading it."

Yes, that would be me. I'm right in the middle of it. One of the characters in the novel, an aesthetician, goes to a Western restaurant and plays a trick on the waiter and orders a made-up dish called "tochimenbo". The footnote says it's a pun on the pseudonym of a haiku poet.

Mum Komaki overheard their conversation and leaned over to look in the Mamemon notebook.

"Isn't that 'topinambour'? It's French for Jerusalem artichokes. It used to serve as a substitute when other foods were scarce, and now it's good for dieting – a root veg that doesn't make you fat, unlike potatoes. It has inulin, which isn't digested – same as burdock roots . . . You want to know what it looks like? Hmm, not pretty. Like a botched attempt at an artichoke."

I guess what Kagami wanted to tell Dumpling Girl was this: if she doesn't want to end up looking like a topinambour, she'd better eat some topinambour.

4

Summer

Lunch and Snacks for the Tiny Tots

Pumpkin potage with soya milk

Summer vegetables in kanten jelly

Stir-fried rice with lettuce and lots of other vegetables

Marinated scallops and mixed beans

Blueberry smoothie

+

Cold aubergine braised in dashi

Norimaki is whizzing around the corridor, looking for a place to hide. Today is the day when the dreaded "Hug Squasher" will come to the house. For him, this monster is as terrifying as the "Pitch Black Soot Sprites" or the "Piggyback Ghost".

I guess I don't need to spell it out at this point, but Norimaki is still scared of ghosts, spirits and monsters. When *I* was his age – about seven months old – I was already roving the streets and taking care of him, so I can't help feeling jealous. It's like baby brothers get a free ride through life.

Pitch Black Soot Sprites hide out in the gloom of the staircase or the corridor at night. Actually, they're the shadows that sway and swell up on the wall, cast by himself or someone else nearby, shapeshifting with the angle of the light. But Norimaki simply can't wrap his head around the fact that the

SUMMER

shadow is stretching from his own four feet. The moment he catches sight of one, his hair stands on end.

As you might expect, the Piggyback Ghost isn't a real ghost, either. When Norimaki is romping around in the garden, a teenage crow (not a crybaby like Yoake Junior, but a cheeky young hooligan) shoots over him, flying low on purpose and throwing a dark shadow on the ground. To Norimaki, the shadow looks like a ghost trying to grab onto his back.

The Hug Squasher comes riding on the back of Tekona's city bike. Compared to the other monsters, she's a little bit cuter, but she's also a bundle of trouble. And she comes astride a fancy child seat with a giant backrest.

She used to come about twice a week until recently. Every time we heard the squeak of Tekona's brakes near Mum's house, Norimaki and I would brace ourselves.

Luckily for us, the Hug Squasher started elementary school in April, so now she doesn't come along with her mum on school days.

"I'd completely forgotten how good it feels to ride a bike by myself. A whole different speed," Tekona had said, the first time she came alone to discuss the next Komakoma Diary with Mum. "I couldn't help 'going bei' down that slope just back here. I felt relieved that I can still do it."

Going bei means riding a bike like a yajirobei – that balancing toy with a small body in the middle and long arms

LUNCH AND SNACKS FOR THE TINY TOTS

spread out on both sides – as in, she took both hands off the handlebars while going downhill. Tekona thinks it's a phrase that everybody knows like it's common sense, but of course it isn't.

She's old enough to know better, but sometimes she's rather reckless. Mum was quick to talk some sense into her.

"You think you're still young, but let me tell you as someone who's gone through that stage already: your muscles have got weaker than you realise. You're in for a nasty surprise if you think you have enough muscle to keep your balance just like you used to ten years ago. Because you don't. There's nothing left – trust me. I suppose you'll say you're fine, you used to be in a sports club at school, but that's different."

"I'm still pretty confident about my muscles, though."

"Nope. Muscle melts away. Those hard biceps you used to have just mutated into droopity-droop and squishity-squish that cling on to you."

"There's plumpity-plump in there, too."

"See? Told you."

Sounds like Mum and Tekona are haunted by monsters, too.

We'd been living in peace since school started in April. But there is a thing called summer holidays for elementary schools, and the Hug Squasher loomed on the horizon again.

SUMMER

"Hi Chimaki, hi Norimaki!" she calls out whenever she comes. "Did you miss me? Koko's here. Let's play together!"

Kokona is missing something – she always thinks we've been eagerly awaiting her return. If she catches us, she'll squeeze us so hard we can hardly breathe. That's why Norimaki calls her the Hug Squasher and dreads her visits.

As soon as we hear her voice, we make a run for it, but Norimaki slips and falls in the corridor, and that's when she grabs him. She really does wrap you hard like a sushi roll – if you're not careful, something will splurt out of you.

Today, we heard Tekona's bike coming inside the gate as usual. Norimaki scampered about in a panic, trying all the hiding places where he'd surely be found right away: burrowing into our bed one moment and sticking his head in Mr Dodo's slipper the next.

Even Norimaki's too big now to fit in the teapot by the kitchen window. Plus, someone's found the missing lid, so it's not so easy to slip in anymore. Weirdly, just the lid is cast iron, so it's too heavy for Norimaki to lift up or even nudge out of place.

In the five months we've been living in Mum's house, Norimaki has grown quite a lot. Though he's still a big baby, and there's lots of things he's scared of and things he can't do. He runs over to Kagami whenever he needs help. Mum helps him too, but she rarely comes downstairs in the morning, so he can't really count on her.

LUNCH AND SNACKS FOR THE TINY TOTS

But this morning was different: Mum was already sitting in the small dining room, having a cup of good coffee brewed by Kagami and a bowl of kiwi, cucumbers and broccoli sprouts tossed in balsamic vinegar. A vitamin C super bowl, with adlay millet sprinkled over it.

Norimaki clambered onto Mum's lap. "The monster's coming," he cried. In Norimaki's world, the Hug Squasher is categorised as a monster, and Pitch-Black Soot Sprites are "yokai" or supernatural spirits. No matter how urgently he appealed to her, though, she probably only heard something along the lines of *"Myamyamiaowmrrrmiaow!"*

"You're surprised I'm up so early, aren't you?" she said, laughing. "I'm going out today. There's going to be a neighbourhood festival, and I'll have a booth at the flea market with Tekona and the others. Koyomi and I will sell books and booklets we made ourselves along with second-hand books; Tekona will bring the goods from her shop; and Rika from Seishiro Farm will open her mobile café-and-diner-in-one, where people can enjoy lots of fresh veg from their farm. All the mums are going to be so busy today. So, our little ones will have a play date here. Sacchan will be our sitter, and Kagami will take care of the food. Tekona, Rika and I hired them. Hope you'll be a good boy, too, Norimaki, and play nice with everyone." (*Wrrmiaowmomyu.* ← Norimaki's reply.)

This was all news to me! Before I could even think *Now*

SUMMER

we're in serious trouble, someone lifted me up. I'd let my guard down.

"Chimaboo, I caught you!"

This was Hako, Tekona's oldest daughter, who was nine years old, also in elementary school. She had come along with her mum and sister on her own bicycle. I'd been so preoccupied with Tekona's bike that I hadn't seen her coming. What was I thinking?

Hako calls me Chimaboo. Since Kahoru, Dumpling Girl's mum in Paris, calls her daughter Hikaboo instead of Hikari, Hako thought it must be some French way of coming up with a nickname and mimicked her.

With a light kick against Hako's belly, I jumped out of her grasp and bolted towards the front door. A flashy cherry red camper van had just pulled up in front of the gate. It was "Rika's Diner": a kei-truck remodelled with a kitchenette. If you open the side door, it turns into a standing bar with a sunshade attached. There's a foldable table and stacking chairs loaded onto the van too, so she can park anywhere and set up a stall right there.

Though the highlight of Rika's Diner was vegetables, she included meat on the menu for today's festival to cater for non-vegetarians, too. The main menu went like this: Light & Cosy Croquettes with pumpkin, white beans and chicken;

LUNCH AND SNACKS FOR THE TINY TOTS

Fresh Summer Veggie Fritters & Pea Curry with more than ten kinds of vegetables and peas; and Creamy Soup Vitamin Boost with julienned peppers.

Seishiro will be selling vegetables at the same venue, so he went earlier to get a head start. Tekona's Darling is on the event committee, so he was already there. In short, the dads were too busy to look after the kids, too.

While the grown-ups were bustling to and fro like they were going on a field trip, the kids had assumed this was going to be just another slow Saturday. But then their parents rushed *them* into getting ready and whisked them off, so they were obviously sulky.

Saturday was one day when they could go through their morning routines, like washing their faces and brushing their teeth, without racing against the clock. But now, this precious morning of relaxation was ruined.

A boy with a rucksack slung over his shoulder dragged himself out from Rika's camper van, grumbling, "Promise you'll take me to Disneyland next week. Pinky swear, mum!"

"I *told* you, we're going to see granny next week. I said the same thing yesterday, remember? Familyland is closer from her house, so we said let's go there – and *you* said you were happy with that the other day, Konchi. Don't drag it up again."

"I want Disneyland."

SUMMER

"What about the grape-picking then? Didn't you say you wanted to have tea at the château with mixed berry ice cream cake?"

"Disneyland!"

The one complaining was Konsaburo, Seishiro and Rika's son, who's turning three soon. Since both his parents are tall, he's already pretty big, but still a baby inside. A girl climbed out of the van, too; she was wearing wellies even though it was a sunny day. This was Konsaburo's elder sister, Yuria, five years old. She was probably rebelling against her mum too, refusing to wear the sneakers she was supposed to.

She was dressed up in a cute outfit – a shirred tunic in strawberry pink and vegetable green over indigo denim – but her face was sour. Plus, she had wellies on.

I saw how little kids give their mum a headache back when I used to hang out at Auntie Meowko's, so I have a fairly good idea of what must have gone on between Rika and the kiddos before they set out.

As the small dining room filled up with people, Sacchan came in from the back door. Today, he wasn't here to hang out with Kagami; he was working as a babysitter. Everyone's eyes flew to his shirt. On the white background, there were rows of maroon-coloured dots like the beads of an abacus, and

LUNCH AND SNACKS FOR THE TINY TOTS

inside each bead was a tiny yellow sunflower. From a distance, the shirt looked chic; up close, it was cute.

"Wow, Sacchan, that's a stylish print," Tekona said. "Is it imported?"

"It was made in Japan for export sometime between 1955 and 65," Sacchan said.

"Amazing. Where'd you find it?" Tekona sounded a bit jealous; it was her line of work to hunt for things like that for her shop.

"My relative used to be a textile wholesaler. This one was just lying around in their warehouse, so they gave it to me. It was only a sample, so there was just enough to make one shirt out of it."

"So you made it yourself? You're *good*."

"I hardly ever find clothes I want to wear in shops, so . . ."

"I can't wear off-the-peg stuff, either — for a different reason. My shoulders are broader than average. With muscles."

She demonstrated with her thumb and index finger. It's true: her shoulders do look rather sturdy compared to the rest of her body, which is on the slender side. That's why she's good at lifting heavy things, but I've yet to find out why she has muscles only on her shoulders.

Anyway, it sounds like a bother when you don't have your own fur to wear.

*

SUMMER

The three mums and Koyomi piled into Rika's Diner with all their goods and headed to the flea market venue together in high spirits, while the group of kiddies were left at home.

Hako is a fourth grader in elementary school, so she's the oldest of the bunch apart from Dumpling Girl. She's in an awkward limbo now: she isn't really a little kid anymore, but she hasn't seen enough of the world yet to flex her real powers as a young girl. She doesn't understand things the way Dumpling Girl does. Put another way, she's tactless. She just blurts out whatever pops into her head.

"Hang on, Konsaburo, you're still wearing *nappies*?" she asked.

She'd spotted the change of diapers that was peeking through the open zip of Konsaburo's rucksack. He'd taken out his favourite towel a moment ago and forgotten to close it.

He was going for a cool look with his outfit today – an army-style shirt and cargo trousers, complete with a camouflage bandana – and nobody would've known he was wearing a diaper underneath if he hadn't forgotten to zip up his rucksack and eagle-eyed Hako hadn't broadcast his secret.

If you ask me, it's really puzzling that someone could become so engrossed in playtime that he forgets to go to the toilet. Even baby Norimaki can do his business on his own. Auntie Meowko, who gave him milk when he was tiny, taught him how. That's why Norimaki thought he was a big

LUNCH AND SNACKS FOR THE TINY TOTS

boy compared to Konsaburo and puckered his face, prim and proper (which is his idea of a grown-up look).

Konsaburo burst into sobs.

"Hey, you lot." Dumpling Girl, who had been writing something quietly until now, interrupted them in a bossy tone. "Do you mind? I'm trying to do my homework here. You're distracting me."

At Dumpling Girl's school, learning about food and nutrition is part of the curriculum, and she's been given homework over the summer holidays. She's supposed to record everything she eats for breakfast, lunch and dinner over one week.

Besides the ingredients for every meal, she has to submit three recipes with a photo (or drawing) of the dish: Our Family Classic, My Original Recipe and The Yummiest Dessert. When you get to fifth grade, the teachers assign you rather elaborate homework (which is also a pain in the neck for the parents who have to help out).

When Dumpling Girl told her mum about it on a video call, Kaporin (that's how it sounds when I try to say Kahorun) said, "Ugh, you can't be bothered to do all that, can you? You could just go to the library and find a recipe book from ten years ago or something – copy down a week's worth of recipes. Be careful not to choose the winter dishes. Make sure they're all summer ones. I doubt any normal child would follow the

SUMMER

instructions to a T. Your teacher must know that's how it'll go down. They're just going along with it so the Ministry of Education won't badger them."

"It'll be okay. I've got Kagami here."

"Bringing in Kagami is a no-no, remember? And don't go out of your way to write things like how your parents have different surnames because they're not really married and both work full-time, and on top of that, one is in Kyoto, the other is in Paris. I'm sure I don't have to tell you this, but just in case."

"By the way, I didn't get around to telling you 'cause you were busy, but there's this thing called family cooking class in second term. We can pick a weekend that works for the parents and sign up. The nutritionist will teach us how to make something, and we'll eat it together. Should I ask Kagami to sub for you?"

"Not Kagami. They'll get suspicious about what kind of family we are, if they aren't already ... Would you mind asking Tohoru? He went as your father for that parent–teacher meeting, so who better than the conman for a silly event like that?"

"Can I? The nutritionist is a young woman, though. She's not like the teachers who wear woollen knee-high socks even in summer because they'll get too cold from the air con. *She* wears shapewear stockings that only go up to her thighs."

LUNCH AND SNACKS FOR THE TINY TOTS

"How do you know they only go up to her thighs? Surely she doesn't wear a microskirt to a school?"

"She puts out one leg at a time when she gets out her car."

"Ah . . . I forgot about that. Young women in Japan put their legs out first when they get out of a car instead of swivelling around on their bottom. And they don't let their knees rendezvous when they sit in a chair, either. Oh well, never mind. Anyhow, Itsuki and I definitely won't be able to come, I can't bring myself to think it's worth adjusting our schedules for. Sorry, but can you ask Tohoru? If he says no, tell him I'll spill the beans. He'll change his mind."

". . . What beans?"

"Beans are beans. He'll get it, so don't worry."

"Hmm. So, I can eat at the lesson?"

"Well, that's what you do in a cooking class, isn't it? Polish off the whole feast on the table. Of course it's fine."

"True. I'll try asking Sakuragawa." That was Dumpling Girl's plan from the beginning; she'd just wanted Kaporin's permission. "Talk to you later," she said, fully satisfied, and hung up.

When Dumpling Girl asked Kagami what the family classic recipe for her assignment should be, he said, "It's summertime, so how about something refreshing: stir-fried rice with lettuce?" So that was settled.

SUMMER

For her original recipe, Dumpling Girl picked her favourite bird's nest toast. And for the yummiest dessert, they chose one with brown rice amazake, a sweet drink made from fermented rice. The amazake they'll use won't have added sugar or additives; its sweetness will come just from the rice koji.

The original recipe is Kagami's, of course, but her classmates are sure to snatch their recipes off the Internet and claim to have put their own spin on it, so it's fair game.

It was a bad habit of Dumpling Girl's, though, to pick the most complicated time to do something, and she decided her cooking class with Kagami should happen today of all days, when the small dining room was packed with kids.

With his pale, slender face, Kagami gives the impression of having a sensitive, nervous temperament, but he sprung from Mum Komaki and Mr Dodo, after all, so he's much stronger and more ballsy than he looks. (Sakuragawa did say that he tried to make Kagami cry when they were at school, but never succeeded.)

Kagami is also patient and generous, at least when he's dealing with younger people. So even when his stony expression makes him look like he's annoyed with Dumpling Girl, he's actually happy to accommodate her single-minded ways.

Since he has to teach her how to make the lettuce fried

LUNCH AND SNACKS FOR THE TINY TOTS

rice anyway, that's going to be the lunch menu for the other kiddies, too. That way, he can cook for everyone together.

Though Rika had picked croquettes and curry on her menu at Rika's Diner today – the kind of dishes that will appeal to anyone – she'd asked Kagami to make something much lighter for the kids.

She wants her children to be able to appreciate the different flavours of each vegetable, so until they learn to do that, she's trying to avoid dishes that make everything taste good with the umami of fat.

"We're farmers, after all," she explained. "They should get to know what veggies really taste like."

Besides the lettuce fried rice, Kagami is making a pumpkin potage with soya milk, scallops and mixed beans marinated in kiwi sauce, and kanten jelly with summer vegetables.

Here's a little secret: the scallops are actually leftovers from my breakfast. This morning, Norimaki and I had crunchies topped with a paste of mashed pumpkin and soybeans, along with scallops grilled in butter and dressed with grated kiwi and frozen lemon once they cooled. I wonder if you've ever tried it. If you put kiwi and lemon together, you might expect it to be doubly sour, but it actually give you this subtle, sweet flavour.

The sourness of the lemon is a perfect match with the butter, and when they melt together in your mouth, it makes

SUMMER

the scallops feel so much bigger than they really are, so soft and delectable. According to Kagami, Norimaki and I need to get a decent amount of the amino acid called taurine, and scallops are a great source. Eating it with vitamin C helps your body absorb it better.

Norimaki loves butter with melted lemon, and he races to the kitchen whenever he catches a whiff of it. He just can't wait till it cools down: he dances on his hind legs, crying out, "It's mine! Mine! Ahh, give me!"

When it was time to dig in, he lapped up the butter with every bite of scallop, so he got it all over his face, dripping everywhere. As always, Kagami had laid the Cheburashka picnic blanket underneath Norimaki before he started eating. (Cheburashka is that cartoon character with big round ears, and this blanket is Norimaki's favourite because somehow he thinks Chebu and him are alike. Chebu has brown fur and looks pretty different if you ask me, but oh well.) Soon the waterproof blanket got greasy with butter, and since Norimaki walked all over it, his paws got buttery, too. And then he got carried away licking his paws and rolled over on his back, so in the end, he was just a buttery ball of fur.

But Kagami took care of him well. He carried Norimaki to the linen room and wiped him with a warm towel, then wrapped him up in a fluffy clean one. He stayed like that, snuggling in the towel inside a basket woven from chocolate vine, and drifted off to sleep. He has it easy. But then the kiddies arrived in the middle of his nap, so he had to scurry around looking for a hiding place, still drowsy.

He couldn't find a good spot in time, though, and he ended up getting snatched up by the Hug Squasher.

Now, back to Dumpling Girl's cookery assignment. She's wearing a white tablier today, like an apron a schoolchild would wear in France, buttoned up at the back. The top part is sewn onto the bottom part, which fans out like an airy A-line skirt. Instead of a bandana, she's sporting a hat with an elastic band that makes her head look like a mushroom. It's better than a bandana because it holds in her fringe and stray strands of hair.

With a handkerchief, you can't cover all your hair; it's okay when you're just cleaning the house, but it's a puzzling choice of headgear for cooking. Well, not that *we* can talk, when we go around rubbing against everything and leaving trails of fur.

They're going to use brown rice for the stir-fry. Not freshly cooked, though – Kagami cooked it earlier and kept it warm in the wooden rice tub. And she'll use his homemade spring onion oil for frying. To make it, he chopped some spring onions, sprinkled herb salt over it, and left it out to dry a little on a sunny day. Then he put it in a storage jar and poured in the oil. After about three days, it's ready for use. The juice

SUMMER

from the spring onions seeps into the oil and gives it a delicious aroma.

Kagami continues his lecture in his usual deadpan delivery. It's not like he's in a bad mood, though; he might sound indifferent, but he's still very thorough.

"Since you're using spring onion oil, you only need some dried whitebait and roasted sesame seeds for the flavouring. You get enough salt from the whitebait, so you don't need more. Usually I don't put in eggs for Komaki's portion, though it also depends on what the menu looks like for the day. It's good to eat eggs to help prevent you going senile, but they're high in calories, so we have to be careful. But you have to eat well to grow, Hikari, so in your case, it's better to put in the eggs."

Lettuce looks yummy when it's lightly stir-fried in oil. Back when I lived with Mademoiselle Rocco, I met a pair of sisters who *loved* crunching on raw lettuce – that was when we visited her friend Rena. They used to halve a head of lettuce between the two of them. Rena would tear the leaves into smaller pieces by hand, and they'd gobble up the whole thing for breakfast.

If they knew what stir-fried lettuce tastes like, they might want some, too. One time, Mum wrote in her Komakoma Diary about a recipe where you boil an entire head of lettuce in a pot. It's something they make at Matsu Sushi for their employees. Their workers get free meals as part of their pay,

LUNCH AND SNACKS FOR THE TINY TOTS

and sometimes they go Western-style, even though their catering business specialises in Japanese food. I'll copy down a passage from the diary here:

For those of you who think lettuce is best enjoyed raw and crispy in a chilled salad – or for those of you who think it's just something you find at the bottom of the bowl to pad out the little side salad that comes with your lunch, not even worth eating – allow me to present a dish that will make the scales fall from your eyes.

I'd rather keep it to myself if I'm honest, but a special treat is there to be shared; if I'm stingy, I'll get bad karma. So, I'll lay it all out on the table today. Lettuce is in season towards that time of autumn when there's a chill in the air. If you think about it, it makes sense to have it as a steaming hot dish, doesn't it?

Enough preamble – I'll get on with it. It's such a simple recipe, really. The pot makes it for you. You know that enamelled pot that comes in pretty colours? Yes, that one. That world-famous pot that makes France proud. It's time to put it to good use. First, you pop in a whole head of lettuce in boiling water and let it cook for about five minutes. (Before you put in the lettuce, add about a teaspoon of salt. You can also cut the lettuce in two and boil one half at a time.)

Haul it out and pour soup into the pot until it's about an inch high. You don't have to measure it, though. Imagine the

SUMMER

lettuce is having a footbath – like that. Anything goes for the soup, too. Chicken broth, kombu dashi, you name it. Next, you toss a bouquet garni into the soup. These days you can get a mix of herbs like that in a teabag, so it's easy peasy. Whatever you have to hand. Then a slice of butter. Cultured butter would be my pick.

If I were French, I'd line the pot with bacon or drop in half a cup of butter like it was nothing, but I can't possibly be so reckless. I put in just enough to get a whiff of it.

And then, open one can of your favourite beans. Empty the whole can, about 250 grams, right into the pot. All in one go. It can be one kind of bean, or it can be a mix: whatever you fancy.

Instead of sugar, scatter some orange or lemon peels in there. A pinch of herb salt. If you have grilled chicken in the freezer, or something like that, you can pop that in, too. Grilled chicken skin, say, or breast fillets would go well. And finally, just put the lettuce on top of that, close the lid, and let it simmer and steam. Give it time – about half an hour.

Trust me, it's worth the wait. Once it's ready, cut the lettuce apart and serve it in a bowl with a big heap of beans. A Spanish-style bowl would go wel – a slightly thick one with blue birds and clovers and things like that painted on it.

You might be wondering, "Why not cabbage?"

Well, the word "lettuce" derives from lactūca, *and* lac *means milk. Just like the white milk that comes out when you*

LUNCH AND SNACKS FOR THE TINY TOTS

snap a stalk of dandelion or thistle, lettuce has its own milk, too. And there's the added bonus that this lettuce milk lulls you into a good night's sleep.

To put it the other way around, it's best not to eat too much lettuce during the day. Especially when you have to wrap up a manuscript!

Led by Sacchan, the kiddies went out to explore the neighbourhood. Well, just to play in the Marukos' garden really. Mr Maruko's family used to be ume plum farmers, so their plot of land is so much bigger than the other houses around here. The family haven't sold their ume since Mr Maruko's father's generation, but they still have a few trees just for themselves.

Uncle Bear is out today; he's attending Miss Oisa's dieting workshop with Mrs Maruko. It's obvious what his problem is, though. He's having too much fatty food, like veal and Gruyère cheese pie, or white fish in creamy béchamel sauce. He just has to quit having stuff like that with Mr Maruko, and problem solved. No need to ask for Miss Oisa's advice.

But for him, the workshop is just an excuse: the only reason he's more than eager to step into his carrier and head to Miss Oisa's is that he'll get to see Lila there. (Lila's a stylish girl with a nice pale lilac coat and lilac-pink in her nose and paws. Though he should know by now that she doesn't like big food guzzlers.)

SUMMER

The ume trees are lush with green leaves now. The family doesn't prune them anymore, so they've grown tall. Where there's a dozen or so trees clustered together, they offer big patches of shade that make a perfect playground for a summer morning.

The sisters, Hako and Kokona, started a game of elastics under the trees to see who can jump higher. Since there weren't that many of them, they tied the elastic rope between two trees. First they started at ankle height; even Konsaburo could jump over that one. Then they moved it higher after each round.

Midway through the game, Dumpling Girl joined in. They quarrelled a bit over the rules at first. They go to different schools, so the versions they play aren't exactly the same when it comes to the little details, like whether it's "safe" or "out" when your leg snags on the rope as you jump from inside the oval to the outside, or whether it's "out" when you don't land with both feet together.

Dumpling Girl, being older, backed down. But that didn't stop Hako from getting grumpy. That was when I learned that girls around nine years old can be the trickiest to deal with.

It should've been Sacchan's job to keep the peace, but he was off changing Konsaburo's nappy. When they came back, Sacchan showed us all kinds of tricks, like a true master: skipping over the rope with a handstand, or doing cartwheels, or a super jump. Even Hako perked up at Sacchan's performance and excitedly clapped her hands.

Only Yuria had her back turned on the rest, busy making mud dumplings by herself. Her shoulders had the determined set of an artisan. She was bent on not being a good girl today no matter what: going her own surly way with a permanent pout on her face.

Peering down at the young dumpling-maker, Dumpling Girl complimented her handiwork. "Quite a masterpiece you're making. Mixing in pieces of plum, huh? The colours look realistic."

Yuria, who had been working in grim silence, looked up and flashed a wide grin. Even a tetchy artisan has a soft spot that can loosen her up.

Dumpling Girl came over to me and whispered in my ear: "They look just like when Norimaki's stomach is a bit upset. She might have a hard time trying to take them home with her when she's done, though."

So that's what she meant by "realistic"!

Soon it was time for lunch. Since the kids had been woken up fairly early for a Saturday and eaten early breakfasts before getting dropped off at the Horai house, they were all starting to get restless, peeking into the kitchen to check what was going on.

SUMMER

Kagami and Sacchan put their heads together and decided to have an early lunch, so Sacchan shepherded the kids to the table.

To start off, Kagami brought out the soya milk pumpkin potage that he'd made in the morning and chilled in the fridge. The thick soup was served in soba chokos – small handleless cups normally used for soba noodles. He'd mashed the pumpkin with the skin on, so there was a faint tinge of green in the bright yellow, but since he'd pressed it through a strainer a few times, the soup was really smooth, like a more fluid version of soft-serve ice cream, even though it didn't have any cream, butter, sugar or egg in it. Instead, he added a bit of tofu to the pumpkin, and turned the switch on and off when he gave it a spin in the food processor: that's how you can get a texture like this. All you need is the deep flavour that comes from the soya milk and the sweetness from the kabocha pumpkin.

Next up was kanten jelly with vegetables. Kagami, who's good with his hands, had cut the jelly into neat lozenge shapes. The red cherry tomato and the black soybean floating in the transparent jelly made an eye-catching contrast. For grown-ups, he would've put in black olives, but since his guests today were little kids, he substituted them with kuromame soybeans for a bit of extra sweetness – though to make up for that, there was no sugar in the jelly itself. Besides the

LUNCH AND SNACKS FOR THE TINY TOTS

red and black veg, he also put in pieces of okra and lotus roots because they have interesting shapes when they're cut.

Sacchan got a phone call from Tekona, asking if everyone was behaving. He gave her an update: so far, so good.

I, for one, however, was a little uneasy about how quiet Yuria had been. She's usually a bouncy entertainer whenever I see her at Seishiro Farm, clambering up onto the cargo bed of their kei-truck and singing a medley of Hibari and Harumi at the top of her lungs. (You might be surprised that a little girl like her knows Hibari Misora and Harumi Miyako – well, she takes after her grandad.)

Tekona passed on a message from Rika: "Konsaburo isn't really reliable yet when it comes to going to the toilet; even if he says he's fine, he's usually on the brink of an accident. So if either you or Kagami can take him with you when you go to the bathroom, that would be great. Yuria can go by herself now. I don't think she'll accept assistance from gentlemen, anyway."

While Kagami cooked lettuce fried rice for the kiddies, Dumpling Girl made her own portion next to him. (This house has two gas hobs: a big one with four rings and a smaller one with two.)

She heated up Kagami's spring onion oil in the pan, then sprinkled in a handful of dried whitebait and fried it until the fishy smell was gone. Next, the warm rice went in along

SUMMER

with sun-dried slices of aubergine and cucumber. To make the egg version of the dish, you'd pour in the beaten eggs at this point, but she skipped it for today. She's a fan of crunchy okra, simply grilled, so she added some of that to the pan, too.

Whitebait makes a nice dashi by itself, so there was no need for salt or pepper. For the last step, she tore some lettuce by hand, stirred it in, quickly turned off the heat, then grated some frozen lemon zest over it while it was still hot. It looked like grated cheese, but it was actually lemon sorbet. Just another stir around the pan, and it was done.

"Lettuce goes well with anything in a stir-fry: you can cook it with small shrimp and broccoli too, or courgette and octopus. Or with walnuts and olives pickled in vinegar. Tomato and parsley, or red pepper and cashew nuts would work well, too," Kagami said. "If you want it to be more filling, you can add chicken mince or breast fillet, or thin strips of pork. Julienned carrots and tarako roe are another nice combo, but watch the cholesterol and salt levels when you cook with fish roe. Just try out whatever pops into your head, and you'll have your original recipe."

"Aww, but you said all the combos already."

"I've barely scratched the surface. There's hijiki seaweed and burdock root, lotus root and—"

"Stop!"

"Anyway, since both of your parents are working out of

LUNCH AND SNACKS FOR THE TINY TOTS

town, it's a good idea to know how to rustle up a little something – then you can fill yourself up as long as you have some rice to hand. I was in the same boat as you. Canned food was a lifesaver when I was too hungry to wait. You can't go wrong if you keep a ready stock of tins just for yourself, like tuna or asari clams in water. Even if the salt concentration's a bit high, it's fine if you don't use all the water in the tin. Besides, if you compare it to buying fast food or bread with savoury toppings, it's still a lot healthier. One thing to watch out for when you buy canned food is to avoid the kinds with oil. You can't do anything about the fat content there. And it smells weird. Try checking if it's got any additives, too."

The lettuce fried rice was ready, and the kiddies dug in with their utensil of choice: chopsticks, a fork or a spoon. Since they were already done with the pumpkin soup, they each had a cup of black soybean tea to go with the rice. The kids and their dishes took up the whole table in the small dining room, so there was no space for Dumpling Girl to write in her notebook.

Besides, the kids had as much table manners as Norimaki, and they'd spread their "goods" all over the table, so it was safer to keep her school notebook well away. I'm sure her assignment didn't include submitting a "scented" recipe.

Instead, Dumpling Girl stayed in the kitchen after cooking. Sitting in the chair with the side table attached to it, she

SUMMER

ate her fried rice and jotted down the ingredients in her Mamemon notebook hanging from her neck.

Early next week, she's going to meet up with Itsuki, who managed to get some time off, and Kaporin, who'll be flying back from Paris, to stay in a bungalow near Lake Biwa. That's why she wants to finish all her nutrition homework today.

After a quick meal, she got down to making the bird's nest toast. She's made this one a few times before, so she can manage on her own.

Kagami went over to the table to help Sacchan, who was so busy helping the kids that he hadn't had a single bite to eat himself.

Yuria toddled out into the corridor from the kitchen and headed for the entrance hall. The house has a slightly unusual construction: there's a bathroom attached to every bedroom upstairs, but (or maybe because of that) there's only one guest toilet downstairs, even though it's a big space with a living room and two dining rooms.

The kids were told to use the toilet in Kagami's semi-basement room because it's closer to the small dining room. But Yuria chose to go to the guest toilet that's further away. Clearly she'd made up her mind to do everything her own way today.

"Are you okay by yourself?" Dumpling Girl asked. She was

the oldest of the group besides Sacchan and Kagami, so she seemed to feel responsible.

Yuria's hair was parted in the middle and twisted into buns above her ears, wrapped in chocolate brown scrunchies with blue polka dots — which made her look like she had a pair of pointy ears. She nodded at Dumpling Girl in response and disappeared down the corridor.

But she came back in no time. When I glanced back, thinking she'd been too quick even for a toddler, I saw that it wasn't Yuria but Sakuragawa. He hadn't rung the doorbell, so I didn't notice him come in. He's supposed to be acting as a sort of security guard for the house, so he has his own key for the front door.

"I passed a munchkin just now — since when was this house a Bambi Garden?" he asked.

"We're looking after them today 'cause everyone's at the flea market," Dumpling Girl answered. After a pause, she asked, "Why 'Bambi Garden'?"

"Wasn't there a kindergarten called something like that in the next town over? The place Kagami went to when he was a kid."

"That was ages ago," she said.

"I'm surprised they asked *you* to babysit, Hikari."

"Not me, obviously — they hired Sacchan. Kagami's

SUMMER

in charge of the cooking. So, what are you doing here, Sakuragawa?"

"Well, I'm going to go gallery hopping later, so thought I'd grab a bite to eat before heading out."

"Here? But you know lunch isn't part of the deal."

"Food goes off faster in the summer – there's bound to be something in the fridge that should be hoovered up sooner rather than later, right?"

"I guess in a normal house, there'd be a bunch of 'unidentified objects' forgotten in the fridge, but not in this kitchen. There's plenty of mouths to feed, and Kagami is super on top of *eh*-verything. No scrap of food goes wasted on his watch. Besides, the house is gonna be pretty empty next week, so the kitchen's probably less stocked than usual."

"Empty? Is everyone going somewhere?"

"Komaki and Koyomicchi are going on a trip to Hokkaido together. And I'll be on holiday with my parents. Kahorun's coming back from Paris, and we'll go to Kyoto to see Dad."

"What about Kagami?"

"He'll stay home. We've got Makimaki to take care of, so we can't all go at once. Gotta take turns. Kagami said he doesn't mind going last."

"Huh. So, he'll be here by himself then."

She paused for a moment. "Are you plotting something?"

"Oh, nothing. It's news to me, that's all."

"Hmm, are you gonna think something up later?"

"Think what up?"

"That's what I'm asking – you tell me. I mean, isn't it your hobby to bully Kagami?"

"*Tease*," he corrected her without missing a beat. Bullying is bad, but teasing is different, seemed to be his point. He wandered over to the fridge to peer inside.

As I said before, the fridge here is in the corridor instead of the kitchen. When they first built the house, they got a huge fridge as wide as a chest of drawers because the international tenants would surely want to roast whole chickens, casually devour bucket-sized tubs of ice cream, and stock up on steaks as thick as the sole of a trekking shoe. And a fridge like that was too big for a fitted kitchen.

Now the Horai family has a different fridge, but it's still rather big. Mademoiselle Rocco's was tiny by comparison. Its contents were completely different, too. Rocco kept all her creams inside her fridge: both the cream she'd put on her face and the one for eating. Sometimes she'd have a spoon of face cream by accident (she was near-sighted).

She liked mayonnaise, too. No-one in the Horai family would even touch mayo. Instead, they use a soybean dip blended with plain or wine vinegar, adding a spot of mustard or pesto to taste.

The bird's nest toast that Dumpling Girl was about to

SUMMER

make usually calls for mustard mixed with mayo or butter, but for her version, she uses the soybean dip instead, spread over sandwich bread with the crust still on.

First, she makes four perpendicular cuts on each slice of bread: one cut on each side of the square, starting from the crust and going halfway towards the middle. Then she takes two baking cups that are normally used for pudding and pushes a slice into each of them, arranging the four corners so they make a tulip shape. Then she pops them into a preheated toaster oven and waits until the tips of the tulip petals turn a crisp golden brown. It's down to your preference, so you can stop when it's a lighter colour, too – as long as the bread stays in the tulip shape when you take it out of the cup.

All that's left is to spread the soybean dip flavoured with mustard or pesto on the inside, then stuff it with boiled vegetables like a bouquet, and voilà: you have your bird's nest. Today, Dumpling Girl prepped two kinds of soybean dip for each bread cup: one mixed with chopped cucumber and walnuts, and another with mustard.

Kagami came out and found Sakuragawa by the fridge, taking out a container of aubergine nibitashi, braised in dashi and soy sauce, that Kagami had made and set aside for his own dinner tonight.

After the flea market, Mum and the others are going out

LUNCH AND SNACKS FOR THE TINY TOTS

together to have a little post-event party. They've already made a reservation, and they're going to bring along the kiddies, too. Sacchan will join them because he likes going to parties like that, but Kagami said he'll pass, and set aside some food for himself in the fridge.

"Mind if I have this?" Sakuragawa asked.

Of course, Kagami couldn't (or didn't) say no to his senpai, so he simply said, "Please help yourself," and added, "There's rice in the tub, too."

"Do you have any ginger?"

"Would you like me to chop some?"

"Nah, I can do it myself. I'll cut off a bit more than usual, if that's okay. And can I borrow a pot? This looks sharp."

He was talking about Kagami's chef's knife, which is always honed and pristine, as you might expect. That's why he stows it away somewhere Norimaki and I can't reach.

With the knife, Sakuragawa sliced the ginger into needle-thin splinters. Then he brought kombu dashi to a boil in the pot, added some sake to it, and scattered the chopped ginger into the soup. After adding a few drops of soy sauce, he let it come to a boil one more time and quickly turned off the hob.

"You might think this is messy, but it's the way I like it. Thanks to gramps' bad influence."

Sakuragawa topped his bowl of rice with the chilled aubergine — which were cut lengthwise in half — sprinkled on some

SUMMER

pieces of roasted nori seaweed, then poured the ginger soup over it, straight from the pot.

In the meantime, Kagami brought out the chair with the sidetable and put it down where the corridor widens a little into the storeroom on the other side of the accordion curtain, which is usually kept open during the day.

"Thanks," Sakuragawa said, sitting down. "Gramps used to grow aubergines in the garden. He cooked them himself, too. He'd take out the big pot and simmer about fifteen all in one go. First he'd have some for lunch while it's steaming hot, then he'd keep the rest in the fridge. At night, it turned into a nice companion for sake. He'd skip it in the morning – he was a bread kind of guy at breakfast, so soy sauce flavours had no part to play. He usually had some bread and butter, mini pancakes, and a bowl of *salade* with lots of tomatoes, broccoli and beans (he always said it like the French: sala-*de*). Then, back to aubergines for lunch. He'd put the ice-cold leftovers from the day before on top of chilled rice, dust it with roasted nori, and pour hot ginger soup all over it. The best way to have aubergine, in our book. Sometimes he'd swap the nori for fine shreds of oboro kombu, or bonito flakes. Or it could be dried whitebait, or thin strips of dried horse mackerel, or chicken breast fillet, too. Whatever you pick, it's still amazing. Depends on how good the braised aubergine is in the first place, but if you made it, Kagami, I'm sure that's no problem."

LUNCH AND SNACKS FOR THE TINY TOTS

There it was – the killer chat-up line! Dumpling Girl mouthed, "You devil!" at his back. I mimicked her.

Kagami's face remained expressionless – in fact, he seemed rather cool and poised for such a hot summer's day – but his hands stopped moving in the middle of washing up. Maybe he was imagining a pot full of aubergines, or he might've been picturing Sakuragawa's perfect slices of ginger, as thin as needles, and secretly squeeing inside.

"It's good," Sakuragawa said, polishing off the aubergine rice. The way he ate was as smooth as everything else he did: he didn't seem to be paying any particular attention to it, but there wasn't a single stain on his white broadcloth shirt.

Getting up to wash his bowl, he asked Dumpling Girl to let him borrow an apron. Kagami went into the small dining room to check how the kiddies were getting on with their lunch.

"Cute or retro? Pick one," she said.

"How about the one you'd recommend?" he answered.

Clearly, Sakuragawa knew how to handle little girls, too. If he'd picked either one himself, he would've walked right into her trap. No doubt she'd bring him a cute frilly apron, or a dark old-school waist apron with a big fat logo on the front (you know, the ones they wear in shops like Mikawa-ya and Yamato-ya). The right answer was to let *her* pick her own favourite. That's the rule when it comes to girls like her.

SUMMER

In the end, Dumpling Girl brought him a navy apron with white lettering on it that said "Makkujira" (まっ鯨); the kanji character for *whale* (鯨) was drawn in a unique shape, and you could make out a whale swimming inside it. Like the lettering on Kagami's apron, this was Dumpling Girl's calligraphy, too. There was a stamp on the side, which contained a stylised drawing of her name.

"What does that mean?" Sakuragawa asked.

"It's a pun on 'masshigura'. Kagami told me that Ryunosuke Akutagawa liked to say 'makkujira' when he really meant 'masshigura' – going 'full *whale* ahead' instead of 'full *sail* ahead'. I got a compliment from Master Kujira for this one."

I forgot to mention, but Master Kujira – or "Master Whale'– is Dumpling Girl's calligraphy teacher as well as her great-grandfather on her mother's side. In other words, he's the same "gramps" that Sakuragawa was talking about.

"You know, Hikari," Sakuragawa said, "if you put your calligraphy out on the market, you'll get buyers. It's only because Itsuki hasn't given you permission yet that just the family's enjoying it now."

"Whispers of the devil." She clamped her hands over her ears and ran away. Kagami came back just as she left, carrying the dishes from the kids' lunch, all empty: the kids had gobbled up everything.

"Gochisosama," Sakuragawa said, thanking Kagami for the aubergines, and headed for the front door.

In the afternoon, there was a short arts and crafts session led by Sacchan, who showed them origami at the table in the small dining room. After that they moved to the living room for nap time. For a while, they romped around making a racket, until everyone except Hako started nodding off. Even Yuria, the defiant artisan, was still too little to shake off the drowsiness. Sulking really does use up a lot of energy.

Only the fourth-grader, Hako, was still wide awake. She sat leaning back on the sofa, writing and drawing in a diary. Jean Paul passed her on the way to the small dining room.

"Hello, mademoiselle," he said.

"Hello," she answered out of habit. She didn't remember Mr Dodo's face, and she thought it was natural to see someone she didn't know in someone else's house, so she wasn't surprised by his presence.

Meanwhile, Dumpling Girl worked on the last part of her homework, the yummiest dessert recipe, with Kagami's help.

"When you use the food processor, be careful of the blades – watch out you don't cut yourself, of course, but you've also got to make sure Chimaki and Norimaki don't climb up on the sink. They can easily press the buttons, so it's a real safety hazard. If you can, keep them out of the kitchen. Just

SUMMER

give Norimaki a small empty bag, and that'll keep him busy for a while. Chimaki doesn't fall for that anymore, so you'd need something else . . ."

"We could leave a couple of books open on the floor, like colourful picture books, or photography books, especially the ones with high-contrast pictures," Dumpling Girl suggested. "I think Chimaki's interested in that kind of stuff. He likes travel brochures, too. He can easily spend half an hour or so staring at them with this serious look on his face."

"I wonder if he's missing the nomad life."

"Maybe it's his age? Maomao *(Chima-note: that's our vet, Miss Oisa, whose real name is Mao Yamao)* said Chimaki was about nine months old when he came here. It's been five months, so he must be at least a year old by now."

She was right. Mademoiselle Rocco told me that I was born in June. Rocco was born in June too, so we made a promise to celebrate our birthdays together – but as I said, we got separated in the chaotic bustle of the airport in the New Year's season, and we haven't seen her since. I wonder if we'll ever see her again. If I can find a way to get in touch with her, I'd love to let her know that Grandad picked us up off the streets, and now we're living in Mum's house and doing very well.

The other day, Tekona brought us freshly picked blueberries from her mum and Kagami made a compote out of

LUNCH AND SNACKS FOR THE TINY TOTS

them. That's what he'll use for dessert today. When you make compote, you have to use heaps of sugar to make it last longer, but he went easy on the sugar this time, so he's planning to use it all up within the next week or two.

Dumpling Girl wanted to make her own portion, so she scooped up fifty grams of blueberry compote. To this she added 100 grams of brown rice amazake and one teaspoon of black vinegar, then mixed it all up in a food processor. After that, she just has to let it sit in the fridge until it's nice and cold.

Before they set up the food processor, Kagami filled an empty paper bag with air and flaunted it in front of Norimaki. Norimaki fell for it and followed him into the corridor. Dumpling Girl spread a travel brochure on the floor of the corridor, showing pictures of the trulli from Alberobello. I played along and pretended to be distracted. Jean Paul came to peer over my shoulder, too. (In fact, the one who likes these holiday brochures is Jean Paul, not me.)

"These pointy roofs are so picturesque. Wish I could see them in person," he said with a smile.

Now it's time for a snack, so the tiny tots gather in the small dining room again. The sweets for the little guests that Kagami prepared yesterday and chilled in the fridge overnight are already waiting for them on the table; the kids munch on them without so much as a peep.

SUMMER

"This is so good," Sacchan says. "It's like a totally guilt-free dessert. Your recipe, Zaku?" He's got a real sweet tooth, so he's even more excited than the kiddies.

Norimaki is crawling forward into the linen room with his head still buried in the bag. The moment it slips off, he spots an even better toy and pounces on it. Yuria's wellies. He's never read *Puss in Boots* – though I guess he would've done it anyway even if he had. He sticks his head in one boot and goes right in.

He burrows deeper into it, his upright tail sticking out of the boot. Then he pokes his head out and stays there like he's enjoying a boot-bath. I'm wondering whether I should tell him or not.

It turns out Yuria the artisan was also a partisan who hid her mud bombs inside her own boots.

5

Autumn

Picnic

All-you-can-stuff picnic basket

Black tea & coffee, herbal water

Cucumber sandwiches & meat pies

*Steamed pork meatballs with mochi rice coating
& pressed anago sushi*

Ohagi (with mochi-awa)

Fig confiture & pomegranate vinegar

+

Crispy-grill of small horse mackerel (meow-food)

Every year around mid-October, Mum visits the cemetery to remember her late husband and the meow-friends who used to live with her before we came. People usually visit their ancestors' graves in September around the Autumnal equinox during the week known as Higan, but her Higan visit happens a month later. Why? Because it's still hot in September, with lots of mosquitoes buzzing around, so it's not a great time for a picnic.

Whoever heard of putting together the Higan graveyard visit and a picnic? It's a funny thing to do, but also just like Mum to think of it. There's lots of green around Tama Cemetery, where Mr Dodo is sleeping. The park across the street has a wide grassy field, and a clump of tall trees called momijiba-suzukakenoki (also known as London planes) stands right in the middle of it. That's her favourite picnic spot.

AUTUMN

If it was just greenery she's after, there's a park near the Horai house, too. But Mum is especially fond of this park across from the cemetery because of the interesting topography, including a river, a terraced hill, a shallow valley and even a small mountain.

"But if you squint above the hill, you can make out the logo of a supermarket chain you can find anywhere in the country. It's okay, though – we can just pretend we haven't seen it. People formed dwellings here in the Jomon period, and the shape of the land, with all the ups and downs, hasn't changed much since those prehistoric times. Of course, I suppose it doesn't compare to where *you're* from, with your Japanese Alps."

Mum was talking to Tekona.

"You know what, though? It's embarrassing to admit it, but I actually never noticed the scenery around me before I moved to Tokyo," Tekona said. "I had zero interest in flowers and birds; as far as I was concerned, all the small ones were sparrows, the big ones were hawks and the black ones were crows. I couldn't tell apart apple blossoms from cherry blossoms. And I was completely fine like that. My school was far away, so I had a long commute – and on top of that, I had club practice all the time. In the winter, I used to leave the house before dawn and get back after sunset, so I never hung out anywhere on the way. My friend and I just kept cycling on and on, yakking it up at full volume. And over the summer, I went on trips with the team for away games, training camp and things like that, so I wasn't even home most of the time."

"Er . . . was it handball you did?"

"That's right. The girls' team at my school was really strong. The school Darling went to was pretty strong too, so I'd see him often at national competitions."

"Ah, so that's how you know each other. I thought you'd met when you were travelling somewhere Czech or Nordic. When you picture someone like you – who deals in aesthetic, crafty goods – crossing paths with a photographer, that's the sort of place you'd imagine, don't you think?"

"Well, we did meet again during a trip, actually. I fell in love with the world of zakka: all those little things that you use around the house that enrich your everyday life. I travelled through Russia, collecting handicrafts and tools from their folk culture along the way, and I was heading for the Caspian Sea. And I just happened to run into Darling during the never-ending waiting time for the ferry. Did you know, the Caspian Sea is surrounded by wetlands, so you can only reach it by boat? He'd kept on playing handball in a corporate team after graduating, but one day he picked up a camera by chance and realised that was what he was really meant to do. He might look kind of laid-back and spaced-out, but once he gets an idea into his head, he doesn't let go of it. That's the sort of guy he is."

"That's why you two get along well together, I think. Seems like an overseas reunion is the magic ingredient for tying the knot. It was the same thing with Itsuki and Kahoru, you know. But they met again in Paris, so I can see that happening. The Caspian Sea, though? If you were after cute crafts and things, why not somewhere like Estonia or Lithuania? They're also former Soviet countries, but closer to Scandinavia."

"I got inspired by this film called *The Colour of Pomegranates*. I was drawn to the title, so I borrowed a DVD from a rental shop, and it really opened my eyes. I was like . . . what *is* this? Those colours, those movements, those buildings . . . And on top of that, everyone in it had sturdy, broad shoulders – ideal for handball. But my trip ended before I reached Parajanov's hometown, once I met Darling. And I ran out of money."

"Oh, I saw that at the cinema. It made me hungry – when I saw that scene where they put a weight on the wet documents, I thought it looked like pickling hakusai cabbage; and the shelves crammed with books were like crunchy chocolate. And the pomegranates were so perfectly ripe. You know that bit towards the beginning where they're washing the carpets by rubbing their feet on it, and there's a close-up of the feet? I heard some lady in the audience murmur, 'Oh, that person's got a bunion.' And people around her giggled – I just can't forget that moment. I never even saw this lady's face or anything, but I still remember her voice so clearly."

I don't know how far they wandered from the subject after that. Grandad came over and took us in a willow basket to a neighbourhood park. Inside the basket were a thermos with cold barley tea in it and a datemaki bento. Grandad's datemaki is different from the egg-and-fish-cake omelette roll that you have at New Year's, and it's not the sushi roll wrapped in egg omelette that you find in fishing towns. *His* datemaki is a supersize sushi roll wrapped in two layers of nori seaweed, and for the filling he puts in a thick egg omelette called atsuyaki tamago, along with fluffy fish flakes called denbu, dried gourd strips called kanpyo, and mangetout.

That's what they call datemaki (伊達巻き) at Matsu Sushi. The smaller version is called futomaki (太巻き). Grandad and his father have the kanji from these rolls in their name: Grandad's father was Tatsuma (達巻), and Grandad is Tamaki (太巻) – I know, so confusing! To add to the mix, the American shorthair uncle who liked to gnaw at Troy (the horse head carved on the armrest of the chair in the small dining room) was called Tatsumaki, spelled in katakana: タツマキ.

It was Jean Paul who taught me about London plane trees. They grow fast, reaching impressive heights even when they're

AUTUMN

not so old. The leaves are shaped like a human hand, and in autumn they bear fruit like pom-poms. Though they resemble prickly burr, each spike is actually a seed. According to Jean Paul, these trees are planted in the gardens at the Palace of Versailles, too.

Mum likes to spread two or three big picnic blankets in the shade of the trees and makes things cosy with round and square cushions and long pillows with tassels. Then, taking off her shoes, she puts a few of the cushions and pillows together and stretches out on top of them. With a basket of bento on her side, she's good to go. She spends half the day lounging there, having a bite to eat or a sip of her drink when she feels like it – and she couldn't be happier.

So, back in September, when everyone else was doing the usual Higan things, she just munched on the ohagi (those sweet mochi rice balls people have during the Higan week) that Tekona had brought for her.

"Don't worry, he's not the kind of person who gets mad because his family won't follow the calendar and come to bring him home right on the dot," she said. "If he has something he needs, *he'll* be the one to come and visit *us* – I'm positive."

Jean Paul gave a deep nod of agreement.

This autumn, Dumpling Girl's school is going to have an extra day off to make up for sports day, which will be held on a weekend. So everyone decided to take the same day off and go for a picnic together.

"Perfect timing. Looks like I can make it, too," Jean Paul remarked, studying the whiteboard with everyone's schedules on it. But he always looks like he's got all the time in the world. Who knows what he meant by "perfect timing"?

They're going to take Norimaki and me to the picnic, too. We'll ride in Koyomi's car to the park. That's yet another reason to postpone the cemetery visit by a month. During the real Higan in September, there are traffic jams from all the visitors – not just cars, but also extra taxis and buses that do laps between the cemetery and the nearest train station – and it's impossible to find a parking space.

Norimaki and I are used to going in Koyomi's car. That's how we get to our regular check-ups at Miss Oisa's. Besides, after we got separated from Mademoiselle Rocco, we drifted from town to town by hitchhiking along the national highway. So we quite like going for drives, actually.

We used to hide in the shadows in the service areas off the highway, carefully observing each truck that rolled in. When we saw a driver we felt we could trust, we went over to talk to them. I can tell by instinct when someone's got meow-family. People like that can catch our meow-talk, too. It's not like we can have a proper conversation, but we understand each other. Usually they'd say something like, "Sure thing, come right in. You're headed for the next rest stop, yeah? Gotcha, I'll take you there. What happened to your mama? You lost?"

Every time they asked, I told them about how we got separated from Mademoiselle Rocco at the crowded airport in the New Year's season. Rather than milking it (I mean, shedding crocodile tears), it was more effective to sound a bit like a lost foreigner (speaking in a faltering way).

"*Miaoaowowo . . . Nmiamyumyumyumo. Mumumyamo.*"

"You had a tough time, huh? You can come to mine, if you want. I've got Jones and Etsuko staying with me right now. I don't know their real names, but that's what I call them. They're both in the middle of a trip. I'm based near Lake Hamana, and it's linked to the sea, you know? So I get all sorts dropping by. You're welcome to come over, too – though it's a bit far from here. I'll treat you to some good anago eel. Or do you still want to get off at the next service station?"

"*Miaunmya* (we'll get off). *Miaunya* (thank you so much)."

"Alright. Your lady Rocco's probably out looking for you somewhere. Poor thing. If only I knew her number, I'd call her myself, but you kitties don't even have collars on."

In the beginning, we were wearing the collars with the jewel charms that Mademoiselle Rocco had given us, but we gave those away to the uncle who looked like a travelling performer and his sidekick, Jonathan, on the big blingy truck.

PICNIC

(Looking back now, maybe they tricked us.) I wonder if those collars had any hints for tracking her down.

Sometimes I have a peak at the newspaper that Koyomi reads; there's a Lost Pets section in the corner. The other day, I saw one that said: "Marron ♀ 1.5 yr old; mixed; maroon cream fur with faint stripes; white socks on front paws and one hind paw on the right; dark brown sock on the left hind paw."

Tekona and her Darling are going to join us at the park, too. They don't have any family graves at Tama Cemetery, but Darling's all-time favourite novelist, Edogawa Ranpo, is buried there, so they thought it would be a good chance to visit his grave. They'll pay their respects to Mr Ranpo first, then head to the park. Hako and Kokona have school, so they won't be coming. Thank goodness.

Dumpling Girl seems more excited about the picnic than about sports day at school. Now that she's a fifth-grader, she apparently can't be bothered to march or dance with everyone, and she doesn't care who wins in the silly competition between team red and team white.

"But I'm looking forward to one thing," she said. "Sakuragawa's coming to sub for Kahorun in the scavenger hunt race, so he'll have to dress up in one of those old-timey aprons with puffy sleeves."

Kaporin (I can't say Kahorun to save my life) must have

AUTUMN

some real serious dirt on Sakuragawa if he agreed to *that*. By the way, there's actually a seventeen-year age gap between the siblings.

According to the story that Kaporin told Dumpling Girl, Kaporin was in senior high when she came home from school one day and overheard her parents talking in the living room. Her mother, Mrs Meowko, murmured, "Scary how one thing leads to another," and her father, Mr Kai, replied, "It's kind of like winning the lottery."

Kaporin called out, "I'm home," and was about to go to her room when her mum said they had something to tell her.

"You're going to have a little brother," Mrs Meowko said. "We know already. When we had you, we were telling ourselves, 'Who cares about the fire horse superstition in this day and age?' but we still couldn't help worrying about it – then there you were, a girl. Every time someone called to wish us well, there was that undertone in their voice that said, 'A girl born in the year of the fire horse? Oh dear.' It got on my nerves. But this time we know it's a boy, and anyhow, it'll be the year of the boar by the time he comes out."

And so, that was how Kaporin became a big sister at seventeen years old. She still huffs when she talks about it. "People gossiped that *I* was the mother, and I almost got kicked out of school! And to top it off, I'm a fire horse!"

*

PICNIC

For the picnic, they're planning to bring plenty of tea and coffee, as well as herb-infused water. Mum says she turns into a glutton when she's outdoors. She has a big picnic basket which holds a set of plates and teacups, and she stuffs it with sandwiches, meaty finger foods and sweets. Mid-October weather is cooler than the lingering heat of September, so the food doesn't spoil as easily.

"We should still be careful what to take, though," Kagami says. "It still feels summery during the day."

Kagami has made a list of everything that Mum Komaki has asked for, and he crosses out the items that he doesn't deem suitable.

When she gets going, Mum really keeps the requests rolling. Even just for drinks, she wanted four different kinds: black tea, coffee, herbal water and bancha. She wants simple cucumber sandwiches in the British style, but accompanied by sausages with herbs like basil and rosemary, and egg jelly, too.

Her egg jelly goes like this: first, you pour about half an inch of chicken stock with gelatine into a cup and let it solidify in the fridge. You add a shiso leaf or two on top of that, and a slice of ham as thin as lace. Gently drop a poached egg on top, then pour more gelatine soup up to the brim of the cup, and chill it again until it's set. She'll take these in a cool box.

AUTUMN

There's hot food on the list as well. Mum wants to bring a mini fondue pot that's fired with solid fuel tablets so that they can indulge in melted cheese outdoors.

They make a good pair: Mum, who thinks "the more the merrier" and just says whatever pops into her head, and Kagami, who's more of a minimalist. I'm sure they'll cancel out each other, and the menu will settle at just the right place on the day of the picnic.

I don't know what the Horais' picnics were like in previous years, but from what Mum says, it sounds like a cheat day where they put aside all thoughts of calories for once.

"Autumn is the harvest season, after all," Mum says. "A time to be grateful for nature's gifts – and it's nice to have at least one day in the year when you let yourself go and eat whatever you like without a care in the world."

At least on the day of the picnic, she gives herself permission to have sweets made with generous doses of sugar, butter and eggs, as well as spicy sausages.

"Besides, Kagami probably wants to cook proper rich dishes once in a while, going all out on butter and egg and things like that," Mum goes on.

"I'm not so sure about that," Koyomi says, joining the picnic committee. "I think he gets enough fun anyway. I feel like he goes out of his way sometimes to test our restraint. You know how he makes those indulgent snacks that he's planning to eat all by himself and leaves them somewhere obvious with a note, like, 'Feel free to help yourself'?"

Her slipper, hanging on her toes, wags in the air. Norimaki crawls under her chair with his eyes fixed on it, ready to pounce.

"There's a stream near the trees – it's only a small, shallow one, but we better watch out Norimaki doesn't fall in," Mum says. "Chimaki's a big brother, and he's always cautious about everything, so he'll be fine, but Norimaki doesn't know how to stop when he goes shooting off. He's the type to climb a tree on the spur of the moment and get stuck on a high branch."

Mum and Koyomi launch into a discussion on whether to put a leash on Norimaki. It's true that Norimaki likes to run around all the time – he's that kind of age – and he's a lot faster now than when he was a baby. But I'm sure he'll be fine because he sets himself these random rules. All they have to do is to put him down on his favourite outdoor Cheburashka blanket (it's a different one from his mealtime blanket), and he won't take a single step beyond the edges of that square, not even by a fraction of an inch.

And if he wants to go somewhere else, he'll cling to Kagami and ask him to carry him. That's his rule when he's playing outside. He feels safe with Kagami because, unlike the others, he never forgets that Norimaki is sitting on his shoulder or back.

"We shouldn't have anything with onions in it – they

AUTUMN

might eat it by accident," Mum adds. "That means no stuffed shoes, and no golden soup, either."

Mum draws a row of onion heads on the piece of paper in front of her. In the Horai family, "stuffed shoes" means dishes like stuffed aubergines or bell peppers. You scoop out the insides, stuff them with mince meat and chopped onions, and sprinkle panko bread crumbs over it. Then you roast it in the oven until it's crispy golden brown.

"Golden soup is so good when you have it outdoors, but I'll live," Mum goes on. "Better safe than sorry – the boys usually don't ask for snacks after breakfast, but you never know what'll happen outside. If we just steer clear of onions, we won't have to worry about it, right?"

Koyomi requests pork meatballs with mochi rice: one of those things that stay just as tasty even when they cool down. You roll up the mince meat and coat the balls with grains of mochi rice, then steam them. They turn into crunchy meatballs that sort of pop in your mouth. The cooked mochi rice is still good even when it's re-steamed, so they're great for storing in the freezer, too.

"We can't use garlic chives, either – they're in the onion family – so I'll sub it with celery. Is that okay?" Kagami asks Koyomi, adding the mochi rice meatballs to the list.

"Yep, fine by me. It'll be nice with celery, too."

*

PICNIC

In her latest Komakoma Diary column, Mum Komaki wrote about the pure delight of going on a picnic, bringing along plenty of drinks, nibbles and sweets to enjoy to one's heart's content:

Finally, picnic season is here. Rice fields ripen and trees bear fruit. I feel bad for the farmers who have to harvest their crops in a flurry around this time of year, but for me, these are the most luxurious days, when I slow down and savour everything that the season has to offer.

I like to pack a big feast and go on an outing. But the days are short in autumn. Just like they say: the sun drops as fast as the bucket in a well. If I get carried away and roam too far, I'll have to worry about getting home in time, and it could spoil a perfect autumn day. A casual destination is best: somewhere less than an hour away.

When it comes to picnics, the list of things I want to take keeps growing longer and longer, so it helps if we have a car. When Holmes and Dr Watson travel beyond the city in a carriage, Mrs Hudson prepares a bento for them to take on their journey. An English picnic basket that can hold plates and a whole set of cutlery, and even a teapot.

Just because you're having tea outside doesn't mean you have to use paper plates and throw them away before you go home. That's not for me – and I never bring plastics, either. An ordinary meal turns into something a little more special

AUTUMN

when you take it outside; all the more reason to use ceramic or porcelain crockery.

Of course, you don't have to bring your most precious china. I just take the plates and cups that I normally use, picking out the sturdy ones that are harder to break. I prefer something simple: plain white ceramics with one or two blue lines around the rim, perhaps.

The cutlery is important, too. Disposable chopsticks and plastic forks put a damper on things. But bringing stainless utensils for everyone would be too heavy and a bit over the top, even by my standards. I like to bring bamboo cutlery instead. And bamboo chopsticks, too – the kind that taper to thin tips and can easily hold silken tofu without making it fall apart.

Speaking of tofu, I just remembered something from childhood. Every year, on the night of the mid-Autumn harvest moon, we made white tsukimi dango dumplings to offer to the moon, stacking them up in a pyramid shape; and for dinner, we had tsukimi tofu. Our "moon-watching" tofu went like this: you scoop out a round hole in the middle of the tofu (the scooped part is used for other dishes like shira-ae salad), then drop an egg in and steam it until the egg is half-cooked. The grown-ups had chicken eggs, and the kids had quail eggs. Smaller tofu, too. The soft, melty egg sitting in the little tofu bath was simply wonderful. It warmed us up from inside.

Back then, nights in September were still cool even in Tokyo, and children could catch a cold in their sleep. Nowadays, it's too hot and stuffy around the harvest moon. Global warming has advanced, sadly.

Anyhow, back to the picnic.

One time, I travelled to the UK on a holiday – this was back when I still worked at a company, before I went freelance – and I stopped by the refurbished Covent Garden. It was packed with elegant shops, and it had been turned into a popular tourist destination. I was so happy when I stumbled across a picnic basket there, charmingly quaint but not too old, that I bought it without a second thought. It was a little too big to take with me on the flight, so instead of using some packaging material, I bought an old blanket and wrapped the basket in it, tying it with string.

When I tried to check it in with my suitcase, it looked suspicious, so there was a bit of a drama with the attendant at the counter. I had to untie the strings and show them what was inside the blanket, then wrap it up again, but eventually, it passed the test.

It was worth all the trouble: that picnic basket is still doing very well. One thing that bummed me a little bit, though, was when I noticed later on that it was actually made in the US. And in the sixties, on top of that. Americans like barbecues, so their tableware of choice for picnics would be enamel, which can be used for cooking on an open fire.

AUTUMN

It did cross my mind when I bought the basket that the belts for holding the crockery in place looked slightly flimsy. With enamel crockery, you don't have to worry about it clattering against things, so there's no need to secure it so tightly. I fortified the straps myself so the basket can carry ceramics.

But sometimes I shake my head at how silly I am: my favourite set of crockery for picnicking (Nordic plates with rust-coloured glaze splattering the surface like stars, with a blue line on the rim, which looks lovely under chunky golden brown scones and slices of spice cake, or things like cold chicken) are, in fact, ceramic plates that mimic the look of enamel ware.

At my top-choice picnic spot that we go to every year, there are a few London planes growing close to each other, which offer a pleasant patch of shade. The grassy field stretches out all around. Tall yomogi plants that look completely different from the young leaves in springtime flourish everywhere, swishing and swaying in the wind.

Lots of plants that look like the fluffy tails of a white fox are growing there, too: bugbane flowers. And burnet bloodworts, like small crimson lamps.

Since I'm a big glutton, I want to have a little bit of everything: sandwiches, sushi rolls, pies, dango. Everything tastes better when you're sitting outdoors.

For sandwiches, cucumber is all I need. Ones with ham or egg spoil more easily, so we don't take them. You toast the

PICNIC

bread (I like it toasted), spread some mustard, arrange thin slices of cucumber, and put the second piece of bread on top. Very simple. The key is to use fresh cucumbers.

Anyone can join in our picnic – just jump right in. The definition of a picnic in the first place is a shared meal where guests contribute some food. If you bring a dish or dessert, you're one of us.

When my father comes along, he always brings anago bo-zushi. It's a gem that everybody looks forward to. And no wonder: this particular sushi with saltwater eel is the speciality at Matsu Sushi, the catering business my grandfather founded. Nowadays, you can get saltwater eel even in early October. Unlike freshwater unagi eel, they say anago with a plump stomach tastes bad. It means it was an over-eager eel that ate too much, and the food it couldn't digest rotted in its intestines. An eel like that is bound to taste off even when it's grilled with a sauce.

At Matsu Sushi, they procure slim anago through a broker. To make bo-zushi, they brush their secret sauce on the dressed eel, grill it over a fire, lay it lengthways on a long mound of sushi rice, and roll it tight with a bamboo mat.

If not the bo-zushi, my father brings grilled anago and cucumber marinated in vinegar, or dried chicken meat. Both are more than welcome. This chicken, which he coats with honey and dries in the wind multiple times, is beautiful when

AUTUMN

it's slow-grilled in a frying pan; it takes on a glossy shine, with a roasty, mouth-watering fragrance.

Tekona brings us ohagi every autumn during Higan. She follows a family recipe passed down to her by her mum, using a generous helping of red bean paste. I imagine my late husband sitting next to me and pour two cups of kukicha (I always have twig tea with these ohagi). These special rice balls have a certain kind of foxtail millet called mochi-awa mixed in, and the chewy grains add a delicious texture to them. Besides the ohagi, she also brings us figs, berries and other fruits, both fresh and as confiture.

Tekona's family are fruit orchard farmers. Kiwis are their main produce, she tells me, but they also grow other fruits like apricots, quinces and mulberries to have at home.

Best of all, they grow pomegranates. It's an extravagant tree whose blossom resembles a crown, and whose fruit wears a crown on its head. But for most of my life, I'd only known a few ways of eating pomegranates: mainly just loosening the seeds and sprinkling them over yogurt and things like that.

Ever since Tekona's mum sent us a bottle of pomegranate vinegar two years ago, that's been my go-to method for enjoying this fruit. Not only does it have a pretty colour, it's also rich in polyphenol. We use it for making salad dressings, of course, as well as stewing chicken. (Chima-note: By "we" she means Kagami. Mum just eats.)

Tekona's hometown is in a rich land: the water is clean and fresh, orchards flourish, and delicious honey is harvested. Once, when I mentioned that I'd love to try living there, she said, "But it's freezing in winter. Back when I was little, we used to get about twenty inches of snow in one night; it kept snowing the next day and night too, and before I knew it, our front door was completely buried, and we had to go in and out through the upstairs window." Oh, but Tekona, that snow is what makes the most delicious water.

On Saturday, the day before Dumpling Girl's sports day, Kagami went out with Sacchan after finishing his breakfast duties. When they came home in the afternoon, they moved the sofa in the living room in front of the TV (it's usually by the window). They were going to watch a DVD they got at the rental shop.

That meant switching on the "Flash Machine", as Norimaki calls it. TV programmes and DVDs are all the same to him. I tend to watch just the scenes I like (that's what everyone does, right?), but for some reason, Norimaki freezes in front of the TV, just staring at the screen. Before long, his eyes start feeling prickly, and he tries to blink away whatever it is that's bothering him; his nose starts twitching, too. And he gets hiccups and can't stop, weirdly enough.

He's fine as long as he doesn't look at the "Flash Machine",

AUTUMN

so this time, he trotted over to Kagami for a nap, cradled in his arms. When the movie started, Jean Paul came into the living room to watch it, too.

Dumpling Girl was making teru teru bozu in the small dining room – those small, ghost-like dolls made of tissue paper that you hang up to keep the rain away – so I went over to take a look at her handiwork. If sports day was cancelled or postponed, she would have to go to school on the day of the picnic. So she was making a doll to make sure sports day actually happened and she'd get the weekday off.

The doll looked stern, with a thick unibrow drawn in a straight line across its round head. She hung it by the living room window. Just as she was passing the low chest of drawers with the mirror on top, she jumped backwards in surprise.

"Phew, that scared me," she said. "I thought something was on fire. But it's just a reflection."

In the film that Kagami and Sacchan were watching, a barn was burning. The dancing flames turned into water. I thought the water was going to put the fire out, but then it became the water dripping from a woman washing her hair.

Jean Paul taught me it was an association of images. Next thing I knew, the windowpane turned into a mirror. You know how a mirror gets cloudy when you use it for a long time? That's called "growing scales". The white scales came into focus, but they turned into raindrops. Water fell from

PICNIC

the eaves, stretching in long streaks like starch syrup, and I could see the scenery through a hole.

Sakuragawa came in. He walked over towards Kagami. Kagami obviously knew he was there, but he only looked up and said hello when Sakuragawa was right next to him.

"Watching old horror movies again? You like the weirdest things," Sakuragawa said.

"A horror movie? It's Tarkovsky."

"I know, it's the story where the guy keeps seeing his wife's face when he's remembering his mother from childhood, right? Nothing more horrifying than that."

Kagami was inscrutable as usual, but he seemed to be lost in thought. He probably didn't quite get what was so scary about a wife's face.

Sacchan said hi, glancing at Sakuragawa, and turned back to the movie. I guess Sacchan and Kagami have totally different tastes in men. That's my hunch, at least, because Sacchan always keeps his cool when Sakuragawa's around.

"It's definitely not a chick flick, anyway," Sakuragawa said. "Don't you get bored? A man showing you the contents of his dreams and imagination."

"You don't like Tarkovsky, senpai?"

"That's not what I'm saying. But it sure was boring for a school kid. Whenever a guy asked Kahoru out on a date to watch Tarkovsky (what kind of guy asks a girl out like that?), she'd make her little brother come along with her instead of saying no. When all I wanted to watch was stuff like *The Terminator* and *Indiana Jones*."

"What film did Kahoru like?"

"*Stranger than Paradise*. She never got tired of it, even when she watched it over and over. Once she got started, she'd keep the disc in the player for days. It didn't have much of a storyline. Not much dialogue, either. A standoffish woman and a man who's got no money but plenty of time to kill. And nothing happens. New York, Cleveland, Lake Erie, Florida. Then Budapest. A black and white movie."

"So do you like it, too?"

"Are you kidding? Why would I want to watch a surly woman and an old lady who shouts at people in Hungarian?"

"I'm starting to get a feel for what kind of things you don't like."

"Thought you'd have known by *now*," Dumpling Girl cut in. She had hung her teru teru bozu near the window and had been gazing at it in total satisfaction. Clearly, she couldn't help grinning at the thought of Sakuragawa participating in the scavenger hunt race tomorrow, subbing in for Kahoru.

"Never mind, Hikari," Sakuragawa said. "Run along and make some tea for me, will you? Otherwise, I won't hand over your present."

PICNIC

"What present?"

Sakuragawa gave her a glimpse of the box. She did a little dance like Norimaki when he catches a whiff of lemon and butter in the air. Girls these days have specific tastes, so she rushed over to check the brand and the item inside.

She undid the ribbon and peered into the box.

"Yayyy, Pink Fairy!" She threw her hands in the air. Sakuragawa would know exactly what to get her, of course. "Thank you, Sakuragawa. I'll make the tea."

Holding the box close to her chest like a precious treasure, she pattered over to the kitchen. Sakuragawa watched her go, then turned to Kagami again.

"Alright," he said, "while the kid's gone, let's have a little chat, just between us. I wanted to ask you something . . ."

Sacchan kept his eyes on the screen, but he pricked up his ears at that. Kagami was reclining on the sofa with his arms crossed loosely around Norimaki, who was fast asleep.

I don't know if he was trying to keep it a secret from Sacchan, or just because he's a mischievous devil, but Sakuragawa leaned down and whispered something in Kagami's ear.

Kagami blinked a few times. He opened his mouth to say something, but he changed his mind and simply nodded.

"Great, you're a big help. Thanks."

I didn't hear what the favour was, but Kagami never says no to Sakuragawa, so it must have been a breeze for the cheeky

AUTUMN

senpai. Judging by how he'd just bribed Dumpling Girl with luxury chocolates, it was probably something he didn't want Kaporin getting wind of.

I bet he asked Kagami to sub for him on sports day. The original substitute for Kaporin unloading his duties onto a second substitute: Kagami.

Whether Dumpling Girl's teru teru bozu magic worked or not, the sun shone bright on Sunday, and sports day went ahead as planned. Kagami participated in the scavenger hunt race, wearing a frumpy apron, and finished in second place. Since this particular event was organised by the PTA, the top participants all got a prize. Kagami seemed quite happy with his new raspberry-coloured tongs and spatula.

Today is the holiday that everybody's been waiting for. Grandad came first thing in the morning when Kagami was still the only one out of bed, bringing with him the precious anago bo-zushi, specially made in the Matsu Sushi-style.

These days, Grandad only has a tiny tipple in the evening and goes to sleep at nine or so; that's why he wakes up before everyone else. In fact, he gets up so early it's basically still nighttime. His son Tsukune – who took over the business after Grandad retired – is in charge of making the anago bo-zushi for customers, but Grandad himself made this one especially for the Horai picnic.

PICNIC

Grandad doesn't call it bo-zushi, which means "stick sushi" because of the shape it's got before you cut into it. Instead, he calls it damakura-zushi, which basically means "bamboozle sushi". His hands and fingers aren't as nimble as they used to be, but he somehow hoodwinks himself into thinking he's still got the moves, and that's how he can make it happen: so, "bamboozle".

Kagami made clean cuts into the oblong sushi and carefully placed the portions into one tier of the jubako, the set of lacquered boxes. In the meantime, Grandad gave Norimaki and me a treat for breakfast.

For Mum and the others, the sushi with the grilled anago, flavoured with the family's secret sauce, is a special indulgence. As for us two, we still have a soft spot for Grandad's fluffy fish balls and sun-dried small horse mackerel, since they're the first thing that filled us up when the Horais took us in.

Today, he grilled dried fillets of small horse mackerel for us. He prepped them specially for us, so there was no salt on them. We tagged along behind him out the back door and sat around the shichirin, a small charcoal grill. Actually, he was luring out Norimaki (and me for company), so that he wouldn't get in the way while Kagami was busy making the picnic bento.

Grandad grilled the fish until the bones were charred and

perfectly crisp. He'd already removed the small ones that might get stuck in our throats. Uncle Bear from next door wandered out to the edge of their garden, attracted by the aroma. But, following meow-rules, he didn't cross the borderline.

Still, Grandad is fond of Uncle Bear – which goes to show how generous and good-natured a man he is. He also happens to know that Bear's real name is Maroko; he heard it from Mrs Maruko herself.

"So, he's chubby Maroko living with the Marukos," he said once when he was talking to Mum Komaki. (Maru means circle, so the names sound round, you see.)

"They might as well call him Marco, then. Maroko sounds like a girl," Mum said. I kind of agreed with her.

"No no, Maroko's nice," Grandad said. "His parents are called Maro and Roko. That's what Mrs Maruko told me."

"Ah, that makes more sense now."

Mystery solved. By the way, a tiny one peered out from behind Uncle Bear's back today: someone I hadn't seen before, but with a similar pattern on his fur as the big Bear. A Chibi Maroko!

To my surprise, Uncle Bear had become a father. When did *that* happen?

At eleven in the morning, we arrived at the picnic spot underneath the London planes after a stop at the cemetery, which

PICNIC

was our first mission for the day. The family spread their blankets and arranged the cushions, pillows and throws on them. It was a bit far from the car park, so they carried the picnic basket on a trolley, like you do with a stack of suitcases. We might've looked like an odd bunch to other people at the park, but Mum didn't care a whit.

"I'm starving," she said, reaching for a meat pie first. Knowing how she likes to try a bit of everything, Kagami had baked mini versions. "These don't have onions in them, either, do they?"

"I used minced celery instead."

"Then why do they have an onion mark? Or is it supposed to be a watermelon?" She was talking about the incisions in the top layer of the pie for letting out the steam.

"That's a zakuro," he replied. Which by the way, means pomegranate in Japanese.

"Really?"

"Pies need air vents, so I thought I'd use my trademark."

"Trademark . . .? You mean the thing you always draw on your stuff in the house is a zakuro, too?"

"Yeah, why?"

"I always thought it was an onion. I've been wondering what it means for years."

"I thought about drawing a mirror, as in a kagami, but then

AUTUMN

it would just look like a random circle or square, so I went with a zakuro instead."

"Wait, so is that why Sacchan calls you Zaku? It's short for zakuro? I can't believe I never realised before. But why a zakuro of all things?"

"I heard that in ancient times, people used to polish bronze mirrors with zakuro. That's why the Edo people called the entrance into the bathing room at the bathhouse a 'zakuro mouth'. The opening was narrow to keep the steam in, and they had to crouch to get through. Crouch, as in 'kagamu'. Kagamu sounds like kagami, and kagami were polished with zakuro – so, 'zakuro mouth'."

"I get it – 'kagami mouth' would've been too straightforward, so they gave it another twist and made a pun on zakuro instead. Wouldn't expect anything less from Edo folk. But . . . I have to say drawing isn't exactly your strong suit, Kagami."

"Look at Delftware: they started out copying the pomegranates painted on Chinese porcelain, but everyone thought they were onions, and that's how the pattern came to be called Blue Onion."

"Where do you get all this obscure trivia from? Well, I know where. From your father, of course. You must've been having lots of secret conversations behind my back."

PICNIC

"Uh-huh. Like on Sunday mornings over breakfast, when you were sleeping in."

"Oops. Touché."

Tekona and Darling, who had paid their visit to the grave of Mr Ranpo, came to join us. A little way off, an unfamiliar girl with a maroon cream coat was trailing behind them, hiding in the tall grass.

Tekona looked back and beckoned her to come closer. Flustered, she shrank back into the grass.

"She's been following us since the cemetery. She hides when we look back at her, but once we start walking again, she tags along. And now she's come all the way here. She's a cutie, right?"

"Hey, she might be . . ." Koyomi said, recalling the missing pet advert in the newspaper from the other day. "Better take a photo." She rummaged in her bag and pulled out her phone to take a shot of the girl, who was looking the other way.

"Do you have the owner's number noted down?" Mum asked. Peering at the photo, she added, "She looks pretty from the side, too."

"I'll call the Marukos and ask Mariko to look into it."

It turns out Mrs Maruko's first name is Mariko. This was news to me. What a confusing family. Mrs Maruko found the phone number of the owner and passed it on to Koyomi, and Koyomi rang them up.

Koyomi's intuition was spot on: the one who'd followed Tekona was almost certainly the same maroon cream girl who'd gone missing. She was wearing a dark brown sock on her left hind paw, just like in the description. She strutted up to Norimaki's Cheburashka blanket.

"May I intrude?" she asked.

She sounded a little bit pretentious, but not in a bad way. Before Norimaki could answer, I blurted out, "Of course." I didn't mean to say anything, but it just came out!

6

Late Autumn

A Hearty Feast

Oyster rice, or oyster tofu

Stewed chicken, apple, and gingko seed

Grilled aubergine in red dashi soup

+

Baked apple sandwich (Mum Komaki's brunch)

+

Apple vs. Marron

Last night, Norimaki and I got a fluffy extra blanket for our bed. Now that it's November, the chilly air lingers under the floor all night long. Daybreak is getting later, too, so when Kagami gets up around half past four, it's still pitch black like it's the middle of the night.

The ground floor of Mum's house has underfloor heating. The pipes run beneath the living room and the two dining rooms. It's an old system where a boiler heats up the water, and it circulates through the pipes, so when Kagami switches it on, it takes a while to get going. It sounds like it's heaving itself out of sleep, clunking into life with exaggerated grunts and groans.

The colder it is in the morning, the louder it bangs, so it really is a harbinger of winter. Mum says the boiler is getting

LATE AUTUMN

on in years and it might be time for it to retire. A maintenance person is coming to take a look at it this afternoon.

I heard a different sound this morning. It came from somewhere around the entrance hall: *clonk, tumble-tumble, thump!* Norimaki, who was trotting eagerly to the kitchen to ask Kagami for breakfast, stopped in his tracks.

"It's the horse chestnuts from the tochinoki tree in the neighbour's garden," Kagami explained to us in his usual indifferent tone. "It gets heavy with nuts every year, and about half of them fall on the western roof over the atelier. They roll down and hit the ground. This house is old, but that tochinoki has been around much longer. Maybe it was already there long before our neighbour built their house."

Kagami was wearing a shell-white knit jumper with a pretty design: it had two light blue lines running around the cuffs and the hem. Since he has pale skin, whitish clothes suit him.

Norimaki kept meowing, "Pet me!" Before putting on his apron, Kagami obliged him by squatting down and playing with us for a bit, while he went on telling us about the horse chestnut tree. Norimaki wasn't even listening. I don't know why, but he loves getting rubbed on his cheeks and massaged on his shoulders. He gets this dreamy look on his face that says, *this is what I'm talking about.*

The sounds came again: *clonk, tumble-tumble.* There was

no *thump* this time, so the nut must've stopped halfway down the roof. The *clonk* comes when the hard shell of the nut hits the roof; then it rolls down and thumps on the heap of fallen leaves on the ground. The part that piques my curiosity most of all is the faint *rustle-rustle* of the leaves that comes after the thump. It awakens my hunter's instinct and makes me itch to pounce on something.

That tochinoki tree just happens to be the house of Mr and Mrs Crow and their Junior. Though Junior was born in spring, he still hasn't flown the nest. Only yesterday, he was staying behind by himself, and when his parents still weren't back at dusk, he started whimpering. The parents, on the other hand, seem to be getting more independent from their son, so they're often away for long stretches. Yoake and Higure each go to different gatherings (a.k.a. "Gripe About Your Husband or Wife Groups"). Maybe because of that, no-one attacks Tekona these days even when she shows up wearing a knit hat that basically covers her whole head and shoulders – to shield herself from the northern wind, she says – making her look like a ninja.

When he's done playing with us, Kagami takes the seiro steamer out from the cupboard. Maybe he's going to steam the rice this morning. Norimaki is already skipping around by Kagami's feet in the shape of a lopsided 8, pleading to be allowed to curl up in the steamer.

LATE AUTUMN

Kagami always tells him that it's for steaming rice, so it's off limits, but Norimaki gets his hopes up every time, thinking, "He just might say yes today."

He's almost a year old, so you'd expect he'd have grown out of games like this by now, but in his case, maybe it's become more of a habit than a game. Back when we were roaming the streets, we had to find hiding places all the time, wherever we went.

All the same, he doesn't look like he's preparing for danger now: he makes too much of a racket every time the steamer comes out. In the end, Kagami gives him a leg-swing, moving his leg back and forth while he hangs on, and that calms him down.

Dumpling Girl has been gone since yesterday. She's on a school trip to an island called Enoshima. According to Rika at Seishiro Farm, the Shonan coastline gets epic waves rolling in around this time of year.

She's chummy with Koyomi, and I heard her talking about it when she came to deliver some vegetables yesterday afternoon.

"The kids won't get to touch the seawater, let alone ride any waves," Koyomi said matter-of-factly.

"Really? On a trip to Enoshima?" Rika asked, taken aback.

"They'll go up to an observation deck to look out at the sea, then to an aquarium to observe marine life like the local coastal fish. After that, they'll head to Kamakura, where they'll put their hands together in prayer in front of the handsome Buddha, visit the Hachimangu Shrine, shop for some souvenirs along the path leading up to the shrine and go home."

"They might as well just go on Street View with an itinerary like *that*."

"The school doesn't want to risk getting into hot water if the kids get hurt or something on the beach – that's why they're playing it safe."

"I get where they're coming from, I guess. When I take Konchi and Yuria to the beach, they always want a drink of water, a towel, a plaster or something else every five minutes, and I just end up pulling things out of our bags and shoving them back in the whole time, and the day is over before I know it. If one of them says pee-pee, I'd try to take both of them at once, but then the other one says they don't feel like it right now. But then, after I get back, the other one asks for the toilet within five minutes. Makes me want to tell them just to dig a hole somewhere and do it in there."

"Oh, but be careful – you'll get in trouble for things like that these days. Any little camera has a zoom function. Parents need to watch out."

"I know, I know."

LATE AUTUMN

Rika used to be a surfer when she was in college. Her plan was to work as a lifeguard, but one thing led to another, and she became the wife of a farmer. Seishiro and Rika used to surf together, and back then she never even imagined that he came from a farming family. Incidentally, Rika's family are farmers, too.

Though he didn't let Norimaki play in the steamer, Kagami made a paper boat for him by folding a flyer. It was a big, sturdy piece of paper with a model illustration of a high-rise apartment that's going to be built near the next station down the line. The part with the blue sky turned up right on the bow, and there it was: a blue boat for Norimaki. The boat had an awning, so Norimaki stuck his head right in and started pushing it forward. It's pretty much the same game he does with slippers, but oh well.

Then Kagami started prepping breakfast for us. He took something out of the fridge: the oysters from Uogin that Nanao delivered to the house yesterday. Woohoo!

Nanao is the daughter and heir at Uogin, the fishmongers (the name of their shop means "Fish Silver"). When she was born, the young chief was over the moon, and he had the idea of putting together two kanji characters for *fish* for her name. But on his way to the ward office, he had a celebratory drink with every friend he met, and ended up so drunk that he couldn't even straddle his bicycle anymore. And so, the big chief (Nanao's grandad) went to the ward office to submit the notice instead, and he spelled her name with plain katakana letters – much more sensible than *fish-fish*. What a close call for Nanao.

Mademoiselle Rocco treated me to oysters last autumn. She didn't like eating them raw; she preferred them deep-fried. Since the oysters curled up too much when she fried them at home, she used to get them from Joshu-ya near the station, where they fried them on the spot in front of the shop. They were so hot you could hear them sizzling inside the bag. She would hurry back home, squeeze a bit of sudachi juice right into the bag, and dig in.

She used to say that Worcester sauce or ketchup is too strong, and they'd drown out the subtle flavours of the oysters, which would be a total waste. Besides the tart, refreshing citrus juice of sudachi, she also liked having them with a spot of grainy mustard and balsamic vinegar.

Whenever she got the oysters, she would set some aside for me. Once they'd cooled down enough, she'd peel off the crispy batter and give me just the oysters inside. When I bit into the soft, squishy flesh, the juice burst out, filling my mouth. And then there were the chewy, frilly bits around the meat. That was another highlight.

I hadn't had oysters yet since we started living in Mum's

LATE AUTUMN

house. It got too warm soon after we arrived. But I was craving them all through summer.

Kagami dusted the fresh, plump oysters with potato starch, then carefully roasted them without any oil or water in a yukihira saucepan. Oyster tofu was on the menu today. But not the one where you just stew the oyster and tofu together; he was going to put oyster and tofu in egg and steam it. You beat some eggs, drop the soft tofu and slices of roasted oyster in it, mix it a little, then pour the mixture into soba choko cups, until they're about seventy per cent full. Then you steam the cups in a seiro basket.

For everyone else in the house, he'll flavour the mixture with dashi and pour thick kuzu syrup over it before steaming. That way it's even tastier, because it keeps in the heat and melts on your tongue. And as a finishing touch, he'll squeeze a dash of lemon or sudachi over it. Having it with vitamin C helps the body absorb the oyster's iron and taurine better.

There was no dashi or kuzu syrup in our portions. And the lemon or sudachi juice would've been a little too sour for Norimaki (he puckers his mouth just at the sight of them), so instead, Kagami mixed in soft pieces of ripe persimmon when he beat the egg for us. It lent a nice subtle sweetness; plus, persimmons are rich in vitamin C.

Kagami often tells us stories while making our meow-food,

A HEARTY FEAST

so I listen closely like a good student. Norimaki is usually too busy playing. Today, he was engrossed in pushing around the paper boat with his head inside the hood.

Besides oyster tofu, there was oyster rice for breakfast, too. Everyone could pick whichever one they liked. Well, it was also okay to have both, but eating too much oyster isn't good for you, apparently. For me, a big oyster sliced into small pieces is just the right amount. For Norimaki, Kagami slices a smaller oyster and mixes it into the egg.

This steamed tofu-in-egg dish also works well with other ingredients – prawns and crab meat are an obvious alternative, but anago eel, asari clams and white fish are nice as well. Oh, and chicken soboro! You know, the crumbly mince chicken simmered in soy sauce and sake? Mum Komaki likes to garnish it with a bit of wasabi. She swirls it into the kuzu syrup and scoops it all up together.

Dumpling Girl likes putting in fish cakes like hanpen or naruto, and even a hunk of Camembert. But that's a no-no for us brothers or Mum because it's too much salt.

Kagami steamed the portion for Norimaki and me in one bowl, and once it was cooked, he served it in separate shallower bowls so it cooled faster. When the steam started rising in thick billows, Norimaki cast aside the boat and came running.

If only we could eat things steaming hot, just like Grandad

LATE AUTUMN

or Mum do. Then we wouldn't have to wait so long with the tantalising aroma wafting into our noses.

Norimaki was so keen that he sprawled out on his belly on his Cheburashka blanket, flapping his paws. Ever since he flipped over a soupy egg dish doing his little dance of joy and learned his lesson (he got a little burn on his paw), he's been going flat on his belly so that he won't get closer to his bowl when he's too excited. I promise, he's not actually practising frog-style swimming.

I was the first to start eating. (Norimaki has even more of a "cat tongue" than me – he can't take hot food – so he counts to fifty after I dig in. While I ate my oyster tofu, he sat next to me with a furrowed look of concentration on his face, puckering up his lips and counting in his head. You know some kids pull a weird face when they're focusing on something? Norimaki is one of them.)

He finally reached fifty and pounced on the food.

"You like it?" Kagami asked.

I looked up and nodded eagerly. Norimaki mumbled through mouthfuls, "*Uryaruaunyamm* (super yummy)!" At least, that's what I *think* he said. I'm not really sure myself.

I heard footsteps coming down the corridor. Nobody else in the family wakes up this early, so we all turned our heads to stare at the kitchen doorway (the door is left open) . . . And what do you know! Sakuragawa walked in. And get this:

A HEARTY FEAST

unlike on other days when he'd already be dressed up for breakfast, he was still in his *pyjamas*. But that doesn't mean he looked dishevelled; he'd shrugged on a long cardigan, and his pyjamas weren't wrinkled in the least. They looked like they were made of soft fabric, which probably doesn't get creased easily. And they were cocoa brown in colour, with pearl white piping on the edges of the collars and sleeves.

"The tiny tots are down here, huh ...?" Sakuragawa murmured.

He still calls us that, but he should know we're big boys now: even Norimaki is almost one.

"Then who's running around on the roof?" he added. "The American shorthair from next door?"

(Does that surprise you? Uncle Bear is actually an American shorthair. He has blackish fur, but if you look closely, you can make out those distinct patterns. But I think his nickname suits him because his coat is so bushy and unruly. The other day, though, when he scrubbed up at a pet salon, he looked so much like grand nobility that I hardly recognised him. I even wondered if his real name, Maroko, comes from "Maro", the first-person pronoun that court nobles used to use. I found out later that the Marukos had been sprucing him up for a photo shoot for next year's calendar and their New Year's greeting cards! Mr and Mrs Maruko are so soft on him you wouldn't believe it. But within three hours, his fur was already

LATE AUTUMN

messed up, and he was back to his usual self. Anyway, *he's* neither light-footed nor nimble-pawed enough to clamber up the drain pipe onto the roof, so he has nothing to do with that sound, and Chibi Maroko still toddles in little baby steps, so he can't even climb a chair.)

When I thought about it, I remembered that Sakuragawa's bedroom is above the atelier, so he sleeps right under that roof. The sounds must've been a lot louder in his room compared to the kitchen. There it was again: *clunk, tumble-tumble, thump!*

"That noise just now. It woke me up, and I couldn't fall back to sleep. I haven't heard it before, so I guess it's something to do with the seasons? Seriously, what *is* it?"

It was spring when Sakuragawa moved in, so this is his first autumn at the Horai house. Just like us brothers.

"It's a Tochimenbo," Kagami said, completely deadpan. Even though he told me it was a tochinoki nut earlier this morning.

"A Tochi . . . what?" Sakuragawa repeated dubiously.

"A supernatural creature that appears around the end of autumn."

Really? I was puzzled. In Soseki Sensei's *I Am a Cat*, "tochimenbo" is the name of a made-up dish in the aesthete's practical joke. What is this about? Kagami's acting weird.

"But it's already the first day of winter," Sakuragawa says, quite logically.

A HEARTY FEAST

"Tochimenbo appear in areas where high-quality honey can be found, so beekeepers welcome them."

"Well, it's not as cold anymore, is it? Not like the old days when they used to call it 'Shimotsuki', the month of frost, in the lunar calendar. Nowadays it's rare to see any frost before the year turns, at least in Tokyo since you were born, Kagami. There might've been a handful of days like that when I was a kid, though. From what Kahoru and Itsuki told me, they used to get crunchy needle ice that looks like it's pushing up the ground even in November. And sometimes thick, solid ice in December. But now the leaves start colouring only towards the end of November, so things have changed a lot, huh?"

"It's said that in some cases, when a tree it dwells in is made into a string instrument, the Tochimenbo will settle inside it."

"Gramps still remembers what it was like in the middle of winter some forty-odd years ago: he says the water in the lotus basin in the garden iced over almost every morning. Really thick ice too, so thick it might've trapped some goldfish. These days you'd only see things actually freezing when the coldest season sets in, and even then only two or three days in a year, right? If what gramps says is true, global warming is progressing faster than it sounds – it's more like 'boiling' than 'warming'. It's not the earth's problem; the sun's the driving factor. After all, if the surface temperature gets as hot as Venus, humans won't survive."

LATE AUTUMN

"Tochimenbo have adapted to urban environments and are rising in numbers."

I was starting to catch on by that point. Kagami sounded as composed as usual, and his stony-faced mask hadn't slipped, but it was actually chaos in his head. The reason, of course, was Sakuragawa – showing up so early in the morning when everyone else was still fast asleep. *And* in pyjamas, to boot. Even though he knew there were other people in the house, they were all alone in the kitchen, and Kagami simply couldn't keep his cool.

One time in the summer when Mum Komaki and Koyomi took a trip together, and Dumpling Girl had gone on holiday with her parents, Kagami was supposed to be left alone under the same roof with Sakuragawa. But then Sakuragawa had to go on an urgent business trip, and Sacchan came over to hang out with Kagami, so in the end, they were never left by themselves.

Today, the troublemaker was Sakuragawa, not Kagami. Sakuragawa must've realised why he kept going on and on with his bizarre Tochimenbo angle, but he was feigning ignorance and ploughing ahead with this asymmetrical conversation.

That's where *I* came in. I dipped my paws into my breakfast bowl and leaped onto Sakuragawa's chest. Then I rubbed the egg on my paws and mouth against his soft, classy pyjamas.

The scenario in my head went like this: Sakuragawa would

A HEARTY FEAST

scold me, and Kagami would quickly grab a wet towel and wipe away the mess (and get close to Sakuragawa as a result). Kagami hadn't moved an inch from the corner of the kitchen so far, so I figured he needed a little nudge.

"Hey, where's your manners?" Sakuragawa said, but he wasn't fazed. He's had meow-friends ever since he was little, so he didn't mind at all. Kagami, though, moved according to my plan: he wet a hand towel and warmed it in the microwave as a quick alternative to sanitising it in boiling water.

But then things started to go wrong. I didn't know this, but Kagami's hands are unusually sensitive to heat. Normally he would remember to use tongs or oven gloves, but he wasn't in his right mind, so he went to pick up the hot towel with his bare hand and dropped it on the floor in surprise.

I don't think I'd ever seen Kagami fumble anything in the kitchen before. He set about preparing a new towel, but Sakuragawa said, "This will do. I'll put them in the laundry anyway," and picked it up from the floor. It had already cooled a little, but it must have still been hot to the touch – yet Sakuragawa seemed completely unaffected as he squeezed it to wipe his pyjama shirt.

Kagami watched him, looking like he wanted to say something but didn't know how.

"I have thick skin," Sakuragawa said. "My sensors aren't as sensitive as yours, Kagami."

It was obvious he was about to add, "Want to feel it?" – of course *he'd* know what to say in a situation like this – but just as he held out his hand and opened his mouth to speak, Kagami cut him off:

"Good effort. Seven out of ten, I guess."

"What do you mean?" Sakuragawa asked.

"'*Sens*ors' and '*sens*itive'."

I knew Kagami was wired a bit differently, but how could he miss such a clear signal . . . ?

Anyone could see that wordplay wasn't the thing to focus on here. Sakuragawa was just making light of the situation in case Kagami felt embarrassed about his clumsiness. But I guess Kagami's brainwaves are controlled by "the Vertical Fusulina Electrical Switchboard" from another of Mr Kenji's poems; unfortunately a circuit must have connected where it shouldn't have.

He should get Sacchan to fix his switchboard!

I'm not sure if Kagami ever realised that he'd let the moment pass, but in any case he busied himself making tea for Sakuragawa from a blend of black soybeans and barley.

With his blunt manner and poker face, Kagami can sound sarcastic when he doesn't mean to; worst-case scenario, people think he's mocking them. Your average guy (with a big ego but a small mind who gets bothered by little things) might have been put out, but, as he said himself, Sakuragawa is

A HEARTY FEAST

thick-skinned, so the needle of his temper gauge doesn't swing into the red zone so easily. Which could be why he's such a charming devil.

"Never mind," he said after a long pause. "So ... the tiny tots had oyster tofu, huh? What's on the menu for the grown-ups?"

"You have a choice between oyster rice and oyster tofu. There's also chicken wings stewed with apples and gingko seeds to go with it. And grilled aubergines in red dashi soup. For the stewed chicken, I usually use soybeans, but today I put in gingko seeds that we got as a seasonal gift. If you choose oyster rice, please make up for it by including one soybean dish in your lunch to get some plant-based protein: it can be tofu, ganmodoki patties or okara simmered with vegetables, for example."

"I'm having lunch with a client today – we're supposed to be going to a Japanese–Italian fusion place."

"Then think about ordering a seafood appetiser. If it comes with a lemon wedge, please use it. Vitamin C will help your body absorb minerals."

Kagami was finally starting to sound like himself again, but he was out of time now. Sakuragawa went back to his room to get changed. So, this morning's "near miss" encounter didn't amount to anything, for better or worse.

A short while later, Sakuragawa returned to the small

LATE AUTUMN

dining room for breakfast in his normal attire: his signature broadcloth shirt, which he always buys from the same shop, and the long cardigan he had on earlier, which he only wears at home. He keeps his jacket and coat in the closet by the entrance hall, by the toilet with the mirror and sink where he gets ready before heading off to work.

A pool of sunlight glowed on the terrace outside the living room. Kagami opened the window for us, so we went to play in the sun. I could see the tochinoki tree standing tall in the garden of our neighbour to the south. Another *clunk* came from the roof over Sakuragawa's room. Startled, Norimaki fell on his bum.

Next came the rumble of the nut rolling down, followed by a heavy thud. It sounded like a big one.

"They ripen later and later each year. They used to fall at the beginning of October, in fact, way back when. You'd think they'd be delicious, with their ruddy brown colour, but they're inedible, no matter how you cook them. They're just about tolerable if you soak them in water to take the edge off, leave them out to dry, grind them into powder and steam it mixed with mochi rice."

That was what Jean Paul told me. I didn't notice him until he spoke, but he was standing right behind us. He picked up a round nut from a mound of fallen leaves. The outer shell, which was smooth unlike the spiny burrs on normal chestnuts, had split open from the impact of hitting the ground, and the nut had rolled out: it looked very similar to a chestnut, but it was a deeper brown, with a delicate silver-leaf sheen around the edges. But according to Jean Paul, not even bears can eat them raw.

Around half past ten in the morning, as Mum was enjoying her brunch, Tekona came by, lugging a big cloth sack over her shoulder. She'd cycled here as usual, of course, so she's only had to carry it from the front door to the small dining room, not all the way from her house.

The sack was filled with plump chestnuts. Her mum had delivered a huge heap that they'd harvested at home, and now she had so much to spare she could've opened a shop. Some of them were still inside the spiky burrs with twigs and leaves attached.

Norimaki tried to burrow into the sack, but Mum held him back by the nape of his neck.

"Phew, that was close. You could've hurt yourself on the spikes. They're sharp, you know. See, they can go right through a kitchen cloth, like this," Mum said, putting a cloth over one of the burrs and showing him. "Is it your first time seeing chestnut burrs, Norimaki?"

"*Mnyanya* (does it bite)?" he asked.

Don't be silly – it's just a chestnut, I tried to tell him. *It's wearing armour to protect itself. Remember we saw them on the grove of chestnut trees next to Seishiro Farm around the beginning of summer? It's the same thing. Well, back then they were still green and soft, less than an inch wide. Gindoro stuck one on his chest like a brooch and marched around with his flunkies in tow – Oguri and Aguri (his next-door neighbours) – remember? He'd convinced himself that it was a medal of honour. These spiky balls that Tekona brought are the riper version, and they've switched on their battle mode.*

"Chimaki's staying away, though," Mum said. "I guess he's not interested – it's neither edible nor alive. Maybe Norimaki thinks it's some kind of living creature."

Bingo. She saw right through him. As for me, I *am* a little interested in *roasted* chestnuts. They were Mademoiselle Rocco's big favourite, and we used to go and buy them in a shop nearby around December. I was still small, so she'd put me on a leash and carry me in her arms. (Norimaki was a little baby, so he stayed with Auntie Meowko.)

Someone wearing a red apron roasted the chestnuts in a big pot. They let you sample them on the spot, so pigeons would gather around in search of the crumbs people left behind. Now *that* was exciting: I'd pin my eyes on the triangle flag of one of the pigeons (that is, the soft spot on its back between the wings) and dive out from Rocco's arms.

Of course, the pigeons would take off all at once, and

they'd be well out of my reach before I could even blink. Not even swallows can fly like that, from what I've heard. The vertical take-off is a unique skill that only pigeons have. Once, one of the feathers that fluttered down after they took off fell on my nose and covered my nostrils, which made me open my mouth, then another one fell right on my tongue, and I couldn't stop sneezing. It only settled down when Mademoiselle Rocco let me borrow her handkerchief.

Her handkerchief had a nice smell, like sweets, or honey – it's hard to put into words, but I'm sure I'd recognise it if I smelled it again.

Norimaki circled around the spiky burr on high alert. He probably still thought it would bite him. He paused now and again, pricked up his tail, and waggled it at the burr (that's his idea of a mild threat). But just like a windsock on a calm day, his tail dipped down in no time. Then he started circling in the opposite direction, stopped again, and leaned forward, his little paws planted in front of him like a sumo wrestler about to strike, glaring at the burr.

Eventually, he decided to use his paws. He gently touched the tips of the spikes. They pricked him, and he shrank back in an instant. He cautiously held out his paw again, hovering just a hair's breadth above the spikes, to see how the burr would react. He was convinced that it would attack him. His enemy didn't move (obviously), so he slowly lowered his hand. It pricked him again. He did the same thing over and over, then turned towards the table, where everyone was sitting, and crinkled up his face.

That's the look that means: *Ahh, what do I do?!* He cries without making a sound.

Kagami, who had been watching his antics, took out a pair of tongs, plucked up the burr with them, and walked off to the linen room. Norimaki trotted along behind him without a care, as if nothing had happened. Kagami changed into thick-soled shoes at the back door and stamped on the burr. Using the tongs, he extracted the chestnuts inside. They were round and plump, with a glossy shine on their smooth shells. He rolled them across the linen room floor. Norimaki shot off, chasing after them.

The chestnuts were unevenly shaped, so they rolled around every which way. Norimaki got hooked on the game: he pounced on the nuts and whirled around the room. He probably thought he was playing with living creatures, like crickets or grasshoppers. I let him do what he wanted.

I went back to the small dining room and decided to take a nap on the sashiko-stitched seat cushion on Mr Dodo's chair. Tekona was in the middle of telling Mum Komaki about yet another episode of her mum suddenly turning up in Tokyo.

A HEARTY FEAST

"She calls me *right* before getting on the bullet train – unbelievable. What if I wasn't home? What would she have done with the chestnuts then? Seriously. She's already standing in our kitchen two hours after she calls. And when I ask her if she'll have lunch with us, she says she'll just go to the museum in Ueno and treat herself to lunch with dessert at Brasserie L'écrin inside the station. It's supposed to be the kind of restaurant you can casually visit, even if you're a party of one. She says it's full of people like her. They let you sit at a proper table even if you dine alone, so you can relax and have a slow meal . . . Wish *I* had the luxury. When I go to Ueno, it's always with the kids, and we head straight to the zoo or the Nature and Science museum, either one. And for lunch, we just eat the bento I packed – though I barely know what I'm eating, since I'm too busy looking after the kids."

"But you know, your mum had to go through the same thing in her time, and now she can finally enjoy her freedom. You told me yourself how your parents took you to Ueno countless times. It must've been hard work for them, coming such a long way with kids, especially back then when there weren't any bullet trains. You know how kids fall asleep on the train back? Maybe you don't remember when you got home, either, Tekona. You might've been already in your dreams, no? I bet your mum and dad took turns carrying you on their backs, and they must've been absolutely knackered by the time you all made it home. So your mum knows Ueno well from those trips you took, right? And now it's a breeze for her to pop over there anytime she likes."

"She has this routine she usually follows when she visits: she stops by Ameyoko to get a little souvenir for my dad and gets home before five in the evening, so they can have dinner together."

"Hats off to her. And thanks to you both, we got lucky with these lovely chestnuts, too – what a treat."

"Thank *you* for taking them. We can't possibly eat them all just by ourselves. I could give some to other friends too, but not many people are happy to receive raw chestnuts. It's too much effort to boil them, let alone stewing, grilling or steaming. On top of that, they're hard to peel, and the shells pile up in your bin, and sometimes you get a jolt when you find a worm in there. So I think when you cook rice with chestnuts or make kuri kinton with mashed sweet potatoes, it's easier to buy those jars of pre-cooked ones in sweet syrup. That way you always get big chestnuts, and they're already flavoured. And there's just enough for one meal, so you won't have any left over. The only downside is the high price. But it's okay to splash out a bit, since it's not something you'd eat every day. Cooked chestnuts are a different story, though; when I steam them myself and make a big batch of unsweetened paste out of them, everybody loves it.

A HEARTY FEAST

It turns into a nice little snack: I like to spread it over bread and toast it until it gets a bit browned and crispy, then have it with maple syrup. If you get a pack of plain American muffins and squeeze the paste over it with a piping bag, that's an easy-peasy Mont Blanc cake. It's a big hit with all the kids. Mont Blanc from shops are too rich for them, but there's no way a kid would want to halve their cake with someone, is there?"

"Do you know how they make the classic French Mont Blanc? They put a big dollop of whipped cream to make a snow-white mountain, then pipe the chestnut purée on top, going round and round like a turban. It's delicious, but oh so heavy."

"And the purée looks different too, right? The French one is coloured like marron glacé, but the Japanese one is golden yellow, like the pre-cooked kanro-ni in syrup."

"Exactly – they go to the trouble of dying it yellow with gardenia seeds. A lot of people in Japan think that's what 'chestnut-coloured' means, actually. It's *supposed* to mean the warm-brown colour of the hard shell. But apparently, half the people you ask – or most young people, I should say – picture that bright yellow colour of Mont Blanc cake or the kuri kinton we have for the New Year's feast. It's a headache for us translators."

"In my family, we have a different recipe for kuri kinton: we

LATE AUTUMN

steam the chestnuts and squeeze them with a light tea cloth. The colour is closer to the French Mont Blanc."

"We've been eating chestnuts since ancient times, so there's a lot of regional variety in how we cook them. Take kuri yokan, for example – it's a classic sweet, but there's all kinds of different recipes. The region you come from is famous for producing chestnuts, so your idea of 'chestnut yokan' is like a block of pure, one-hundred-per-cent chestnut, isn't it?"

"Are there other kinds of kuri yokan?"

"Most people think of a block of red bean jelly with whole chestnuts inside."

"Oh, right. The steamed ones are like that, too."

"At Matsu Sushi, they have a special dish for the autumn they call 'kuri datemaki'. You beat some eggs, mix it with chestnut paste, and roll it up in the pan just like tamagoyaki."

"Mmm, that sounds amazing."

The whole time they chatted, Mum was tucking into her favourite baked apple sandwiches. To make them, melt some cultured butter in a frying pan, wait until it starts bubbling, then arrange apple slices in neat rows. Be patient: cook each side slowly without jiggling the pan or stirring with chopsticks. When they're ready, line the slices on a piece of simple white bread, dust it with cinnamon, and pop it in a toaster oven.

The juice from the apples melts together with the butter,

A HEARTY FEAST

and a tantalising aroma wafts through the kitchen. The butter makes a sort of film over the bread, so the juice doesn't seep in. The apples turn soft and moist; the bread nice and crisp. You hear a light, airy crunch when you cut into it with a knife.

She used wedge-shaped apple slices today, but when she makes these sandwiches with English muffins, she opts for thin rings.

It was Kagami who had prepared the apples for her sandwich in the morning and kept them in the fridge. Since he uses top-quality butter, it seeps into the apple slices over time, and when you heat it up again, you can enjoy a new flavour that's different from the freshly cooked version.

Mum added a drop of crème de cassis to her strong black tea. Taking a sip, she murmured, "This is something special – never gets old."

Tekona, who was having the same, nodded in agreement. "I didn't know tart liqueur goes so well with black tea."

"It goes with any tea that's fermented. Lovely with oolong. You can use umeshu instead of crème de cassis, if you like."

For this week's issue of *Mamateko* (short for *Maman tekona*; that's what I've started calling Tekona's magazine, following Dumpling Girl's example), Mum wrote about chestnuts and apples in her Komakoma Diary:

You can find chestnut sweets all year round, but when I start seeing the phrase "Fresh Chestnuts" attached to the

LATE AUTUMN

usual labels, I can't help reaching out for it, thinking, "It's a bit pricey, but . . ." I love all kinds of kuri yokan: the simple ones made with just chestnuts, kanten jelly and sugar; the red bean ones with chunky chestnuts trapped in the azuki jelly; the steamed ones that are so nice and chewy. It's impossible to pick a favourite.

Back in the day, I used to cut a couple of inches from the block and savour it with a cup of bancha – that's what I call pure joy – but nowadays, I keep it to less than half an inch. It's a pity to cut the chestnuts into small pieces . . . but I remind myself that I must be disciplined if I want to stay healthy and indulge in chestnuts again in a year's time.

It's one way to live, though: eating what you like as much as you like, and waving goodbye to the world with no regrets.

Once someone gave me a souvenir that I thought was slightly unusual: white kuri yokan. It was made from white azuki and haricot beans mashed together and solidified in a mould along with chestnuts. If the steamed kuri yokan – with the rich purplish brown of the red azuki paste and the golden yellow of the chestnut – is like a classy kimono with thick vertical stripes, then the white kuri yokan is like a white han'eri collar lining embroidered with raw silk thread. Its delicate, soft hues have a subtle allure, calling to mind the flesh of a young woman. It's not as firm as the normal azuki yokan; it crumbles lightly in your mouth with an airy texture. I once heard that geisha used to give out this white kuri yokan to their special patrons. If you look at it again in that light, the pale colours start to take on an even more seductive air.

From autumn to winter, it's also the season for apples. Fruit with a bit of sourness taste even better when you cook them a little – the same goes for apricots and plums. Stew them with meat or stir-fry with vegetables: both delicious.

Slice an apple into apple rings without peeling the skin, then cook them in cultured butter, nice and slow – and you get baked apples. Place one slice of pork loin ham on each half of an English muffin, arrange a few apple rings on top of that, sprinkle with cinnamon, and cook in the oven toaster. I put a sheet of aluminium foil underneath, and I like to toast it until the muffin halves turn crispy.

Instead of apples, grilled broccoli or courgettes go well, too. Red bell pepper adds a splash of colour.

If you put a green shiso leaf on top just before you bite in, it gives another unique twist to the flavours. Make sure to put the leaf back-side up! I won't pretend to be an expert –somebody taught me. Who knew flipping the leaf around would change how it tastes? Just try it!

Apples steamed in that pride-of-the-French enamel pot is another seasonal treat. (Of course, you don't need the French pot for this – you're free to use any old steamer, too.) The Jonathan apple works best. Plumleaf crab apples make for a

LATE AUTUMN

cute mini-size version. First, wash the unpeeled apples (if the wax on the skin bothers you, you can rub it with baking soda and rinse it off), then scoop out the core. A core remover is always handy, but a fork works just as well.

Careful not to make a hole on the bottom. All the good stuff – the butter and juice that seep out when you steam them – will drain away, and that would be a sad sight. You can also wrap the bottom with aluminium foil, if you like.

Stuff the hollow with cultured butter. How much is up to your preference, but I'd say about thirty grams. In the meantime, melt more butter (a separate dose from what you use for stuffing the apples) in the pot. Place the stuffed apples inside and close the lid to let them steam. Wait until the butter inside the apples starts bubbling; when it's melted, add the sugar. Beet sugar would be better for your health. Again, how much you put in is up to you. We'll be adding jam later, so you might want to hold back a little bit.

Depending on the size of the apples, the juice will start bubbling up to the brim after about fifteen minutes of steaming. Stuff a spoonful of your favourite fruit jam into each apple – take care not to let the juice spill over – and steam it a tad longer. Last but not least, splash a bit of Calvados over the pot if you have some. And if you flambé it, you get a lovely glossy finish.

As for the jam, marmalade is common with this dish,

but if you'd like to try the French way, you can pick groseille (redcurrant), cassis (blackcurrant) or framboise (raspberry).

Then, you have the whole apple while it's still piping hot, all by yourself!

With a dollop of whipped cream, it turns into an even more lavish feast . . . but I'd better keep myself in check. How about some homemade cottage cheese instead? Just a little scoop wouldn't hurt . . . right?

In the afternoon, the boiler maintenance person came by: a lady named Ms Noe. Mum asked her to park in the garage in front of the house. Just as she was taking out her tools, she cried out, "Oh! What are you doing in there?"

Guess what she found! A little meow-girl sitting in the middle of a coil of rubber tube in the boot of her car. She stared back – not in a dazed, startled-out-of-sleep kind of way, but as if she'd been lost in thought. She looked like she'd be a clever student.

"Ah, she's a pretty one. What's her name?" Mum Komaki peered in, smiling.

"I'm sorry. This is Apple. She disappeared last night, but I was sure she must be somewhere in the house – she's the type who's bossy at home, but shy outside, you see. I looked everywhere for her until it was time to leave for our appointment. I had no idea she was hiding here."

LATE AUTUMN

She had semi-long hair with a blend of cinnamon powder and blue; with her apple green eyes, she seemed very intelligent. I'll call her Miss Apple, since she has a scholarly air.

"They all love new rubber tubes, don't they? If she went missing last night, I suppose she hasn't had breakfast? We could give her something here, if you'd like. Though we feed our boys homecooked food."

"She's a real glutton, so she'll gobble up anything yummy."

"Well, I hope it'll be to her taste."

"I'm sure it will. It's written on their faces that their meals are delicious," Ms Noe said, looking at me and Norimaki.

"Would you like to try our breakfast?" Mum asked Miss Apple. Miss Apple glanced sideways at us. Norimaki hid behind me in a fluster.

"Yes, please, I would love to," Miss Apple answered, speaking like a graceful lady.

Mum led her to the small dining room and said, "Make yourself at home – sit wherever you like." Miss Apple chose Koyomi's chair, which had a crocheted cover, and leaped lightly onto the seat. I went to see what was going on in the kitchen.

Kagami was making butter-steamed oyster in the microwave. Oyster tofu would take too long, you see. When the oyster was cooked, he garnished it with homemade cottage cheese. What a feast! But it was too hot for her to eat right away.

A HEARTY FEAST

While I was focusing on the oyster, Miss Apple slipped into the kitchen and started trotting up and down restlessly. She must've thought it was bad manners to wander around in someone else's house, too eager for food to sit still, so she turned to ask me, "May I enquire as to where the powder room is?"

The one for meow-girls is in Madame Hinako's atelier. Why? Because of Marron, whom we met at the autumn picnic. Her mum, Chitose, is an artist who dyes and weaves textiles, and she started attending Madame Hinako's embroidery classes. Marron tags along and plays with us.

I took Miss Apple to the atelier. It wasn't the day of the class, but – surprise, surprise – Chitose was there to see Madame Hinako. Apparently, she'd come in her capacity as a textile artist today, not just a student. Marron was with her too, as always.

"Look, Marron – it's Chimaboo and Noripee." (That's what Chitose calls us.) "Oh dear, there's a new girl with them. Here comes a rival. What are you going to do, Marron?"

A rival??? Before I could react, Marron's back went round like a ball – or that's what I thought until I realised her hair was bristling! When I turned around, I saw Miss Apple doing the exact same thing. Whoa, meow-girls can be scary.

7

Early Winter

A Special Gathering

Rice with mushrooms aplenty
Chicken skin and tofu stewed in bonito dashi
Onion tart

+

Crystal tofu
To-œuf à la steak!

December feels hectic for one reason or another. Both Mum and Komaki are bustling about, chased by something called *dead lines*. Even Tekona – who usually stays for tea when she comes around – rides her bike straight to the back door, has a hurried discussion with Mum, and off she goes like the wind.

Still, they all seem excited about something. Whenever they have a spare moment, they put their heads together about some kind of plan. Every day, Koyomi reverently opens each flap of her handmade advent calendar, humming a tune. Whatever it is, they must be *really* looking forward to it.

It's in the Horai family's nature to be restless with eager anticipation on the days leading up to any big event, whether it's a dim sum party or a picnic. What could it be this time?

I counted the days leading up to this mystery event on

EARLY WINTER

Koyomi's calendar, but the date doesn't quite match up with Christmas. For Mademoiselle Rocco, Christmas seemed like a bigger deal than any other festival, but the Horais aren't so fussed about it. And New Year's is still too far ahead.

From what I've managed to piece together, it sounds like they're having an end-of-year gathering they call the "Fun Party". There'll be Mum and Tekona, and Koyomi's usual circle; Rika from Seishiro Farm and Miss Oisa will come, too. Nanao from Uogin said she wants to join if she can – but the end of the year is when business booms for a fishmonger, so she added, regretfully, "I probably can't make it."

Matsu Sushi is crazy busy at this time of year, too: so much so they could even use some help from a cat, as the saying goes. That's what Grandad said when he came over the other day. So Norimaki and I wanted to go and pitch in, but he just thanked us, saying, "Don't worry, it's the thought that counts."

Back when he was head chef, Grandad used to get up extra early and go to the fish market. He still wakes up early even though he's retired, so he often drops by at the Horai house around the time Norimaki and I are having our breakfast. In fact, he has an ulterior motive for coming at that particular hour: he wants to have breakfast with us. I don't mean with us as in sitting next to us – I mean he wants to eat the same breakfast we're having. That's a crucial difference.

Let me explain: the breakfast menu for us brothers has

A SPECIAL GATHERING

all these things that Grandad isn't supposed to eat (though he loves them), like chicken skin, chicken wings and butter-grilled fish. So, Grandad comes along right around the time we eat so that he can sneak a bite or two from our bowls.

On the one hand, Tsukune, Grandad's son, has asked Kagami not to "feed him". On the other hand, Kagami can understand how Grandad feels, so he doesn't know what to do. This morning too, Grandad showed up when Norimaki and I were having chicken skin and tofu stewed in bonito dashi. There was a big heap of bonito flakes on top, so it was fun to blow on them, huffing through our noses and watching them flutter in the air.

"Now that looks good," Grandad said, and Norimaki answered honestly, *"Mmmiaofmya,"* with his mouth full. Before Grandad could start pleading with him, Kagami sensed what he was after and served him a bowl. "Ah, just the ticket," Grandad said, his face crinkling into a big smile. Unlike ours, his soup was steaming hot, with black sansho peppers sprinkled over it.

"Mmm, these strips of skin are so plump and chewy. Every bite feels like cheese melting in my mouth. The dashi flavour's seeped into the tofu, too – very nice." Grandad looked positively ecstatic.

Later in the day, I overheard Kagami telling Mum Komaki that Grandad's bowl didn't contain a single piece of real

EARLY WINTER

chicken skin. Instead, he'd made an alternative out of gnocchi dough and flavoured it like chicken. Grandad's palate isn't as keen as it used to be, and the bonito soup was piping hot, so he fell for it.

But maybe he knew all along – maybe he'd only pretended to fall for it because he was touched by Kagami's thoughtfulness. Yep, I'm sure that's it.

Tekona is the main organiser of the big party. The guest list includes people who have something to do with her shop's free magazine, either as a reader, a writer, or a business that buys advertising space.

Last night, there was a call from Tekona, and I heard Mum talking in the small dining room.

"I'm wondering what to do about onions. You can't really do without them for all the homely seasonal dishes I can think of: cream stews, creamy crab croquettes, marinated or simmered fish, all that. Besides, you know the biggest highlight of our potluck party are those special onion tarts that Mao Sensei's mum makes. She always gives Mao Sensei the baked crust and the filling separately, so we can just prep it on the spot, bake it at a high temperature for ten minutes or so, and have it fresh out of the oven. That steaming hot, rich and creamy onion filling paired with the light, crispy tart crust is pure perfection. Isn't it like eating a slice of happiness? The onions get that lovely, roasty flavour when they're a little charred. You know when you're stir-frying sliced onions, you get those little strips that curl up like a thin moustache towards the edge of the frying pan because they're a bit burnt? I always get the urge to fish those out and have them on toast. But since our boys came to live with us" – (Norimaki was dozing in her lap, perfectly snug in the front pocket of her long jumper) – "we've tried to keep them away from the kitchen when we cook anything with onions. Sometimes we make a playground for them in a different room or take them out for a walk . . . That's right, onions are bad for them however you cook them, whether it's finely diced and mixed into Hamburger steak or puréed for a potage. Even a little piece is toxic for them, so we can't take any chances. Especially with our boys – if it's mixed into meat, they'll think it's a feast and tuck right in. Onions have this substance that breaks down the cat family's red blood cells. It's not just onions; it seems like a lot of plants that have a strong smell are something to watch out for, like garlic chives, rakkyo and garlic – spring onions and fennel, too. They're good nutrition for humans, so back in the day, I suppose people used to feed their cats leftover rice porridge with chives or spring onions without realising they were doing any harm. That must be why cats didn't live long in the old days. They can't have raw egg whites, either. Though raw egg on white rice would be a big treat for some humans. I actually don't like raw eggs, but I think there's a lot more people who like egg-topped rice than people who don't, right? . . . See, there you go. What about natto soybeans? I have them with a bit of grainy mustard and balsamic vinegar. I'd have to worry about my salt intake if I used the sauce that comes in the package, and I don't like that bright yellow mustard, either. My dad used to have natto the orthodox way, at least before he started having to limit his eggs – he'd have it with raw egg, soy sauce, finely chopped spring onions and Japanese mustard, but now he goes for black vinegar . . . Anyway, that's neither here nor there. Where were we? Oh yes, onions. You know I gave Kagami a special holiday on the day of the party? So it's up to me and Koyomi to look after the boys, but we're bound to get carried away eating and drinking and chatting, so we might miss something. I thought about asking Kagami to take the boys out, but I felt sorry to ask him on his day off. I think he's planning to go somewhere with Sacchan, anyhow. I mean, if it was something to do with our work schedules, I would've thought about asking him, but this is just a party, so I can't be too pushy. Another idea was to ask Hinako to look after them in the atelier, but she'll have guests that day, so I didn't feel I could. It's a busy time for everyone, so I'm stumped, to be honest."

To put it in a nutshell: they want to eat a hearty meal with plenty of onions, but Mum's at a loss because Norimaki and I might take a bite by accident. Of course, we wouldn't chance

A SPECIAL GATHERING

it if we can see it's onion, but if it's melted in a stew, and if there's a tantalising aroma of meat wafting from the pot, we might forget our manners and stick our heads in. Even if we're feeling full from breakfast, it's hard to resist the smell of meat.

If all else fails, I'd prefer to stay at Seishiro Farm during the party. It's a perfect playground. Though we have to stay on guard a little bit with the formidable artisan Yuria around. (Gindoro is nothing to worry about. He's a simple one, so compared to Yuria, it's so much easier to deal with him. Just flatter him a little, and he'll be putty in your hands in no time at all.)

Sure, I'm grown up now (I mean, in meow-years I'm basically a twenty-year-old). But Yuria's growing fast, too; she'll be in the last year of kindergarten come spring next year. These days, she's added Saori Yuki to her karaoke repertoire. Saori was a popular singer back when Yuria's granny was young, but she's still very much active and hasn't slowed down.

Since the calendar turned to December, deliveries have been coming for someone or other almost every day. Dumpling Girl received an early Christmas present from Kaporin (I mean her mum, Kahorun) in Paris, but she hasn't opened it yet. She's saving it for Christmas.

The Horai family doesn't put up a real tree, but Koyomi drew one as tall as herself and hung it up on the wall in the

EARLY WINTER

entrance hall. And underneath the drawing, a few biggish baskets are placed side-by-side. Whenever a present arrives, it goes in there.

At first, Norimaki didn't seem that interested. But as soon as a few presents went in, and they formed nice gaps between the sides of the baskets, he dived in with a gleam in his eyes that said, *Look at* this*!*

He's snug in there right now – poking his head out with a thoroughly contented expression on his face. I don't know what's so fun about sitting in a basket!

You could say that the entrance hall of the Horai family exists just for Sakuragawa's sake. The closet by the front door is practically his private space. Of course, other people use it sometimes, and when we have guests, that's where they put their coats, but Mum, Koyomi and Dumpling Girl go in and out the house through the back door most of the time.

These days, even Tekona and Rika from Seishiro Farm come straight to the back door. So do friendly neighbours and delivery people. It feels more approachable than the stern-looking front door, and you can see into the kitchen through the window, so it's easier to get someone's attention. There's even a notice board hanging outside the back door so people can leave a message if no-one's home.

On the door, there's a cast-iron knocker with a cat's face on it, and visitors can use that instead of ringing a bell. It's

A SPECIAL GATHERING

surprisingly loud, so you can hear it on the other side of the house, too. Mum found it at a flea market in Paris. The face looks a bit creepy, so Norimaki passes by without so much as a glance in its direction, pretending it's not there.

Mum came downstairs a little later than usual today, past eleven a.m. Around five this morning, when Kagami was serving us breakfast, she came into the kitchen to say a drowsy good night then padded up to her bedroom. It was still pitch-dark outside. Winter nights are long, aren't they?

For breakfast, Mum's having rice cooked with plenty of mushrooms. Koyomi's cooking now – she was planning to have an early lunch before going out.

While waiting for the rice to cook, Mum sets to work on her Komakoma Diary. She writes as if she's cooked everything herself:

In the cold months, there is nothing more satisfying than mushroom dishes. Shimeji are so much more fragrant than in the summer, with sweet notes like a flower. It's no wonder, then, that rice cooked with plenty of shimeji gives off a delicious aroma.

Lightly toss the mushrooms in a frying pan before mixing them in the rice. Spring onion oil is especially good at bringing out the fragrance. It's easy to make a batch of spring onion oil to keep it close at hand, so I'd recommend it for anyone's

EARLY WINTER

kitchen. It's perfect for those times when you feel like putting in garlic, but you think, "better not", because you have to go out afterwards.

Find a jar or bottle – something small enough to keep in the fridge, one that can hold about 600 to 700 millilitres is perfect. Cut one spring onion into diagonal slices and stuff it into the jar. If you sprinkle the slices with herb salt and dry them in the sun first, you'll get extra rich flavours. Then you pour in rapeseed oil, corn oil or any oil of your choice over the slices – and you're done. You can mix sesame oil into rapeseed oil, or come up with your own blend. Just make sure the spring onions are completely covered. The oil will already be infused with the scent of spring onions the very next day. When you use it, you can of course use the chopped pieces in your cooking along with the oil.

As long as you have a jar of this by your side, you don't have to season most stir-fries. You can say goodbye to salt. And soy sauce. That's why it's so useful for people who want to cut back on their salt intake.

Heat up some of this oil in a deep enamel pot, drop in a handful of dried whitebait, and stir-fry until it's light and crisp. This adds depth to the flavour of the rice when it' s cooked. Once the whitebait is ready, stir in the mushrooms. Today, it'll be shimeji and eringi. We have some stored in the freezer from before.

A SPECIAL GATHERING

Mushrooms are really handy because you can buy in bulk and stock them in the freezer. They go well in any kind of dish, and they're great when you want your meal to be a bit more filling (but you're watching your weight!).

To freeze shimeji, remove the base of the bunch and pull them apart with your hands. And for eringi, chop them into thick rings. Keep reading, and you'll find out why I'd recommend rings.

Now, once the mushrooms are lightly cooked, flavour them with a generous measure of sake and soy sauce. You can put in as much as you would when you usually make takikomi-gohan. But with spring onion oil, you'll still get enough umami even if you go easy on the soy sauce. Quickly stir the mushrooms so that they're well coated, then take them out and leave them to rest in a colander. Pour the remaining liquid into a measuring cup. You want a little less than you need for cooking plain white rice – if there isn't enough, you can add water – then pour it back into the enamel pot.

Then, add the uncooked rice – rinsed and drained – in the same pot. Some people have a certain way of preparing rice before cooking: first they rinse the rice and drain off the water, then cover the rice in water again and let it soak for about half an hour.

I usually skip the soaking step and use rice that's been rinsed and drained half an hour or so before cooking. It depends on

EARLY WINTER

where your rice comes from and what kind of texture you prefer when it's cooked, I suppose. Or perhaps there are more scientific reasons, but anyhow, I'm happy with how it turns out with my current method.

Cook the rice in the same enamel pot. First, you let it come to a boil on high heat without adding anything else. When it's bubbling, give the rice a stir, then add the mushrooms from the colander. Cover with a lid and cook for about five minutes on medium heat. When the bubbling sound starts getting louder, turn down the heat to low and cook for another five minutes or so. Lastly, turn up the heat to high again just long enough to evaporate the excess liquid, then turn off the hob and let it sit for about fifteen minutes with the lid on, so the hot steam trapped inside can fluff up the rice.

If you listen carefully to the sounds coming from the pot, and peek in once in a while to check on the bubbles, you'll get it right most of the time. The sitting time at the end is important, so resist the temptation to lift the lid too early.

Voilà! Now it's ready.

Serve a generous scoop in a deep dish and dig in. You can chop up your preferred aromatics and sprinkle them over the rice, too. Look how soft and plump the eringi mushrooms are. They taste so rich they could pass as scallops. Now you see why you want to slice them into thick rings. With real scallops, you need a bit of extra prep to get rid of the fishy smell, and if you buy them fresh, you have to use them right away. If you buy frozen, you have to rinse away that ice glaze. But eringi? Just pop them right in. And *they're easy on the wallet!*

Someone called from the back door: "Hello, I brought some vegetables for you." It was Granny Chikako from Seishiro Farm (she's Seishiro's mum and Rika's mother-in-law). Yuria had tagged along, too!

"Oh, good to see you, Chika. It's been a while. And you too, Yuria – come on in. You don't have kindergarten today?" Mum invited them in for tea. Mum and Granny Chika went to senior high school together; they were in the same year.

"Seishiro and Rika have gone out to sell produce at the local end-of-year market, so I'm taking care of our deliveries instead. And the kindergarten's taking a day off because the flu's going round, as if we weren't busy enough already. But luckily our little 'uns haven't caught anything. Konsaburo's at home with his grampa. He's showing him how to grow bonsai. The boy likes that sort of thing somehow."

"Well, a bonsai tree is like a universe in itself. Maybe that's what he likes about it?"

"I don't know. I feel it's just another way of playing house."

Yuria came into the kitchen. She had her own water bottle, hung diagonally from her shoulder on a strap. Kagami was making samples of new recipes, pickles and things like that while listening to music, but when he noticed Yuria, he took off his headphones.

"Do you want me to make a snack for you? Any requests?" he asked.

"I'll leave it up to the chef," she said.

Acting like a lady at a restaurant!

Yuria clambered up onto the bar stool at the counter. Apparently, she likes it better there than a normal chair because she feels taller. Always stylish, she was dressed in a Scottish blue tartan tunic today, and off-white knit leggings decorated with pom-poms. She came in wearing boots that were fluffy on the inside, but she took them off at the back door. (Needless to say, Norimaki made a beeline for them.)

Kagami prepared a hot smoothie with European pears. He adapted a summer recipe that uses frozen fruit and soya milk, using fruit kept at room temperature instead. You can make this smoothie with any fruit, like apples or bananas. Give them a good whirl in the food processor with soya milk. The trick is to add about half a teaspoon of vinegar when you blend it. (In winter, it's good to use top-quality black vinegar. Why? Because blackish foods are better at warming up your body than whitish foods. Or so I've heard, at least.)

When the smoothie was ready, Kagami warmed up some slices of pear in the microwave, then poured it over them. He offered the bowl to Yuria along with a spoon. Of course, you might prefer a chilled smoothie – it's up to you.

While Yuria ate her snack, Kagami jotted down what he gave her to let Rika know, just like what the Marukos next door do when they give Norimaki a treat. He comes home with a ribbon that says something like "Today's snack was this and that". (Norimaki's been having playdates with Chibi Maroko lately. Looks like he enjoys feeling like an older brother.) Kagami checks the ribbon and adjusts his breakfast for the next day accordingly. Otherwise, Norimaki would end up eating way too much, like Uncle Bear.

Back in the small dining room, the grown-ups were chatting away about the get-together. Granny Chikako suggested having the party in the cyclamen greenhouse at the farm.

"We'll have shipped off all the flowers by then, so there'll be enough space to put out tables and everything. It's a potluck party, so we don't need a big kitchen, do we? Wouldn't Rika's camper van be enough? That way, we can have onion dishes, no problem. Don't worry about our cat – he doesn't like to be around girls outside the family, so he won't come near us if he sees unfamiliar women around. He might run away from home in protest, but most likely he'll go and sit in the next-door garden and grumble at us from a distance. He won't come back until the coast is clear. So, you can have as much onions and garlic and all that as you like."

EARLY WINTER

"Good idea! You're right – I forget we don't *have* to do it at ours. A dinner party in a greenhouse has a nice ring to it. Maybe we can see the stars."

"No, that I can't promise. It's not transparent, so that the plants aren't exposed to direct sunlight. I'd say it'll be a more homely kind of setting, like a market stall – nothing fancy."

Mum and Granny Chikako got all excited and decided on the spot that the party venue would be the greenhouse at Seishiro Farm.

On the day, Yuria will sing her medley of songs, and they'll also have a "debut" performance by Hako and Kokona, a sisters' duet. Imagine *that* coming to the Horai house – the onion problem aside, I would've considered running away from home for the night, too. Such a stroke of luck that Granny Chikako has space in her greenhouse.

The day of the party is finally here: a Saturday. Kagami made breakfast for everyone and took the rest of the day off. Sacchan came over, and they went out somewhere by themselves.

Dumpling Girl is cooking something in the kitchen. The get-together is a potluck, so each participant brings a dish they'd recommend. It can be handmade or bought from a store. The kids don't have to bring anything, of course, but when Dumpling Girl heard on the grapevine that the Hako and Kokona duo will be baking cookies, she suddenly got

A SPECIAL GATHERING

fired up and decided she'll bring a dish too, not wanting to be outdone by the sisters.

She's going for the win (mind you, it's not a contest) with an easy but delicious dish Kagami taught her. First, she'll top chilled rice with chicken chopped into bite-size pieces and seasoned with salt and pepper, along with plenty of spring onions and mushrooms. Then she'll pour soup all over it and steam it until it's piping hot. It tastes the best when it's hot, so she'll prep at home and bring the ingredients to Granny Chikako's greenhouse. It's a simple dish, though – you just have to chop up the toppings and put them on pre-cooked rice. She'll bring Kagami's special soup in a plastic bottle.

I'm not kidding when I say this soup is out of this world. It's a collagen-rich soup broth that Kagami makes by slowly stewing chicken wings on a low heat. It's so good you'd want to gulp it all down at once. He makes the same chicken-on-rice dish for our breakfasts, too, swapping the spring onions with bonito flakes.

At eleven o'clock in the morning, the three of them – Koyomi, Mum and Dumpling Girl – set off for Seishiro Farm in the car, with Koyomi behind the wheel. Norimaki and I stayed behind, but we had Jean Paul for company.

Besides, a sitter came to look after us, too: Miss Oisa's younger brother, Yuji. He's an aspiring vet, and normally he's

EARLY WINTER

in Hokkaido, studying with a research group at a university there. He's on winter break now, so he's back home with his family, and Miss Oisa asked him if he could look after us for the day. It wasn't long before he started playing shogi with Jean Paul. In other words, Yuji has a sixth sense for the spiritual world.

Madame Hinako was also having a gathering in her atelier. The door opening onto the entrance hall was locked. When Koyomi told us this in the morning, Norimaki and I went to scratch on the door to check if it was true. It didn't open. She laughed, as if to say, *See? Told you so.*

Jean Paul dug out an old siphon coffee maker from somewhere and set it up on the table in the small dining room. As it burbled away, a lovely aroma drifted through the room.

I heard the lock turn in the door to the atelier. When Norimaki and I dashed over to have a look, the door was just starting to open. Madame Hinako appeared. "I'm sneaking out," she said with a smile.

With the door ajar, we could hear the murmurs from the atelier. Someone was playing the guitar, and it sounded like a lively party. Madame Hinako looked very chic in a slim dress, long and black, and a pair of small cloth shoes, shaped like ballet flats, embroidered with beads. She slowly glided over the entrance hall carpet.

The fabric of the dress was thinner from the neckline

A SPECIAL GATHERING

down her back and on the sleeves, with embroidery in shiny thread, which glimmered in the light of the corridor. It was beautiful, like silver droplets trailing down in delicate lines. She went into the small dining room.

Just as she stepped in, there was a sharp clack of wood on wood as someone – either Jean Paul or Yuji – placed a shogi piece down on the board.

"Ah, you're back again, I see," Madame Hinako said. "No wonder I caught a whiff of your coffee – takes me back to the old days. Kagami's brew is nice too, but it's more modern. Compared to his, your coffee is retro, even though you use the same beans. May I have a cup?"

"Of course, join us." Jean Paul made to stand up, but she stopped him with a graceful gesture.

"Don't mind me. I'll pour it myself, so you carry on with your game," she said, taking out a cup. "What a quiet afternoon."

"The girls have all gone out today. They're having a get-together in the greenhouse at Seishiro Farm. So I came over to keep the boys company, but they already had a sitter. This is Yuji; he's the younger brother of Dr Yamao, the vet."

When Jean Paul introduced him, Yuji sat up straight next to the shogi board and said with a bow, "Nice to meet you." Not that he was slouching before; he'd had good posture throughout the whole game.

EARLY WINTER

Yuji wore square glasses, and his figure had angular lines to it that matched the frames. His jumper was navy, plain and simple, but he looked good in it. He had short hair and a nicely shaped head.

"So young – such a pity," Madame Hinako said.

"Don't jinx him. He's still on your side of the river," Jean Paul said.

"He has a rare talent, then."

"Like you, Hinako. Once in a while, we come across folks like him, and thanks to them, my kind is saved from boredom."

"Well, glad to hear it. And, are you aware of who he is?" she asked Yuji.

"Isn't he Jean Paul?"

"I see . . . you can talk to cats, too. These boys are the only ones who call him that."

"He's training to become a vet, so of course he can talk to them," Jean Paul chimed in.

"So you have another name, monsieur?" Yuji said.

"Don't worry, anything goes. Just call him whatever you like. After all, he doesn't belong to this world anymore. He's free." She paused. "For such a young man, you don't seem unsettled by anything."

"I'm not the sensitive type."

"I wouldn't say so – people who are really slow on the

uptake don't realise it themselves. I bet you're popular with the girls. Though you probably haven't noticed it yourself. That's the way things are, isn't it? Thank you for the coffee. The host of a gathering needs a refuge from time to time."

Madame Hinako went back to her atelier, waving at us with a radiant smile.

At around five in the afternoon, Kagami and Sacchan came home. Apparently, the city streets were too packed and chaotic on a Saturday at this time of year, so they decided to head back early. Yuji told Kagami that nothing in particular had happened while he was away. When he mentioned that he'd played shogi with Jean Paul, Kagami cocked his head, wondering who that could be.

They discussed what to do for dinner. Yuji had been invited by Miss Oisa to come to Seishiro Farm when he was finished looking after us, and Kagami could see that Sacchan – who's a fan of parties like this – wanted to join, so he prodded Sacchan to show Yuji the way.

Sacchan happily agreed, and the two of them headed over together. I got the feeling that Yuji might be Sacchan's type.

After seeing them off, Kagami didn't go to his room or the kitchen as he usually did, but stayed in the living room and leaned back on the sofa. He really did look exhausted. If only Norimaki and I could make a cup of hot tea for him or bring

EARLY WINTER

him a blanket – but Kagami's room is in the semi-basement, and we can't drag his blanket up the stairs.

Jean Paul had disappeared a little while ago when I wasn't looking. I guess there's a time limit to how long he can be here. Like those superheroes from outer space.

I had an idea to ask Madame Hinako for a blanket if she came to take another break, so I took Norimaki out to the entrance hall – that way he wouldn't pester Kagami to cradle him. We settled down to wait for the atelier door to open.

Just then, I heard a sound from the front door. Somebody with a key had come home. I was trying to think who it could be – Mum and the others would've come in from the back door – when Sakuragawa stepped inside.

"What's up? You look like you're waiting for someone. Is it just the two of you here?"

There was music and laughter coming from the atelier, but our side of the house was dark; the only glow came from the downlights in the corridor.

While Sakuragawa stroked our heads, we tried to tell him, "*Miumomunyanyamo* (there's something wrong with Kagami)."

"You're not hungry, are you?" he asked.

"*Nnyo.*"

"The heating's on, so somebody must be home."

We dashed to the living room. Sakuragawa followed us.

Kagami was draped over the sofa like before; he seemed to be dozing. But he sensed Sakuragawa's presence and opened his eyes – because Sakuragawa was standing right in front of him, peering into his face.

"Senpai," Kagami murmured after a pause.

"You alright? You look tired."

"A little. I went shopping in the city with Sacchan, and it was so crowded."

"What did you expect? It's a Saturday at the end of the year. Where's Komaki and the rest?"

"They're at a party at Seishiro Farm – all three of them. I don't have to cook dinner for anyone tonight, so I was just being lazy ... It's not like you to be home on a Saturday evening."

"There's a cocktail party at a gallery later, so I came back to get changed."

"I see ..."

"Thought I'd have a bite to eat. I tend to get sick when I drink on an empty stomach, so. Mind if I use the kitchen?"

"Sure, please go ahead. But I haven't cooked rice tonight. There's leftover cold rice, though. And a bit of tofu in the fridge, and frozen mushrooms – that's about it. Everyone took all the food for the party."

"That's fine. I don't need a big meal."

Norimaki and I tagged along behind Sakuragawa to the

kitchen. He rarely cooked anything here, so we *had* to watch. Kagami probably wanted to see it too, but he looked like it was too much effort to get off the sofa, so I decided to watch closely for him and report back.

I leaped up on the sink to get a better view. Norimaki managed to come up too, by using the kitchen stool like a stepladder. Sakuragawa told us to stay clear of the knife, so Norimaki pressed himself against the window. Sakuragawa has this "senpai" way of talking – like someone older who knows what he's doing – so I guess Norimaki feels like he's got to follow his every order, word for word.

"I'll borrow this for a bit," Sakuragawa said, taking the navy apron that Dumpling Girl had left hanging on a hook. It was the Makkujira apron: the "full whale ahead" with the whale-shaped kanji on it.

First, he placed a block of tofu on a draining board. While the water dripped off the tofu, he put cold rice and water in an earthenware pot and let it come to a boil. Then he dry-roasted some dried whitebait in a frying pan without any oil or water. Once they were cooked through, and a tempting aroma wafted through the kitchen, he added one cup of water, a handful of mushrooms, and soy sauce and sake for flavouring. Though he didn't use spring onion oil, the steps in the recipe were basically the same as those Kagami would follow.

"Surprised?" Sakuragawa said to me. "My mother picked up some techniques from the older chief at Matsu Sushi; she mimicked their style in her own cooking at home. My gramps was a fan of Matsu Sushi flavours – that's why."

Huh. Interesting, I thought. Sakuragawa's mum is Mrs Meowko, right? I didn't know she cooked, too. She sounds like a super busy lady, so I didn't think she had time for things like that. I still haven't met her in person.

Sakuragawa cut the tofu into flat squares and coated all sides with plenty of potato starch. He dropped them in boiling water, and the starch solidified into a jelly-like coating as clear as crystal. He served them in a bowl with stir-fried mushrooms in a sauce thickened with potato starch, and there it was: ankake tofu, or tofu with thick dashi sauce.

Besides the ankake tofu, Sakuragawa also placed a crystal-coated tofu square deep inside the rice in the earthenware pot, just as it was starting to bubble. He found oboro kombu in the fridge and topped the tofu with the fluffy seaweed. He said it also worked well with roasted sesame seeds, nori seaweed or arare rice crackers. They all sound like things that Grandad would like, so I bet this is another recipe from Matsu Sushi.

I thought Sakuragawa was going to eat both dishes, but he took the earthenware pot with the tofu in rice porridge to Kagami. It was time for his devilish charms to shine. If he had

EARLY WINTER

a hidden agenda, that was one thing, but if he was just being nice, that made him even trickier to handle.

"You look like you're coming down with a cold. Better eat something to fight it off," Sakuragawa said.

Let's see how Kagami's electrical signals were doing today.

After a moment of silence, Kagami said, "It's uzumi tofu."

"Is that what you call it in this house? 'Hidden tofu', huh – sounds kind of poetic."

"At Matsu Sushi, they serve the crystal tofu just by itself in the summer, and when winter comes around, they bury the tofu in rice porridge and call it 'hidden tofu'. Hiding it in the rice helps to keep its shape when they deliver it to customers."

"Makes sense. Now that you mention it, it's true that 'hidden tofu' sounds kind of warmer than 'crystal tofu' – better for the winter months."

Hmm, they're actually having a decent conversation this time. But just as I was thinking that if they kept this up, they might actually get somewhere, someone barged in. Dumpling Girl. Since kids weren't supposed to stay at the party past eight o'clock, Tekona's Darling took the sisters home and had dropped off Dumpling Girl on the way.

"I'm back," she called out. "Oh . . . are you feeling sick, Kagami?"

"I'm just tired out from all the crowds. I'll feel better by tomorrow."

"Hmm." She took a moment to reassess the scene, staring back and forth between Sakuragawa in her apron and Kagami lying down on the sofa. "Am I a total third wheel right now?"

Bingo. It was just like Dumpling Girl to direct the question at Sakuragawa.

"Exactly. We were having an intimate conversation," Sakuragawa answered devilishly.

"What's Kagami eating? Ooh, did you cook something for him?"

"It's too simple to call it cooking," Sakuragawa said. "But when you're tired, it does the trick pretty well. I'm guessing Kahoru makes it, too? It's a classic in the Sakuragawa family. It's crystal tofu buried in rice porridge. Though I just heard you call it uzumi tofu in this house."

"Kahorun calls it to-œuf à la steak."

"To-œuf . . . what even is that?"

"She drains the tofu, then dips it in a mix of beaten egg and soya milk, and fries it in a thinly buttered pan. We eat it by itself, or put it in rice porridge, or on couscous, for example. She named it 'to-œuf à la steak'. It's one of the best entries in my Mamemon notebook. Isn't it sweet?"

Silence stretched on. *I'd give Kaporin a standing ovation, though!*

Come to think of it, Mademoiselle Rocco used to murmur, "œf, œf", when she made omelette. Now I know she was just

EARLY WINTER

saying "egg". By the way, I heard that in correct French, they say "fromage de soja" – "soybean cheese", that is – for tofu.

After Sakuragawa went to get changed, Kagami ate the crystal tofu; seeing the way he savoured it, it must've been delicious. All's well that ends well.

8

Midwinter

Snuggling at Home

Simmered satoimo, deep-fried tofu and kiriboshi daikon
Crab pom-pom balls (meow-food)
Kumquat sushi

+

Baked chocolate & chocolate cake

These days, it's so cold I feel like cuddling up to anyone at all – doesn't matter who. That reminds me: when we got separated from Mademoiselle Rocco in deep winter last year, the first cosy spot we found was inside the fluffy pocket of one of those waterproof jackets that airline staff wear when they work outside.

It was hung on the backrest of a chair in an admin office, and the thick white boa fleece was sticking out of the pocket like a little flag. Both Norimaki and I charged at it. We were a lot smaller back then, so we burrowed into the same pocket together. It was so nice and snug in there that we dozed off. When I woke up, the jacket was swaying back and forth like a swing.

The owner of the jacket had finished work and was on his

way home. He was a really big man, so his jacket was big, too – that's why the two of us could easily fit into his pocket. I decided to call him Mr Boa.

Mr Boa commuted by car. As he was getting in behind the wheel, he shrugged off his jacket and tossed it on the back seat. That sent me tumbling out of the pocket, and I meowed at him in surprise. But the car stereo was turned up, and Mr Boa didn't notice.

Eventually, the car rolled into the car park of a building with a cat painted on it: a pet salon that also served as a hotel. Mr Boa got out and talked to a lady. Not long after, a girl appeared, smelling like she'd just been shampooed. She had a cream-coloured coat and bright white gloves. Even her nails were shiny. She looked a little older than us. She said goodbye to the lady and gracefully sashayed onto the back seat of the car, where we were sitting. The baby pink cushion seemed to be reserved for her. The car started moving again.

My eyes met hers, and she asked me who we were, so I answered, "Marble and Chocolate", That's what we were called back then, you see. Some meow-girls slap you for no reason when you meet them for the first time, but this one wasn't like that. She was friendly and straightforward.

"Mm. I'm Lunée. They gave me this name because my creamy white coat glows like the moon," she said.

It was true – she really did have a gorgeous coat, as smooth and glossy as a pearl. She was a stylish girl with pretty blue eyes.

"Are you brothers?" she asked. "We live with two sisters, Eclair and Charlotte. You can come home with us, but are you ready to fight?"

"With who?"

"The sisters, of course. They're chabo – you know, bantams. They respect me because I kept them warm with my fur when they were little chicks, but they're feisty and they always pick fights with newcomers. Eclair has a dark brown head and a golden russet body like a fox. I don't have to explain where she gets her name, do I? Charlotte's head is shaped like a daisy, like Charlotte cake. It's a mutation. So? What do you want to do?"

I decided to change cars. No way was I going up against a couple of Amazons. Lunée opened the window for us when Mr Boa stopped on the shoulder of a road to take a call.

"So long, sweeties. If you want to hitchhike, go to a service area instead of staying on the roadside. Cat lovers will let you hop in. Do you know the pose? You have to go like this."

She showed us the maneki-neko pose – you know, those cat figurines holding one paw up to beckon good luck. But Norimaki couldn't keep his balance, so he ended up raising both paws like a "Hurrah!" Even then he tottered and flumped back on his bum.

If you think all cats are born with a great sense of balance,

MIDWINTER

let me tell you that's far from the truth. We need experience and practice, too.

For example, you might expect that walking along a garden wall is as easy as pie for our kind, but it's hard work to climb up there in the first place. We have to train our back muscles. You're not thinking we get up there in a single leap, are you? We have a method for scaling a high wall.

Back when we started our nomadic life, I was still little, so I hadn't yet learned the technique. At Mademoiselle Rocco's, she put up a prickly cover over the wallpaper to keep us from scratching it. So we couldn't go near the walls. If we wanted to feel like a climber, all we had were the curtains.

Once I became a wandering cat, I watched my seniors strutting along walls like it was nothing and studied how they climbed up. At first, I imagined they put their legs together and inch their way up like an inchworm. But actually, they spread out all four limbs like a frog, cling to the wall, and quickly move their legs one after the other to make their way up. Sounds funny, right? But that's how we do it.

Once everybody's gone off to school or work, and Kagami has wrapped up his morning duties in the kitchen, it's hard to find anyone to snuggle up to until Mum comes downstairs. Norimaki and I wander around the house, looking for any pools of sunlight. Today, Mum finally appeared around noon.

She sat down at the small dining table, and when we trotted over to her, she called to us, "Come here, my yutanpo." That's her nickname for us because we're warm like hot water bottles. Like us, she isn't keen on the cold. She patted the small blanket covering her lap and held the pocket in the middle wide open, as if to say, *Here you go, hop in.* She told me it's supposed to be where the heat pack goes, but it's a perfect fit for us.

Dumpling Girl came home from school a little later. She had shortened school hours today, so she finished right after lunch. As soon as she put down her bags, she sat at the table in the small dining room. She pulled out her Mamemon notebook and frowned at it, thinking hard about something.

"You know how grown-ups give the kids some money at New Year's, and the little envelopes they use for it are called 'pochi bukuro', like 'a little bag'? And you know how a lot of dogs are named Pochi? Are those the same kind of *pochi*, or something different?"

"Another tough question. Have you looked into it yourself?" Mum asked, making spirals with her pen on the corner of her Komakoma Diary manuscript. It looked like it might be almost out of ink. She always writes her diary in longhand first, by the way – then she types out the final draft for Tekona on her computer. Tiny wrinkles formed on Dumpling Girl's brow. That's her frustrated face.

"I did look into it, but people have different opinions. Some people say the dog name Pochi comes from 'petit' in French. Other people say it comes from 'pooch' in English. And then there are people who say those are both wrong, and that it came from 'Spotty' instead, which is a popular name for dogs in America."

"It's an age-old dispute, you know. Theories like this have been around since I was little, and not a single one is definitive. I mean, it's not the sort of problem that would come up on an exam, and it's not exactly a life-and-death question. You just have to find an explanation that *you* think is convincing. Which one would you go for, Hikari?"

"Well, none of them really clicks for me. They all sound pretty far-fetched."

"At times like that, try going round to the side of the building, or the back. Look at it from a different angle. Then you're sure to discover something you didn't expect – a small door used for inspections that you hadn't noticed before, or a tiny window about the size of a small plate, for letting in the light. Picture the word *pochi* in the Roman alphabet. If you draw out the *o*, you can read it as *pōchi*, too. Like how we call the bag that holds our make-up kit in Japanese: *keshō pōchi*. Pōchi means a pocket or a small bag. In English, it's spelled *pouch*, but in French, it's *poche*. Now try writing that in cursive. It looks almost the same as *pochi*, doesn't it? *Pochi* is an old word that already existed in

Japanese, signifying a small point. In medieval Japan, people called punctuation marks like the dot <·> or the full stop <◦> a *pochi*. But I have a feeling that it was thanks to the influence from the French *poche* that the word became linked to the idea of a small bag. The pronunciations sound nothing alike, but imagine people around the bunmei-kaika years in the early Meiji era, when Japan became rapidly westernised – how they must have studied using dictionaries that were written with a brush. What if they saw an entry like '*poche* – bag', read it as *pochi*, and memorised it like 'pochi bag' or 'pochi bukuro'? It rolls off the tongue, doesn't it? As for the popular dog name Pochi: considering how they used to read the dot <·> as *pochi*, I'm guessing it had something to do with *buchi*, as in 'spotted fur'. But dog breeds that are native to Japan – like Akita, Tosa or Kai – aren't spotted. The Japanese Chin are kind of spotted, but it's not like they have dots in their fur, so they don't really make you want to call them Pochi. It could be that Portuguese or Spanish travellers brought in the Pointer at some point in history, but it's hard to believe such exotic dogs would've been seen often enough by ordinary people to have an influence on the language. Actually, when we hear the word *buchi* now, the first thing we think of are cats, right? There must've been lots of cats named Pochi. Isn't it cute as a cat name, too? Tama is still popular for cats, but I think both Tama and Pochi must've started out as cat names. If Japanese people were naming dogs, way back when, wouldn't they have given them names like Koganemaru, or Chiyomaru, or something old-fashioned like that? Though I've heard of Tsun for a female dog. Maybe it was only after hunting dogs were brought into Japan in the early Meiji period that people became familiar with spotted dogs. I have a feeling that the first Japanese person to see a spotted dog asked what its name was, and the owner – English or American or whatever they were – said 'Spotty', and the Japanese person heard it as 'Pochi'. I'm probably not too wide of the mark. So, back to your initial question, Hikari: the *pochi* in *pochi bukuro* and the dog name Pochi are similar in the sense that they both evolved from a foreign word. But this is just my personal opinion at the end of the day . . . Phew, let's take a breather."

Mum went to the kitchen to boil more water for tea. I hopped down onto the floor and trailed behind her. Norimaki was still buried in Mum's front pocket; he turned around inside it and poked his head out, taking a little gulp of air, as if he'd been diving underwater.

"*Whoa.*" Dumpling Girl was gasping for air, too. She looked full, like her stomach was bulging with all the words she'd just been fed.

"Did that convince you?" Mum asked.

This time, Dumpling Girl exhaled deeply. "I feel like I'm drowning in a sea of words."

She retreated to her room upstairs with her Mamemon

SNUGGLING AT HOME

notebook, whose pages were filled with fresh notes. Right after she left, Tekona appeared at the back door.

"Oh, you're early. I'm not done yet," Mum said. The manuscript paper in front of her was completely blank. Though there were lots of scribbles in the margins. Like "pochi" and "buchi".

"I know, I know," Tekona said. "I just stopped by because there's something I want to ask you. It's about cooking nikkorogashi with satoimo taro. I can't get my kids to eat it, even when I braise the satoimo with beans or turn it into kenchin soup."

"Is it because the chunks of satoimo are still hard in the middle?"

"You got it."

"That's a tricky one – getting them soft and fluffy. But wouldn't you be better off going to the Seishiro Farm with a question like that? I'm sure Rika, the veggie buff, will tell you the secret, complete with a child-friendly recipe." (I knew she'd say something like that! Mum doesn't cook herself, so she can't teach anyone. Though Tekona doesn't know that, of course.)

"The Seishiro Farm lot have gone on holiday. They said it's the only time of year the whole family can take time off together. They've gone all the way to Aoshima, the island in Miyazaki. There's onsen, there's surfing, there's delicious food

275

everywhere, both from the sea and the mountain. I think it's where that myth about Umihiko and Yamahiko comes from – you know, the sea brother who's good at fishing and the mountain brother who's good at hunting."

"Oh, they're on holiday? I didn't know that."

"If they announce it before they go, word could get around where they don't want it to, and someone might try to break into their house while it's empty, so Rika told me they're just going to slip away. She said she'll definitely bring back goodies from the island, though."

"I see . . . And you were saying you want your kids to like satoimo, Tekona – is that it?"

"Exactly. They say that when I cook satoimo, it's too rough and hard, and they don't like it. And I have to say it *is* rather different from the nikkorogashi I used to have when I was little. My mum's satoimo were more sticky and kind of creamy inside. But I can't re-create that texture no matter what I try."

"Why don't you ring your mum and ask her for tips?"

"All she says is wash the satoimo, pop them in the pot, and simmer them in dashi soup with a bit of soy sauce – that's it. What *I* want to hear are more basic things like how much water to put in, or how high the heat should be, and things like that, but somehow we get too embarrassed to talk about it. When I looked it up in a cookbook, it said things like add a handful of rice bran to retain the light colour of the satoimo and give it a refined finish, but it didn't say anything about how to fluff it up. Is it some sort of trade secret? I know I dug my own grave by spending all my time on sports ever since elementary school and never helping out in the kitchen, but still."

"Well then, should I write about it for Komakoma Diary?"

"Yes, please. I'd love that."

Tekona rearranged her shawl, which covered her completely from the top of her head down to her arms, then whizzed away into the north wind. Mum set about interviewing Kagami right away. The following is the result.

When we see a chaotic crowd of people, we say "it's like washing potatoes". We often hear it from news reporters on television when they show the beach during the summer holidays. But I'm not sure if young reporters have ever seen potatoes being washed in their daily lives. Surely they're not comparing the view of a kitchen sink while washing five or six potatoes to a beach resort teeming with people.

People who don't have words of their own don't think twice about rattling off idioms like that.

Incidentally, I asked young people what kind of "imo", or potatoes, they think of when they hear the word "imo". Most of the time, they answer jagaimo, plain potatoes. The second most popular answer was satsumaimo, sweet potatoes.

And what potato dishes do they like? Nikujaga, or meat and potato stew; potato salad; French fries; daigaku-imo, or candied sweet potatoes; and so on. All the dishes they bring up are made with either plain potatoes or sweet potatoes. As an experiment, I tried asking what "imo" do they think we actually mean when we say "it's like washing imo".

If my mother and father heard the results, they would be astounded. The most frequent answer was sweet potato. The second was plain potato. Here in Tokyo, there are still plenty of vegetable patches growing satoimo taro if you just stretch out a little into the suburbs. Ah, but even so, how few are the people who name satoimo as the representative imo! Even fewer people picked yamaimo. Perhaps they don't ever think about what those names signify: the satoimo is grown on the flat, tilled ground of a sato, or village, whereas the yamaimo grows naturally in the yama, or mountains.

And this despite the fact that both yamaimo and satoimo have been eaten by people since prehistoric times – that they have the oldest, deepest connection with human beings out of all the foods we still eat.

I love satoimo. But I hate washing them, which used to be a typical chore that children would help out with. It was boring and your hands got cold. I grew up in a family who runs a catering business, so washing imo was basically part of my everyday routine. I washed them in the little stream that flowed past the back of our house.

Today, our district of Tokyo is just your average residential neighbourhood, but back in the day, there were vegetable patches all over the place. There were cows and horses too, as well as many pig and poultry farms. It wasn't only children whose families had a catering business that washed imo in a stream branching off the river – it was a task for children in ordinary families too, during the winter.

We got our satoimo directly from a farmer nearby, so they were still covered in soil. First, I would wash the dirt off along with the thin roots that grew out of the outer skin like little hairs. Then the whole bunch went in a big colander, and I'd scrub them clean. Some people let the river do the work by making a closed basket that rotated in the current. Anyhow, imagine scores of satoimo packed into a colander or a basket, the clumps of dirt and the thin roots peeling off as they rub against each other in the running water. That's what it's like to wash a throng of imo.

If you soak satoimo in water for too long, they turn hard. And once they turn hard, they don't turn soft again no matter how long you boil or steam them. After you wash them, you shouldn't leave them lying around wet or immersed in water.

Once the dirt and roots are gone, take them out of the water right away and wipe them dry with a cloth. In my family, we *prepare the satoimo in different ways depending on their use: for the satoimo that goes in our catering menu, we peel the thin skin, cut off the edges to make them nice and round, and stew them. But for those we eat at home, we don't peel the thin skin, and we just steam or boil them as they are.*

Some people might not get what I mean by the "thin skin" of a satoimo. Most people must think satoimo have thick skin. That's because people tend to peel the bit that's edible, too.

Actually, some people don't even like that certain sliminess of satoimo taro. But the thick, slippery texture is exactly what gives them their umami, and what's more, it's a treasure trove of dietary fibre. I once saw in a cookbook written by a British chef that the trick to cooking okra is to boil it in a way that keeps the sliminess trapped inside. Then what are you eating okra for, I'd like to ask – but it seems like people who live in dry regions shrink away from slimy, sticky foods. The sliminess of okra is fibre, too, of course.

My favourite way of having satoimo is to simmer them with strips of sun-dried daikon and deep-fried tofu. If you roast dried whitebait in a pot and pour in some water, that gives you a nice dashi base already. Add soy sauce to taste and simmer the kiriboshi daikon and abura-age tofu. In a separate pot, put whole satoimo with the thin skin still on in an amount of water that just about covers them and stew them slowly on a medium heat.

If you cook them whole like this, it takes at least half an hour to get them soft, assuming you have four or five satoimo in the pot. If you'd prefer a shorter cooking time, you can choose smaller satoimo in the store. You can also cook them in a steamer, too. Thoroughly cooked and soft satoimo will become a little bigger than when they're raw because they fluff up. You only need to pinch it with your fingers for the skin to slip off. Then you'll see how thin a skin they have.

Unlike plain potatoes, satoimo don't fall apart even when they're overcooked. When you're cooking just for the family, you can let them get too soft – no problem. If they get extra gooey, then you're in luck. Cut them into bite-size pieces and add them to the first pot where you've cooked the kiriboshi daikon and abura-age tofu.

Sometimes people use sugar to stew satoimo, but all you need is the sweetness that comes from the daikon strips. But there's another secret trick you can use if you want your kids to love it: you can add some sugar-free amazake. The sweetness of the fermented rice, the daikon and the satoimo come together so well, and the whole dish becomes even more delightful. I couldn't get enough of this when I was little. While the grown-ups were having the kenchin soup with sake kasu mixed in, the kids ate the child-friendly version of the soup made with amazake. It's a fermented food, so it warms you up, too.

Though you might expect amazake to have alcohol in it,

MIDWINTER

since it's written as "sweet sake", it actually has zero alcohol, unlike sake kasu, which is left over from the sake brewing process – so it's perfectly safe to feed to children. Amazake goes well with rice, too. If you serve it in a soup bowl like a potage, it's a perfect companion to bread for breakfast. A cup of amazake is just what you need to warm yourself from inside on a cold morning.

Whatever you do, the important thing is to buy satoimo that still have dirt on them. Pre-washed ones are no good. Ones soaking in water are even worse.

For some reason that I haven't figured out yet, the front gate of the Horai house doesn't have a nameplate. But the gate itself is always half-open. The well-informed delivery man, who comes in the truck with the black cats' logo, just walks right in and then goes around the house to the back door. He knows that's where he can find people.

Most visitors step inside the gate more tentatively, listening out for signs of life in the house. Once they reach the front door, they find a doorbell. But even there, there's no nameplate. Since they can't know for sure whose house it is, they hesitate to ring it – the more proper and upright someone is, the longer they hesitate.

In contrast, the entrance to Madame Hinako's atelier has the sign ATELIER HINAKO hanging on it. After much consideration, some people decide to ring *her* bell instead. But Madame Hinako usually doesn't come to the atelier until around noon, so there's nobody there to answer the door in the morning.

Whenever we notice someone hovering outside the front door, Norimaki and I go out to tell them, "You can keep going to the back door." But they rarely understand what we're saying.

That's why, just recently, the family put up a sign on the front door in Dumpling Girl's calligraphy that says, PLEASE COME ROUND TO THE BACK DOOR, with an arrow pointing left.

There was another one of those visitors again today: a lady I'd never seen before was hanging about the front door. She was wearing a parka, the kind you'd take on a casual hike in the mountains. It was a bold green colour with accents of white lines, like a road sign. Black slacks below it, a daypack on her back.

The Madame looked closely at the sign written by Dumpling Girl. First she stared at it for a while, then she took a few steps back, crossed her arms and nodded to herself.

Norimaki and I went up to her, thinking of letting her know that the back door is on the left side of the house. But at that moment, Sakuragawa came down the exterior staircase of the annex – even though it was just before noon on a weekday.

I wondered if he was taking a day off. But he was wearing a suit and carrying a bag that was bigger than usual, so maybe he was going on a business trip somewhere. He noticed the visitor and called out, "You can try going to the back door on the left. There should be someone home."

"Anata koko no uchi no hito desu ka? (You live here?)" she asked, speaking in a choppy sort of way. "Kono calligraphie, spirituelle, moderne, dynamique. Watakushi, taisou kini iri mashita. (I like it very much)."

Sakuragawa was silent for a moment. Once he'd taken in the situation, he started saying something fast, moving his mouth in a different way than he normally did. Then the Madame changed how she spoke, too; this time her sentences sounded flowy and elegant, instead of the jerky, sharp contours she'd started out with. I couldn't tell what they were saying, though.

Sakuragawa opened the front door of the main house with his key and invited her in. Norimaki and I went in together. He offered her a seat and headed towards the kitchen, calling for Kagami.

Kagami appeared in the entrance hall, wearing his navy blue apron that says HAVING SUITON SOUP AT A RAILWAY STOP in white letters. The Madame got to her feet, saying, "C'est bon." She seemed to have taken a liking to the lettering on the apron, too.

"This Madame here likes the 'Please come round to the

SNUGGLING AT HOME

back door' sign that Hikari wrote and says she wants to have it. Sorry, I've got to run – can you take care of the rest? I have a work trip," Sakuragawa said quickly, then dashed out of the house. Kagami didn't get a chance to respond. He stood there, face-to-face with the lady, with his customary deadpan expression (which probably meant he was, in fact, totally confused by Sakuragawa's absurd request).

The Madame flashed him a winning smile. Kagami stepped out the front door, peeled off Dumpling Girl's sign, and placed it on the guest table in the entrance hall.

"Please take it," he said. "Would you like me to wrap it in paper?"

She gazed at the sign admiringly.

"I'll go look for something to wrap it with," he said and walked off to the back of the house.

"Oh? Is that you, Mikasa? When did you get back?" Mum called out, coming down the stairs. She looked fresh, like she'd just washed her face. The colder it gets, the later she gets out of bed. The visitor's face broke into a grin, and she pattered over to Mum, noiselessly waving her hands. So, mystery solved: she was Mum's visitor.

"Komaki! Watakushi, kesa tsuita no. (I just landed this morning.)"

"Have you seen Laurent already?"

"Mada (Not yet). *He sleeps in after night shift, so he wants to meet in evening. But, he asked me to pick up Lunée. She stays at pet salon, when he works night shifts."*

"I can sympathise – it feels safer than having her wait at home all alone. So, I'll introduce our boys to you."

Kagami came back with a paper bag just in time.

"That one in the apron is my son, Kagami; the little ones are Chimaki and Norimaki," Mum said. Kagami bowed, and I said hello. Norimaki made a bow, too.

"*Good boys, good boys.*" The Madame squatted down to pet me, cupping my head, ears and cheeks all in one with her warm hands. She did the same to Norimaki; he must've felt really good because he started purring.

"This Madame is Mikasa – she lectures on Japanese subculture at a university in Paris. Her father adored Japan. He didn't know much about Japanese, nor was he an expert on Japanese culture, but he gave his two daughters Japanese-style names. Or that's what he intended, anyway. I'm told he chose the names because he thought they had a nice ring to them, but unfortunately, he wasn't aware at the time that the family name comes first in Japan. Mikasa's younger sister is called Mikuni. Funny, right? Well, at least he didn't pick Mikado, the emperor. When his grandson, Laurent, was born, he was so excited to give him a name, but as soon as he mentioned 'Genji', everybody rejected his idea. This time he made sure he picked a first name (or so he thought), but it was too old-fashioned."

Mikasa's dad sounded like fun. Mum didn't stop there: the stories kept coming. Back when she was studying abroad, Mum used to rent a room in a flat that he owned. Mikasa, who was an art student, was living in the same flat, and that's how they became friends. It's all "ancient history", Mum said. It seemed like she would keep on talking for ever, but Kagami managed to cut in when there was the briefest of pauses between her sentences.

"Could you explain something to Madame Mikasa?" he asked. "She says she wants to buy Hikari's sign, but it's not fit for sale, and I think if she knew what it said, she'd change her mind."

"I don't think so. Mikasa can speak enough Japanese to hold a simple conversation, and she can read a little, too. Though she's a bit wobbly on the particles. She married a Japanese man and was going to live in Japan, but Mr Kudo got transferred to the US, and then she got divorced soon after that."

As she talked, Mum peered over Mikasa's shoulder at the sign on the table in the entrance hall.

"You're right, though," Mum went on. "'Katteguchi' is a kind of quaint way to say 'back door', so young people might not get it. Nowadays they might not even know that 'daidokoro' means 'kitchen'. I wonder, do people still say 'okatte' for the kitchen? When I was a child, women would say 'okatte-sama' to sound sulky. It basically works the same way as 'oainiku-sama' or 'habakari-sama' when you want to say a sarcastic 'too bad for you'... but come to think of it, nobody says that anymore, do they? They're the sort of phrases Hikari would jot down in her Mamemon book. We're talking the sixties. That time when women wore tight skirts and dressy blouses with balloon sleeves, and backcombed their hair to lift it up, and long lashes were just as crucial as they are now. Back then, they used to glue on fake lashes with grains of cooked rice. Can you believe it? But that was the best way to make them last, from what I've heard."

"It's true, you know. But it hurt when you had to peel them off," Madame Hinako chimed in.

"Nako!"

"Mikasa, are you going on a forest patrol or something?"

"I stand out when I walk on dark street, and it's warm. Perfect for climbing Mount Takao." Mikasa took out a *Michelin Guide*.

"It's not the best time of year for Mount Takao. Cedar pollen everywhere. I heard hay fever is common in France, too?"

"I am fine."

Madame Hinako also studied Dumpling Girl's sign. "Hmm. I have to say, this is a superb piece of work. It's modern. I suppose Hikari dashed it off because it's just a sign. If you try

SNUGGLING AT HOME

too hard to make something look good, you can't get lines like this. You could cut a mat board and make a panel out of it – it would look beautiful on white wallpaper. Just like your house in Paris, Mikasa. That wallpaper with the quirky texture, with patterns like seashells. Did you know, Kagami, she goes everywhere dressed like a forest ranger, but she's actually very well off. Her father owns a château in the countryside. Why don't you name her a high price? She'll be happy to pay it," she said, egging Kagami on.

"Itsuki doesn't seem to approve of selling Hikari's calligraphy, though," Kagami said.

Madame Hinako chuckled. "I'll tell you what that is: jealousy. Itsuki is good at calligraphy too, but his isn't artistic. It's more practical, you could say. Hikari's is bolder – she goes outside the box. But she's not afraid to do that because she hasn't grown up to be anybody yet. Once you start trying to become something on purpose, your expression gets hemmed in. So you shouldn't be too quick to treat a child's drawing as a piece of art. Itsuki's doing the right thing as an adult and as a father. But I'm sure there's an element of jealousy in it, too. He sees that Hikari has something he doesn't."

Jealousy, huh? I used to hear that word all the time when I lived with Mademoiselle Rocco (especially when she was chatting with her friends on the phone), but now that I think about it, I'd forgotten all about it after coming to the Horai house. No wonder – everyone in this family is kind of offbeat.

Mikasa, now the happy owner of the PLEASE COME ROUND TO THE BACK DOOR sign, strolled off with Madame Hinako and Mum to have lunch. Kagami wasn't the type to think about making money, so he just gave it away for nothing!

Kagami was melting chocolate in the kitchen. Chocolate is another thing that Norimaki and I aren't supposed to eat (though it's not so dangerous as to earn a red skull mark sticker), so he told us to go and play in the small dining room. We snuggled up to each other on Mr Dodo's chair and sat like two little loaves, tucking our paws underneath us. The sashiko-stitched seat cushion cover had just been washed, so it smelled nice. Sunlight poured through the skylight and pooled right on the chair. A cosy spot in the warm glow. I started nodding off.

Just as I was hoping someone would come and let us sleep on their lap, the doorbell rang. Koyomi, who happened to be coming down the stairs, went to peer through the peephole.

"Well, this is a surprise, Miyako," she said, opening the door and welcoming the caller.

We heard "Meowko" and dashed to the entrance hall, eager to see her. She looked flawless in her simple snow-white knit and slim-fit denims. This was Mrs Meowko: Kaporin and Sakuragawa's mum.

Norimaki, still half asleep, couldn't stop running and bumped into her foot.

"Oh dear, are you alright? You must be the brothers I've been hearing so much about. So, we finally meet. Hello there. I'm Miyako. Pleasure to meet you."

I was stunned. Since she had the same name as Auntie Meowko, I was imagining a squat, stout auntie with a round, happy face, but she was nothing like that! I'd also had the idea that she'd be the sort of person who wore kimonos on a regular basis, but I was wrong about that, too.

Even though she wasn't dressed up or anything, she still looked so fashionable. She had a slender figure and airy light brown hair with meche highlights that fell just below her shoulders. Sitting down on the chair in the entrance hall, she gracefully crossed her legs. She wore a pair of bluish purple moccasins the colour of violets. Their fringes caught Norimaki's attention: he slowly stretched out his paw, then shrank back without touching it. He did this a few times. There he went again, thinking it was a living creature. Mrs Meowko wiggled her moccasined foot to give him something to play with.

"I brought something to show Hinako, but I see she's out."

"I heard her talking just a minute ago, though," Koyomi

said. "I was upstairs, so I didn't see her, but I heard someone say, 'Which one should I have, soba noodles with grated daikon, or shamo chicken hot pot?' – I'm pretty sure it was Hinako's voice."

Kagami overheard them and popped his head out of the kitchen.

"Hinako went to have lunch with my mother. They should be back soon. They went with Mikasa, who's visiting from Paris."

"Mikasa's here? Shamo hot pot?" Mrs Meowko asked.

Kagami nodded.

"Oh, what did I miss? I should've come a bit earlier. I haven't had lunch yet today – wish I could've gone with them."

"Would you like me to make something?" Kagami asked.

"It's alright, just ignore me. Thank you, though. But what I do want to know is what you're making with this lovely aroma of chocolate wafting from the kitchen. That reminds me, it's almost Valentine's Day. I heard your chocolate cake is sublime."

Kagami's expression didn't change at all, but a faint flush came into his ears.

Koyomi peered into the kitchen, too. "Mmm, it *does* smell good. But it doesn't look like chocolate cake."

"I'm doing a trial run of baked chocolate at Hikari's request. I'm simplifying the recipe so she can make it herself."

"She's making sweets for someone? Sounds like she's got a serious crush," Koyomi said.

"She said she's having a girls' party."

"I wonder. Is that just camouflage?"

Just as they were talking about her, Dumpling Girl appeared. She wavered between the Makkujira whale apron and the apron that looked like it was made for a princess, and eventually picked the princess.

"Hello, Miyako," she said. Dumpling Girl is Mrs Meowko's granddaughter, but she doesn't call her granny. If she says it by mistake, she gets a fine of 500 yen. That 500-yen coin goes in a piggy bank, and when it's full, Mrs Meowko will use it for enhancing her beauty and health.

"You've grown up so fast, Hikaboo, making chocolates for Valentine's already – no wonder I have more small wrinkles on my face," Mrs Meowko said.

"Kahorun says chocolate with nuts has an anti-ageing effect," Dumpling Girl said. "So she tries to avoid eggs and cream as much as she can, but she doesn't cut back on chocolate."

Then we heard Mum, Madame Hinako and Mikasa return: the jolly chatty trio. They burst into a jaunty exchange of greetings with Mrs Meowko. (Sounding just like how Auntie Meowko would chit-chat with her neighbours, when she'd call out things like, "Hullo there, I haven't seen you in ages – going out somewhere?" and they'd say, "Just around the block.")

"Oh no," Mum blurted out. "Mr Collector will come soon. I've got to wrap up my manuscript." With that, she hurried up the stairs. Mr Collector is her nickname for Mr Toritani, who works at a publisher and comes to "collect" her translations.

The others moved to the small dining room. The table there is the most convenient place in the house to chit-chat face to face. No sooner had they sat down than Mrs Meowko said, "I wanted to show you this," and started digging for something in her bag. But it took a while for her to find it.

"You know my father-in-law loves konatsu citrus? They're only in season for a short time, and they don't appear on the market in the Kanto region, so what he does is pre-order them in the autumn and have them shipped directly from a farmer when they harvest in February. And the truck driver who delivers the order for him is always the same man, every year. He comes in this big truck that looks like a palace, decked out in all these glitzy lights. He brings along this cat that's five or six years old – his fur is white on the belly and black on the back, like he's wearing a cape. His face looks like a magician's, too; the top half is black like a mask. His name is Lupin. Besides Lupin, the driver has a tufted capuchin called Jonathan. The monkey is good with his hands, so with proper training, he can help disabled people with little tasks. When they came to deliver the konatsu for us the other day, I went over to say hello to Lupin, and I noticed he had a rather stylish collar around his neck this year. It was an embroidered ribbon – my favourite shade of violet. And it had this elaborate design like your artworks, Hinako. When I asked the driver where he got it, he lowered his voice like he was telling me a secret . . . He said he was having a nap in a restaurant car park, and when he woke up, Lupin was wearing it around his neck. It wasn't just the ribbon that was gorgeous; it had this agate pendant, a slightly unusual one with a moiré pattern in creamy tones. The driver said he'd thought it was a glass marble. Well, what else could I do then? I convinced him to let me hang on to it for now – I told him if it's a stolen object that's been reported missing, he could be accused of a crime, and he got scared. And . . . this is it."

Having delivered this somewhat long preface, Mrs Meowko produced the object in question from a velvet drawstring pouch: the pendant with the ribbon.

I could hardly believe it (so many surprises today!). Never in my dreams had I expected to hear any news of Jonathan and the uncle who looked like a travelling performer. On top of that, Mrs Meowko had found the very collar that I'd given them.

"There's an engraving on the back of the pendant that says 'Marble'," Mrs Meowko went on, "It might be the name of the original owner, or the name of a shop somewhere, but it's not enough of a clue to go on."

Madame Hinako took the ribbon, and after a quick inspection, she said, "This is definitely a ribbon I made. It's the one stocked at a boutique in Ginza. They're sold by length in ten-centimetre units. Which means somebody must've bought the ribbon for a kitten named Marble."

"*Myaumiamo* (that's right)." Mademoiselle Rocco bought the ribbon and the agate pendant, and made the collar herself. She liked the agate stone because the marble pattern on it looked just like mine. I tried my best to explain.

"Hmm, what is it, dear . . . ? I think he knows something about it. I can't speak cat. Anyone here who can?" Mrs Meowko asked.

Right on cue, Jean Paul appeared, beckoning from the corridor. As usual, Madame Hinako was the only one who saw him. "Excuse me for a minute," she said, and walked out of the room. Everyone thought she was off to the toilet, so they didn't look her way. That's the etiquette, you see. So no-one saw her talking to Jean Paul.

Mikasa seemed to have recalled something and was poking around in her daypack. Soon, she found what she was looking for. Much faster than Mrs Meowko. It was a pocketbook. With a little sigh of relief, she opened it, and a piece of paper fluttered out.

It was a photo of Mademoiselle Rocco, rubbing her cheek against mine with a goofy grin. It was before Norimaki was born, so I was still tiny, but the creamy caramel cake swirl on my belly showed that the kitten in the picture was me.

"Hey, look!" The first to notice was Dumpling Girl. "Isn't that Chimaki? Or maybe his brother? He's got a persimmon paste mark right there, just like Chimaki." (I *told* you, it's creamy caramel cake, not persimmon paste!)

"*I thought he looked familiar, but is it possible?*" Mikasa said. "*This* mademoiselle *is Rocco. She works at my* galerie. *She translates Japanese leaflets, interprets for tourists. Sometimes she sings anime songs. With dancing. University students call her to their bar – big hit.*"

Just then, Madame Hinako came back from her whispered talk with Jean Paul and was able to interpret for Mikasa, who, it turned out, had been asked by Mademoiselle Rocco to look out for us brothers while she was visiting Japan. According to Mikasa's story, Mademoiselle Rocco had handed the pet carrier with us inside to her friend in a crowded airport around the New Year's season. But when the friend got home and opened the carrier, we were nowhere to be seen. The last thing *I* remember is hearing Mademoiselle Rocco saying to her friend, "Sorry, this came up all of a sudden," and then I dozed off inside. Next thing I knew, we were surrounded by men in uniform. Maybe the clasp on the carrier came undone, and we tumbled out while we were fast asleep.

While the uniformed men had made phone calls and

announcements about two lost kittens, we started feeling an urge for the toilet. I went out to the corridor with Norimaki to look for one, and when we finally found the right spot to do what we had to do, we couldn't find our way back. We saw a door, so we went in – and that's where we spotted the jacket with the fluffy pocket.

On Sunday afternoon, there was a family meeting at the Horai house. Mum looked sad that we might have to say goodbye. Dumpling Girl said, "Makimaki have been with us longer, so they're basically our cats now, aren't they?" but Koyomi sighed, "It's not about that, unfortunately."

But this question was resolved in no time at all. Since Mademoiselle Rocco was planning to work from Paris for the foreseeable future, she asked the Horais if they could carry on taking care of Marble and Chocolate as part of the family. She was fine with them calling us Chimaki and Norimaki, too.

"What a relief," Mum said, perking up.

Soon after that, the Seishiro family – who had just returned from their trip to Kyushu – stopped by on their way back home.

"We got some souvenirs for you," Rika announced. "We thought the Horais would like this kind of thing more than sweets or processed foods, so here you go." They dropped off a load of kumquats and frozen crabs. Mum invited them in, but they said they had to get Yuria and Konsaburo home – they'd got too hyper on the flight back and were already sound asleep. "We have to bathe them somehow, and tuck them into bed, pronto," Rika said, and they whooshed off to the farm.

"Well, how about golden sushi to celebrate tonight?" Kagami asked Mum, looking at the kumquats. "I'll make a special breakfast for Chimaki and Norimaki tomorrow with the crab."

Woohoo! I can't wait. This crab is a species of the Portunidae family, and it's known as a tiger crab because its shell is striped like a tiger. If you ask me, it looks more like tiger print underwear.

Norimaki was a bit scared of it, mewling, "Tiger?" So I told him the picture book story about how the tigers tried to eat Little Babaji: they circled round and round the boy until they turned into golden butter, and Babaji made pancakes out of that butter and ate them. Norimaki loves butter, you see.

Dumpling Girl got down to making the baked chocolates she'll hand out for Valentine's. Koyomi peered over her shoulder.

"Huh. So you just melt the dark chocolate and add pancake mix – that's it? And you bake it in the toaster oven? It really is an easy recipe," Koyomi said.

Kagami took out a piping bag and inserted a flower-shaped tip in it. "If you put in a little bit of extra effort and squeeze it out into different shapes – like pointy hats, stars or logs – you get these nice bite-size sweets. You could decorate them with sugared violets or silver dragées, too."

"So? Who are these for?" Koyomi asked Dumpling Girl.

"It's a secret," Dumpling Girl said in a sing-song voice.

"I bet it's Master Kujira, isn't it? You know he'll give you something ten times better in return when White Day rolls around."

Once Dumpling Girl's baked chocolates were done, it was time to make kumquat sushi. Kagami asked Sacchan to come over to help; they started peeling the boiled kumquats with Dumpling Girl. The older pair peeled the skin in leaf-like shapes, then Dumpling Girl cut them into thin strips with kitchen scissors.

Meanwhile, Mum was adding a passage on kumquat sushi to her latest column:

When I was a child, kinkan kumquats weren't perfectly round, but shaped more like an egg; the skin was sweet, but the insides were sour, and we couldn't eat them raw. That was the only kind you'd find in stores. And so, people would turn them into a sour drink by steeping them with rock sugar in vinegar, or they'd make a syrup for treating sore throats by steeping them in honey.

Nowadays, kumquats have become surprisingly sweet: as sweet as satsuma mandarins. If they're the round kind, you can eat them raw, skin and all. These sweeter ones are nice in their own way, but I wouldn't want to miss out on the good old sour kumquats, either.

When I want to marinate kumquats in honey or vinegar, or turn them into marmalade, I don't look for those neat packs with fruits of the same size; I want those kumquats sold in bags at a cheaper price, even if the sizes aren't consistent.

A kumquat dish that's a highlight for this time of year is kumquat sushi. Citrus fruits and the sweet-tangy flavour of sushi rice go well together. This recipe works with other kinds of citrus too, but kumquats are special. Because it's their peel that's supposed to be eaten in the first place, it has a gentle sweetness that gives a wonderful fragrance to the sushi.

With this kind of sushi, it's tempting to mix mushrooms and root vegetables into the rice, but to savour their flavours to the fullest, I would keep the ingredients to kumquats only, so that nothing interferes with their subtle sweetness and refreshing relish.

The way I do it is to boil the kumquats first, then cut the peel into thin pieces. If you prefer a crisp texture, you can chop the raw peel instead. Slice a few of the kumquats into thin circles and set them aside for the finishing touches. With sushi, presentation is as important as the taste, after all.

Put the peeled fruits in an empty dashi bag or large empty tea bag and squeeze out the juice, which will be mixed with

MIDWINTER

the sweetened vinegar when you prepare the sushi rice. You can keep the leftover pulp in the bag for later: just pop it in the bath for a homemade scented bath oil.

Prepare sweetened vinegar for the rice with dashi stock taken from kombu kelp. Making good dashi isn't my forte, either. So allow me to introduce a secret trick. You can make a cold brew instead. If you're planning to make the sushi around lunchtime, start the brew the night before; if you'll be cooking at night, start in the morning of the same day. First, pour fresh water into a bottle. Then add a piece of kombu – about a two-by-two inch square – and close the cap. Just let it sit in the fridge, and it does the rest by itself.

You can use the same method for getting dashi from kombu and bonito flakes. And beans as well, by the way – if you soak the beans in water flavoured with soy sauce, sugar and sake overnight, all you need to do the next day is to pour the whole thing into a stewing pot.

But this technique doesn't work with azuki beans. Azuki beans don't absorb water even when you soak them, so you're supposed to boil them right after they're rinsed. In other words, you can start cooking them on a whim without having to prep in advance. There's no need to soak them from the night before, like you do with other beans like kintokimame, hanamame or kuromame.

Now, for the rest of the kumquat recipe.

Once the rice is cooked, spread it in a large wooden tub while it's still steaming hot and drizzle the sweetened vinegar over it to make sushi rice. Then scatter the thin slices of kumquat peel over the whole thing and garnish it with the circular slices. And there you have it! If you'd like, sprinkle some minced white sesame seeds or something similar to taste.

When you have leftovers, stuff them into slow-stewed abura-age tofu pouches and turn them into inari sushi, and your bento lunch is sorted.

The next morning, Kagami made pom-pom balls with crab meat for Norimaki and me. He took the crab meat and crab miso – the innards that look like a paste – and mixed that into a delicious fish surimi, specially made by Grandad. After mashing them thoroughly together, Kagami scooped up the mix with a big spoon and dropped each scoop in a pot of hot soup. He quickly popped them in, like *pom pom pom* – that's why we call them "pom-pom balls". The emptied shell and legs were all in the soup, of course, so it was infused with the sumptuous crab dashi. Even the steam smelled appetising. Once the balls turned a pale pink from the cooked crab meat, they were ready to eat.

They were still too hot for me and Norimaki, though. Kagami told us to wait until there was no more steam, so Norimaki kept a close watch on it. But soon his face got all wrinkly. The steam tickled him and made him pucker up. That's the face he makes when he feels like he's about to sneeze but it won't come.

The steam disappeared, and we finally pounced on the food. One big bite of the pom-pom ball, and the sweetness of the crab filled my mouth like a soft, fluffy cloud. Life is good.

That night, Kagami made chocolate cake – the one rumoured to be "sublime". But it was almost eleven. Why so late?

A sound came from the front door: a key quietly turning in the lock. It was Sakuragawa, back from his business trip. Instead of heading to his room above the atelier, he drifted towards the kitchen.

"The smell pulled me in," he said. *Ah, now I get where the rumour started*, I thought. It must've been Sakuragawa who'd told Mrs Meowko that Kagami's chocolate cake was something special.

"I just finished baking it . . . Would you like some?"

"I didn't get a chance to grab dinner, but isn't it too late for cake?"

"If you're concerned it's too rich, this one doesn't have wheat flour in it, so it's fine. The batter is very light, made with almond flour. It's a recipe that a British person devised for their long winter nights, to go with tea. The cocoa mass in chocolate is rich in polyphenols and dietary fibre, which makes it the most suitable choice for a late-night snack."

"Will the lecture last much longer? I'm starving."

"... Yes, I'll make tea right away."

The night wore on; only the light in the small dining room continued to glow as midnight came and went. Now it's Valentine's Day. Norimaki and I have tiptoed away to leave them to it. Night night.

MAYUMI NAGANO is a writer and illustrator born in Tokyo in 1959. In 1988 she won the Bungei Prize for *Boy Alice*, and in 2015, she received the Izumi Kyōka Prize for Literature as well as the Noma Literary Prize for *On the Path to the Land of the Dead*. The recipes in *Diary of a Cat* are her own.

YUI KAJITA is a translator, illustrator and literary scholar, originally from the countryside in Kyoto, Japan, and currently based in Germany. Her translations include *Run with the Wind*, a classic sports novel by the award-winning author Shion Miura.